SILENT HUM

AFTAB KHAN

This is a work of fiction. Names, characters, places, and incidents either are the product of the author's imagination or are used fictitiously. Any resemblance to actual persons, living or dead, events, or locales is entirely coincidental.

Book cover designed by Elizabeth Khan

First paperback edition September 2021

Paperback ISBN: 9798539380052

Dedicated to
Elizabeth, Prema and my mother -
my inspiration.

Chapter 1
The Case Against Malthus

I know many secretive things because I know many secretive people. Chief among them are Malthus, Mr. Lyell and, well, Chief O'Brian. I was there for the sentencing of Malthus, as was everyone else in Silent Hum on that cold and rainy Sunday morning. He was so convinced of his innocence, that he invited everyone to witness his freedom. Everyone that is, except his father. From the beginning, he has pleaded not guilty to the murder of beloved actress Madison Wallace.

The verdict.

Judge: "Could the defendant please rise. Ladies and gentlemen of the jury, have you reached a verdict?"

Jury: "Yes, we have your Honor."

Judge: "In the charge of first-degree murder of Madison Wallace, how do you find the defendant?"

Jury: "We, the jury, find the defendant..."

The Hat: "Wait!"

That one shrilling word was all that I heard. After I forced myself to the front of the crowd, I saw a meek fellow, standing in a drenched, black raincoat. His face was covered by a top hat but no one was looking at his face. All eyes were focused on the disk in his extended arm. A quiet murmur echoed across the courtroom. The gavel struck the desk several times to quiet the crowd. There was silence.

Judge: "What is the meaning of this?"

The Hat: "Please, your Honor, I have evidence to prove that Malthus did not commit this crime."

With the wave of her finger, the judge signaled the bailiff to retrieve the disc. Both lawyers joined the judge, one carrying a laptop.

After viewing the contents of the disc, the judge announced, "Based on new evidence brought before the court, I must declare Malthus *INNOCENT* of all charges."

The courtroom erupted in shouts of disgust.

The Wallace family was overcome by grief.

After months of expert testimony and intense cross-examination, Malthus was about to walk free.

Chief O'Brian was outraged, though he kept his anger to himself. After all, he had spent six months tracking Malthus around the globe to bring him to justice. With a task force of several hundred, the Chief finally cornered and arrested him in the dense Brazilian rainforest.

The gavel struck the desk again. Silence descended upon the courtroom.

Malthus uttered, with a derisive smile, "Am I free to go your Honor?"

With a slight reservation, the judge replied, "Yes, you are."

With that, it was all over. The most dangerous man in the world was free. Those present in the courtroom were incensed. The Wallace family was inconsolable.

What of the evidence, the evidence that the judge found so compelling? According to the coroner, Miss Wallace died of a gunshot wound at 1 pm on March 5th. It was exactly what the video showed. Yet, the Chief was not so easily convinced. So, he handed the disk over to me. There is not much that a teenage girl can get past a veteran police chief but he has so much confidence in me. He trusted me over all of his officers, especially considering recent events.

I could not find any evidence to counter the judge's decision but all that changed on my fifth viewing of the two-minute video. First, I considered the lighting that day. March 5th at 1 pm was sunny, just as it was in the video. The shadows cast by the sun were almost non-existent, as the sun would be overhead.

Nothing seemed out of the ordinary. The video showed Madison running for her life. Once she was out of view of the camera, a shot was fired. The shooter then placed a plastic bag over the surveillance camera as he was leaving the Wallace estate. His face was clearly visible. It was not Malthus. As he stretched out his hand over the camera, his watch showed that it was indeed 1 pm. But it also indicated **3/4**. This was the evidence that the Chief was looking for. It was the correct time, but the wrong date. The video was taken at 1 pm on March 4th, as indicated by the **3/4**. The murder was committed at 1 pm on March 5th. The evidence presented in court was a dress rehearsal for the real murder. Records showed that Madison was indeed preparing for a movie role. Miss Wallace was unaware that her performance on March 4th would set a most dangerous criminal free.

The Chief rushed over to the judge's house, in the middle of the night, to show her what I had found. Judge Russell was not pleased at first. She did not want to listen to the Chief. She even let him stand outside in the pouring rain. He persisted, and, eventually, she relented. Judge Russell admitted that she knew about the video, long before anyone else. However, the video played no part in releasing Malthus. So what did?

According to the judge, Malthus had planned everything. First, he kidnapped Judge Russell's granddaughter. Then, he filled the basement of the courtroom with explosives. Finally, he invited everyone in Silent Hum to witness his sentencing. Malthus would be free or no one would be free.

But why kill Madison? Well, her parents were very wealthy and very influential. Yet, nothing was stolen from the Wallace estate. As it turned out, Malthus murdered the wrong Wallace sister. While Madison was an aspiring actress, her twin, Samantha, was a gifted scientist. She was working on a secret project at her father's institute, as I later learned from the Chief. He had to provide extra security for her, due to concerns for her safety. He also told me that her work was so secretive that it had the blessings of the Pope. Whatever she was working on, Malthus was very much interested.

Later that evening, Judge Russell's granddaughter was found safe. The next day, the judge was found dead. Those connected with Malthus's arrest and trial were also murdered, except Chief O'Brian. Then, following a break-in at her father's institute, Samantha and everything associated with her secret project went missing. The building has since been left vacant. Shortly after that, the same fate would befall her father. No one has heard from him in months. As for Malthus, he was nowhere to be found. He did not leave the country because there were no records at the airport. He has not used a credit card or cell phone because there were no records of these either. He simply vanished. Coincidentally, his freedom also marked the first of a string of earthquakes and tsunamis which have resulted in countless deaths around the world.

CHAPTER 2
The Tournament

"I know a secret *aboooout* you! It is something you need to know. I will not tell you what it is, but I will give you clues to help you figure it out. All you have to do is arrange these letters in a row: I-L-R-S appears three times each, A-E-T-V twice and once for the other letters. Be warned, however, this one is very hard. It's almost impossible to solve. I hope you are ready because here are the clues:

The Alpha and the Omega precede whiz and shirt;
The 6th and 20th letters are the same;
Sam is directly to the left of James Bond's boss;
The second letter is another name for me;
Mary and Lucy are in alphabetical order but 19 letters separate them;
The Sun is directly before the Umbrella;
One Snowflake has fallen directly behind the last Igloo;
Two Leaves are next to each other, with my friend directly before and me directly after;
G-T-V-E-R is in this order but separated by five letters each;
Only two vowels (me and Epsilon) are between the Arches;
After each Exercise, you must Rest;
The two Valleys are separated by four letters;
B-Y-N is in alphabetical order but not next to each other;
The fifth, plus four, plus three, plus two, 16th, and 24th letters are vowels. Good luck!"

Emma neatly folded the piece of paper, on which was written the exhaustive list of clues, then waited patiently for an answer. She raised her right hand to her face, flicked her wrist, and stared at her watch, counting each second out loud as they ticked by. To listen for his answer, she leaned her head forward, tilted on a slight angle, like a barn owl pinpointing a field mouse.

The afternoon sun glistened off her loosely flowing, long black hair. Her piercing blue eyes were locked onto her victim. Her other senses were finely tuned to any signs of nervousness. After failing so many times before, she finally had him where she wanted. There will be no escape this time.

It was the most difficult puzzle that Emma had ever created and she knew it. It could not be solved. Two others had already tried, unsuccessfully. She was confident that there were too many letters and too many cryptic clues, for anyone to be able to figure it out. Just the idea that someone would even attempt to try and solve it, was absurd, she thought, especially, if they did not use a pencil and a piece of paper. With a word like Epsilon, she knew that he would also need a dictionary. Good luck, indeed!

With his squinting brown eyes fixed to the clear blue sky above, Gilbert pondered the clues. He gently rubbed his chin with his thumb and index finger, as he contemplated a possible solution. He then closed his eyes, one at a time. With a deep breath through his mouth, his chest heaved. He slowly exhaled through his nostrils, meditating on the flow of air rushing out of his body. With each cleansing breath, his focus became clearer. All that remained were the clues that Emma read, each one echoing inside his head.

With a final deep breath, Gilbert lowered his head, eyes still closed. The cryptic clues flew wildly in his mind. While Emma had never used such a clever tactic before, he found them easy to unravel. He instantly solved the cryptic clues and replaced them with letters. The letters began to arrange themselves along a horizontal line. It appeared as one long, unbroken string at first. Then, the letters began to divide themselves into words. A smile came over Gilbert's face, as he read the secret message in his mind. He could not believe how easy it was to solve.

Regarding Emma's puzzle-making abilities, Gilbert admitted, "That's a very clever one." He added, sincerely, "Thank you for the compliment."

Emma's mouth fell open as she glanced at her watch and again at Gilbert. Speechless, she raised both hands with upturned palms, bent at the elbows, as if to demand an explanation.

As Gilbert opened his eyes, he proudly displayed a broad grin across his face. The apples of his cheeks glowed like red roses, separated by an equally rounded nose. Though he was pleased with himself, he was also very much afraid. Nervously, he awaited Emma's response.

Her clenched teeth, flaring nostrils and scrunched eyebrows made Gilbert terrified. The grin quickly disappeared from his face, replaced by a blank expression. Seemingly at a loss for an explanation, Emma demanded angrily, "How did you solve that one so fast?"

Her shrieking words sent a cold shiver down his frail spine. His sweaty palms grew clammier with each passing second. His eyes nervously twitched while his knees shook with anticipation of what was to come.

She informed him angrily, with hands flailing, voice raised to a fever pitch, "It took me almost one week to come up with that puzzle! Charles and Fitzroy gave up after an hour, and they had a pencil and a piece of paper. What do you have to say for yourself?"

"What it is!" he calmly and confidently answered, shrugging his shoulders. In fact, that is always his answer, when he solves one of her puzzles. He could offer no explanation, other than, "What it is!"

They stared at each other for a moment, waiting to see who would blink first. Emma looked furious. Gilbert held his breath. Suddenly, they both burst out laughing. Emma's cackling was drowned out by Gilbert's loud guffaw. Emma immediately grabbed the left side of her rib cage, as she winced in pain. It was caused by a birth defect or so she was told. Gilbert looked concerned but Emma reassured him that she was alright.

Gilbert did not have to reveal the answer to Emma. She knew that he had figured it out from the smile on his face. He had also thanked her for the compliment that she paid him, so she had further evidence that he had indeed uncovered the secret message. Emma knew one other thing: she would never be able to create a puzzle that Gilbert could not solve.

This was the first time, all day, that Emma had seen a smile on Gilbert's face. She could not quite figure out what was bothering him. Maybe someone at school had called him a dirty name again or made fun of the way he walked, she thought.

It took Gilbert exactly twenty seconds to solve the puzzle. He had never taken so long before. Emma was certain that he would not be able to solve it. Yet, she was not surprised when he did.

As Emma continued to question him, Gilbert's gaze drifted to the pendant that was dangling from the chain around her neck. Following Gilbert's eyes, Emma paused and looked down at the sparkling jewelry. She, too, remembered how Gilbert helped her win it.

Every year, Mr. Sedgwick, their history teacher, organizes a quiz tournament at their school. Teams of four players compete against each other until a champion is declared. Emma's team also included Charles and Fitzroy. After three rounds, they were one of the finalists. For the second year in a row, they had to face Beagle Abbey's team, the defending champions.

All of the contestants involved could feel the pressure as they sat before their peers and parents in the full gymnasium. Just before the final round began, Emma, Gilbert, Charles, and Fitzroy all held hands and repeated their motto: "Together, for each other!" It was a saying that Emma came up with two years ago when the four of them became best friends. It was a reminder that no matter what happens they will always be there for each other. While Emma has known Charles for almost eight years, she and Fitzroy have been friends all of their lives.

Once Mr. Sedgwick had read the rules for the final round to the contestants and audience, he promptly announced the first clue. Looking directly at both teams before him, he stated, "He was the original source for the ancient city of Atlantis."

Emma quickly buzzed in. A green light blinked on the buzzer in front of her. Mr. Sedgwick pointed to her.

She confidently answered, "Who is Plato?"

The crowd roused to a boisterous cheer when Mr. Sedgwick indicated that she was correct. Gilbert smiled warmly at her. Charles and Fitzroy were overjoyed. Beagle and his teammates were shocked that Emma pressed the buzzer before they could.

Everyone on Emma's team breathed a sigh of relief. Although they were prepared, Emma and her teammates were still intimidated by Beagle. However, they knew that they were playing for more than just a trophy. Beagle was the primary source of Gilbert's bullying. Emma, Charles and Fitzroy pledged to do their very best to make sure that his team did not win.

Once the cheering from the audience subsided, Mr. Sedgwick continued, stating, "They were the first two people to successfully climb Mount Everest."

While everyone on Emma's team tried furiously to buzz in, a member of Beagle's team was the first to do so. She answered, "Who are Namgyal Wangdi and Sir Edmund Percival Hillary on May 29, 1953?"

Mr. Sedgwick pointed to her, indicating that she was correct. It was received by jubilant cheers from the crowd. Until now, Emma was unaware of Sherpa Norgay's real name. She was also surprised to learn that Hillary had been knighted. She was even more surprised that her opponent knew the exact date.

With the score tied at one, Mr. Sedgwick provided the next clue, stating, "The Ship of Dreams sank in this year."

Beagle Abbey quickly buzzed in and answered, "The Ship of Dreams, also known as Titanic, sank on April 15, 1912."

Mr. Sedgwick pointed to Beagle, indicating that his response was correct. The crowd showed their appreciation by applauding. In the back of her mind, Emma wondered why Beagle gave the exact date and not just the year. She was amazed at how accurate her rivals have been with all of their responses. Yet, she had an unsettling feeling that something was not right.

Mr. Sedgwick stated the fourth clue, saying, "This statue was completed on October 28, 1886, and erected on what was then Bedloe's Island."

Charles quickly hit the buzzer and proceeded to answer, "What is the Statue of Liberty?"

Mr. Sedgwick happily announced, "The score is now tied at two points each!"

It was much to the satisfaction of Emma's supporters, who showered them with applause and shouts of encouragement. Even though they were trailing the defending champions, they showed no signs of quitting. Their determination to win was steadfast, not just for the trophy, but for Gilbert, also.

Mr. Sedgwick continued with the proceedings, stating, "For a brief time, New York was referred to as this fruit."

While Team Abbey was still pondering the clue, Emma buzzed in and answered, "What is New Orange?"

"That is correct!" shouted Mr. Sedgwick, pointing directly at her.

Emma's team was ahead three points to two. Emma received a standing ovation from the audience, for being the first person to give two correct responses. She simply smiled in appreciation.

Always humble, she remained, as her next-door neighbor Mr. Lyell had taught her to be.

Everyone eagerly awaited the next clue. Mr. Sedgwick was all too willing to abide. He stated, "This animal has three hearts, a beak and blue blood."

Fitzroy buzzed in just ahead of Beagle Abbey. He answered, "What is an octopus?"

Even before Mr. Sedgwick was able to indicate whether or not the answer was correct, most of the students in the audience knew that it was. They cheered loudly. Emma's team had a four points to two advantage and they were only two correct responses away from winning. Their opponents were not very happy as they constantly argued with each other.

With both hands raised over his head, seeking silence from the audience, Mr. Sedgwick informed everyone, "The score is now four points for Team Keeling and two points for Team Abbey. The next clue is, before the use of radar, the US Postal Air Service navigated using part of this Elton John song title."

Beagle buzzed in. Charles knew the answer, but he had to listen to Beagle say, "What is Goodbye Yellow Brick Road?"

"Yes, indeed," announced Mr. Sedgwick to the audience. "Pilots followed brightly colored, reflective yellow arrows, painted on cement blocks on the ground to navigate. It was commonly known as The Yellow Brick Road."

Mr. Sedgwick announced, "The score is now 4 points for Team Keeling and 3 points for Team Abbey. Here is the next clue. On this date, he was the first person to reach the South Pole."

Tessship, the only person in Silent Hum with three consecutive letters in her first name, buzzed in and correctly responded, "Who is Roald Amundsen, on December 14, 1911?"

While Emma's team was doing well, everyone expected that Team Abbey would attempt a comeback. It was an unbelievable turn of events, even for Mr. Sedgwick. He was surprised that Emma did not buzz in first. He knew how diligently she and her teammates had prepared. He witnessed them studying in the library daily. Beagle Abbey and his teammates, on the other hand, were not among the most accomplished students in school and they did not study very much.

With the score tied at 4 points each, Mr. Sedgwick announced the ninth clue, stating, "This ruler was the first to tax his subjects for growing a beard in this country."

Gilbert quickly slapped the buzzer and yelled out, "Who is Peter the Great of Russia?"

The audience gasped. They were utterly shocked. While it was mandatory for Mr. Sedgwick to request the answer, Gilbert did not wait. His dislike for Beagle made him do it.

No one knew which team had buzzed in first. There was a green light on for both teams. Charles could not believe that Gilbert yelled out the answer before Mr. Sedgwick pointed to him. If he points to Beagle's team, they could give the same answer and take the lead. However, the cheers from the crowd brought Charles's head up from the table. Mr. Sedgwick responded to Gilbert's correct response with a definitive closed-fist pump in the air and a clenched-teeth grimace of approval. Everyone in the audience stared blankly at him, as did Emma. Never before had they seen him display so much emotion.

Mr. Sedgwick knew that he should not have done that, as he was an impartial moderator. However, he was encouraged by the determination of Emma's team. After composing himself, he addressed the audience, saying, "Peter Romanov or Peter the Great, first Tsar of modern Russia, did indeed tax his subjects for growing a beard."

Gilbert could not stop smiling, as he was congratulated by his teammates. Emma was ecstatic that her team had the lead again.

While Emma's teammates were focused, Team Abbey was constantly bickering at each other. Even the audience seemed restless. There was an exciting energy passing over them that could not be quenched. Never before had they experienced such a thrilling final round of competition. Neither team was willing to relent. To calm everyone down, Mr. Sedgwick raised both hands in the air. There was silence. He announced, "The tenth clue is this: The calendar most widely used in the world today, was introduced in 1582 by this person."

While stating the clue, Mr. Sedgwick paid close attention to Team Abbey. There was something very disturbing that he noticed. One of Beagle's teammates buzzed in before he could finish stating the clue. It was as if he was anticipating the clue.

Alexander buzzed in ahead of Emma. While Emma knew the answer, Mr. Sedgwick pointed to her opponent. He responded, "Who is Pope Gregory the Eight, on February 24, 1582?"

Emma's closed eyes and lowered head made everyone aware that the score was now tied at five. She knew the answer but was not able to buzz in fast enough. Again, Emma was astonished by the fact that Alexander knew the Pope's full title and the exact day. Emma and her teammates refused to quit, however. There was still one more clue.

"After ten clues," announced Mr. Sedgwick, "both teams are tied at five points each. Good luck to everyone. Here is the final clue. This individual is the only named person in the Bible to have been killed by the great flood."

When Emma heard the clue, she was baffled. She could not understand why Mr. Sedgwick chose it. After all, there were only two other people in the room who knew the answer and Mr. Sedgwick knew it. She could not comprehend what he was thinking. Emma did not want to win the tournament this way. Seeing Gilbert reaching for the buzzer, she grabbed onto his hand. He did not resist her. She, herself, refused to buzz in.

Everyone in the audience glanced back and forth, several times, to see who would buzz in first. After an anxious moment, Beagle pressed the buzzer. Emma was certain that he did not know the answer. However, he proceeded, by Mr. Sedgwick's invitation, to respond, "Who is Methuselah?"

"We have our champions!" boldly declared Mr. Sedgwick, as he pointed to Beagle's team. Emma, her teammates and everyone in the audience who supported them, were absolutely devastated by the announcement.

Emma was even more confused now than before. How could Beagle have known the answer? She looked at Mr. Sedgwick. He gestured to her with a slight nod of his head. She was unsure of what it meant but she trusted her teacher.

Emma was gracious in defeat. She stood up and applauded the champions, as did those in the audience. Her teammates followed her lead. Charles and Fitzroy felt that they had let Gilbert down.

A few minutes later, just as Mr. Sedgwick was about to present the championship trophy to Beagle, something fell and crashed onto the gymnasium floor. Simultaneously, everyone looked to see what it was. A small laptop-like device had fallen from the top of the stands.

Mr. Sedgwick went to investigate. Upon closer inspection, he discovered that the clues that he was asking were written on it and so were the answers. There were even answers to clues which he had prepared but did not ask.

While Mr. Sedgwick had suspected that there was cheating going on, he had no proof. Now he did. He stormed onto the stage and wrestled the trophy away from a protesting Beagle Abbey. His teammates quickly corroborated that they were in fact cheating, as they did last year, but that it was all Beagle's idea. Beagle, distraught from being caught, ran out of the gymnasium and never returned.

Mr. Sedgwick declared, with great satisfaction, pointing to Emma and her teammates, "Ladies and gentlemen, I give you your true champions!"

The applause they received was immediate and thunderous. Mr. Sedgwick was delighted to present the championship trophy to the rightful winners. Gilbert could not believe what he and his teammates had accomplished, as tears of joy streamed from his eyes. He had always dreamed of a crowd cheering for him. They did so, wholeheartedly. Mr. Sedgwick then presented Emma with a necklace and pendant for being the team's captain. Inscribed on the pendant were these words: **Be true to thyself**. It was the greatest moment of Gilbert's young life.

Chapter 3
The Third Letter

"Goodbye, Miss Emma," Gilbert said politely, releasing his gaze upon the pendant. With the wave of his hand, he turned and ran to the front door.

Ever since Emma could remember, Gilbert has always called her Miss Emma, even though they were the same age. He greatly respected her, not only for her friendship but also for her intelligence. To Gilbert, Emma was perfect. She had everything going for her. She was smart, athletic, confident, and she had a lot of friends. She was everything that he was not. While Gilbert wanted to be *exactly* like Emma, she reminded him that she is a young woman. He had no reply, except to smile.

Before crossing the street, Emma looked both ways. A blue Mustang suddenly drove past her. She noticed that the driver was wearing dark sunglasses. When the road was clear, she began to cross. As she did, she noticed a large package sitting below her mailbox. Without hesitation, she ran towards it. Her oversized backpack swayed from side to side. When she reached the package, she stopped for a moment to admire it, all the while struggling to contain her excitement.

Even before she picked it up, Emma already knew what was inside. Just the sight of the large box delighted her. After all, she had to wait six months for it to arrive. It was six very agonizing months. It took all the patients of her thirteen years, but the moment had finally arrived and she was very excited. Emma quickly hunted through her pockets. Once she had located her keys, she reached down to pick up the package, only to hear a familiar voice.

"It finally arrived!" he happily announced, chuckling. He spoke in a soft and gentle voice, almost grandfatherly. It was a voice that she knew very well, one that she has heard every day of her life. She often argues with him that she knew his voice even before she was born. It was a voice that she could count on, depend on and lean on.

"Sorry, Mr. Lyell!" shouted Emma. "I have to go!" After she secured the package in her hands, she ran to the front door. With precision, she inserted the key and opened the door without breaking stride. Before she disappeared inside, she yelled, "I'll see you later, Mr. Lyell!"

Even though he was disappointed to see her leave so quickly, a smile overcame his grey-bearded face. He understood her reason for rushing off. He had anticipated it all day. From his porch, he saw when the package was delivered. He even signed for it. Her overly excited reaction was exactly what he expected. Two months earlier, Emma had told him about the package and what would be inside. He was happy that it had finally arrived. At least now, he would not have to listen to her complain that it was taking so long.

The door slammed shut behind her as Emma entered her home. No sooner did she step inside, her shoes were off and across the living room floor she sped towards the stairs that led to her room. Up the stairs she flew, skipping a few steps in the process. Her school bag, all the while, swayed from side to side.

Emma knew her home like a goldfish in a bowl. From the front door to her room, all she saw was a large box in front of her. Her nimble hands and agile feet had earned her the nickname "crazy legs" on the school playground. She was so fast, that when you thought she was going one way, she would stop, pivot, and change direction. No one could catch her in a game of tag.

It was the same agility that her school's football coach noticed. He encouraged her to join the team. She did so without hesitation. Her ability to catch a football and dodge any of the boys on the gridiron was a testament to her nickname.

Emma is the only girl on her school's football team. It is a football team in progress. Two years ago, they only managed to win two games out of ten. That was twice as many as they had won the previous year. However, with the addition of Emma a year ago, they made it to the championship game, although they did not win.

This year's team is much better. They have won all of their games and Emma was voted the most valuable player. However, none of that would matter to her if they lose the next game. It's the championship game and it is only a few days away.

Emma closed the door behind her as she entered her room. She gently placed the package down on her desk. Pulling out the chair and spinning it around, she dropped onto it. While opening the package with one hand, she picked up the telephone with the other. She dialed the number and waited for an answer, all the while busily opening the package. After a few rings, someone picked up the telephone.

"Heaven-o Charles," she greeted him gleefully. Emma knew that it was Charles on the other line, even before he said anything. He always picks up the telephone on the fourth ring. She delightfully proceeded to announce, "My microscope set just arrived in the mail!"

"No way!" he replied, with excitement in his voice. "I was just about to call to tell you that my telescope set just arrived."

"That's great!" she exclaimed.

"By the way," asked Charles inquisitively, "did you figure out what I wrote in the letter?" The excitement over the microscope and the telescope was short-lived.

"Of course," replied Emma. "After all, I was the one who created it. I'm impressed that you've learned how to write it so fast."

It was not that long ago that Emma came up with a secret way for her and Charles to communicate with each other. She recreated the alphabet using symbols to represent letters. Charles was still learning how to decode and write the messages.

"Emma," called a voice from outside her room.

"Oh, Charles," said Emma, "my mom is calling me. I'll have to call you back later. Bye." She hung up the telephone.

"Come in, mom," invited Emma.

The door opened to reveal a woman covered in flour. Unlike her mother, Emma had dark-colored hair, and after thirteen trips around the Sun, she was already as tall as her mother. The features of her face more closely resembled her father, although you could not tell that with all of the flour on her mother's face. From pictures of her father, Emma could see where she got her appearance.

The most unmistakable staple of her mother was a towel wrapped around her left hand, indicating that dinner was being prepared. In her right hand was a dirty, white envelope. On her face was a look of concern.

Holding up the envelope, and pretending that there was nothing wrong with her appearance, Susannah said worriedly, "I found this in the mailbox. Strange, there is no return address or stamp. It must have fallen to the ground. There is some dirt and sand on it." There was suspicion in Emma's mother's voice. She added, "It looks *familiar.*"

Emma gave her mother a reassuring smile. She got up from the chair and met her at the door. Emma brushed her mother's nose with her finger, giggling, "You missed a spot." She then took the envelope, holding it by the edges with her index finger and thumb.

Emma did not know what to make of the envelope, as she returned to her desk. It was the third time that she had ever been sent a letter in the mail. Her mother had her reasons to be concerned, especially considering what happened after the last envelope that Emma received.

Surveying Emma's room, Susannah said, "I see you've made space on your mantle."

The mantle that she was referring to was Emma's trophy mantle, above her computer desk. On it, Emma displayed all of her track and field medals, an MVP award, an athlete-of-the-year trophy, a volunteering ribbon, and a special junior constable plaque given to her by police chief O'Brian. One of her most prized awards, however, was kept on a chain around her neck. The space that her mother was referring to was right in the middle of all of her medals and awards. Hopefully, in a few days, there will be a football championship trophy.

"Do you like it?" asked Susannah, pointing to the package on the desk.

"It looks better than my old one!" replied Emma excitedly.

Before she turned around to leave, she said, "Don't be too long. Dinner will be ready soon." She then added, referring to the microscope, "Let's try to keep this one."

"Thank you, mom," replied Emma with an appreciative smile.

Emma did not take her eyes off the envelope since taking it from her mother. She had received two similar envelopes, one nine months ago and another six months ago. It could not be a coincidence that her new microscope set arrived on the same day as the envelope.

Emma was nervous and excited to see what was inside the envelope. Glancing over at the clock on the wall, she knew that there were still ten minutes before supper, even though the clock was not working.

She began by tearing a small piece of the envelope along the edge, next to where the stamp would be. After inserting a pencil into the hole, she tore open the envelope. Chief O'Brian had told her stories of her father opening his mail that way. Slowly and carefully, she peered inside before pulling out a piece of paper. She carefully placed the empty envelope on her desk. She did not want to get her fingerprints onto it or to disturb any that were already there.

Carefully, she opened the letter. She was amazed as to what was written in it. "What is this supposed to mean?" she asked herself out loud. She read the letter again and again, but could not understand it.

"Emma," called her mother from the bottom of the stairs, "dinner in five minutes!"

Emma quickly folded the letter and carefully placed it back in the envelope. She pulled out the top-center drawer of her desk and gently placed it inside before closing it.

CHAPTER 4
The First Letter

As Emma was putting the envelope away, she remembered the first letter that she received. It arrived almost nine months ago. Except for the sand and dirt, both envelopes looked identical. Neither one contained an address or stamp. Emma knew that they were hand-delivered by the sender because the envelopes simply said: **Attn: Emma**. There were also no identifying marks or fingerprints on the first letter. It simply contained the following:

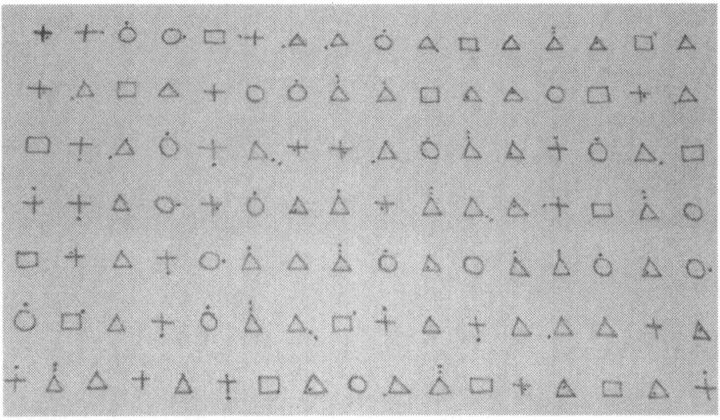

Emma was puzzled by the contents of the letter because there were no instructions. All she saw were a series of hand-written shapes. After failing to crack the code by herself, she enlisted Charles, Fitzroy and Gilbert. They all gathered at Emma's house. Just as Emma was about to place the crypt down on the dining room table, it suddenly began to rain.

Charles and Fitzroy did not know where to begin. Gilbert glanced over at the piece of paper. It did not take long for him to begin unraveling the crypt. Gilbert recognized that there were only four basic shapes: crosses, circles, rectangles, and triangles. The dot or dots in and around each shape created many possible combinations. He reasoned, "Since there are four distinct shapes, this could only mean that the alphabet can be divided into four distinct groups."

Fitzroy thought about it for a second and asked, "How can you divide the alphabet into four?"

Gilbert explained, "Circles, crosses, triangles, and rectangles are made up of one, two, three, and four lines, respectively. Every letter in the alphabet consists of one, two, three, or four lines. We can, therefore, group all of the letters into these four distinct groups."

This is exactly what Emma proceeded to do. She organized all of the letters of the alphabet into one of four groups.

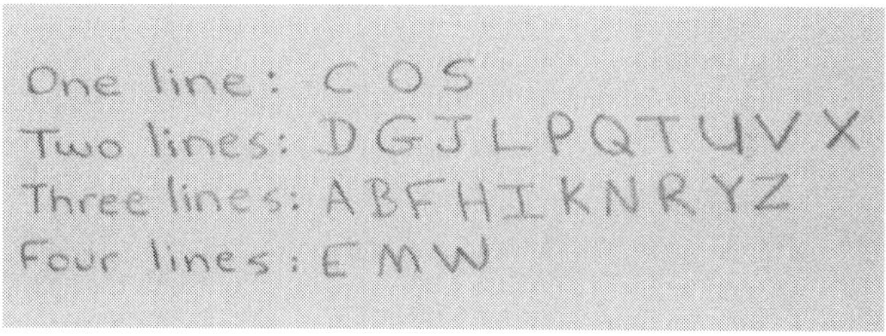

Gilbert then explained that the position of the dot or dots indicates which letter of the alphabet they represent. Looking at the crypt, Charles raised a question of how to interpret the dots.

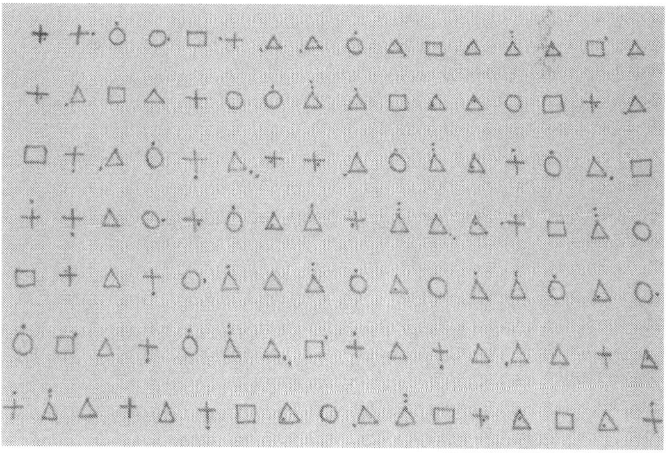

Gilbert's keen eyes noticed that of all of the rectangle shapes that were used in the crypt, only two patterns emerged. Of the three letters - EMW - which are represented by rectangles, only two of them were actually used.

Fitzroy suggested that only the letters **E** and **M** were used. He further reasoned that the rectangle with no dot could be the letter **E** because more of them were used in the crypt. He knew that the letter E was the most widely used letter in the alphabet. Although it was mere conjecture, he believed that he had figured out the pattern.

Emma had to explain it again to Charles, as he seemed confused. She said, "Each shape represents a group of letters. Each dot represents a different letter within that group. The dots go clockwise from the outside of the shape and continue on the inside, in the same manner. Where there are too many letters to be represented by one dot, he has used two dots."

Fitzroy agreed with Emma's explanation. In reality, Charles did not need help to follow Fitzroy's logic. He could see it as plain as day. He simply wants Emma to pay more attention to him. Charles knew that while his relationship with Emma was just as a friend, she and Fitzroy shared something more.

Once they had figured out which shapes matched with which letters, they quickly translated the crypt. While the others called out each of the letters, Emma wrote them under its symbol.

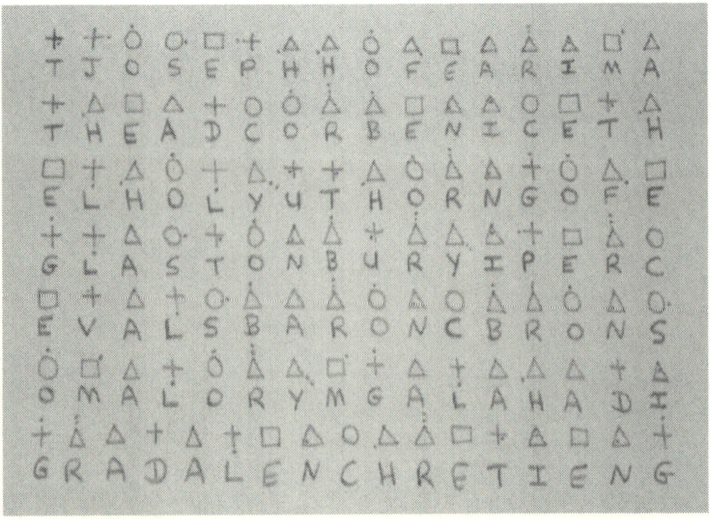

It was indeed a very long string of letters. Emma questioned Fitzroy's logic of how to read the crypt because the solution was still hidden.

While Charles remained silent, he was smiling on the inside because of the manner in which Emma questioned Fitzroy. Even though they were friends, Fitzroy always made him feel uneasy, especially around Emma. It was the first time that she had ever openly disagreed with him. The bright blue bursts of lightning and ear-shattering crashes of thunder coincided with their disagreement.

Gilbert was the most perceptive one in the group. He always solves Emma's puzzles faster than anyone else. If anyone could figure out the crypt, it was Gilbert.

He picked up a pencil and pulled the crypt closer. He began to draw lines under some of the letters. Everyone looked on with interest to see what he had come up with. While Charles did not like what Gilbert was about to say, he was more devastated to learn that Fitzroy was correct all along.

After he was finished, Gilbert informed everyone, somberly whispering, "There is more than one clue here."

Although no one else had figured it out, his tone of voice concerned everyone, especially Emma. Gilbert's eyes guided everyone towards the crypt.

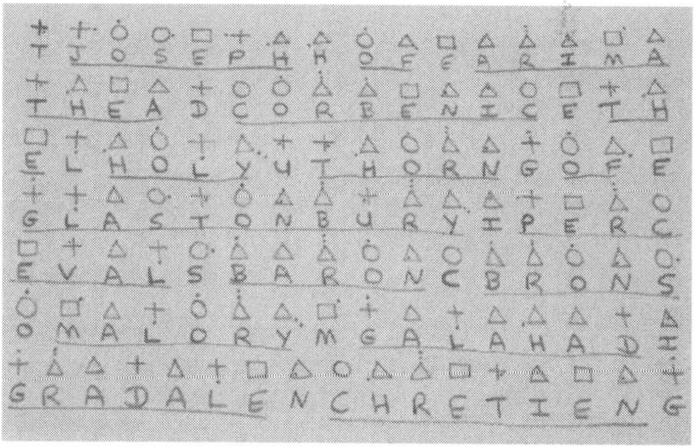

He said, pointing to the underlined words as he spoke, "Here is what I have uncovered so far: **JOSEPH OF ARIMATHEA,**

CORBENIC, THE HOLY THORN OF GLASTONBURY, PERCEVAL, BARON, BRONS, MALORY, GALAHAD, GRADALE, CHRETIEN."

Gilbert had mentioned that there was more than one clue.

Emma inquired hesitantly, "What's the other clue?"

With a shallow breath, he warned, "You guys need to see this!"

"What is it, Gilbert?" asked Emma nervously, as everyone moved in closer to see what he had uncovered. Gilbert stared blankly at the piece of paper in his hand. He pointed to the extra letters that separated the words and names but said nothing. He seemed transfixed.

Emma pried the piece of paper from his hand. She looked at the letters that were not underlined. These letters contained a secret message, a warning. She wrote down all of the extra letters.

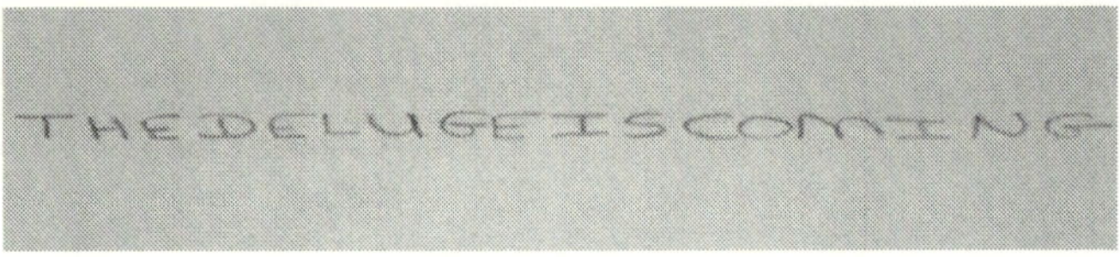

She whispered for everyone to hear, "**THE DELUGE IS COMING!**"

Everyone paused for a moment. They were all puzzled. No one knew what it meant, but everyone sensed that danger was near.

No one said a word until Charles wondered out loud, "What is a deluge?"

"A flood!" immediately cited Emma. She warned, "A great flood!" The crashing thunder high above emphasized just how great a deluge really is.

Everyone glanced to his or her left and right without moving their head. No one said anything. They all understood that it was a warning, but no one knew what it meant.

The silence was broken when Charles inquired, "What are all of these names?"

Everyone looked at Emma. While Gilbert recognized the names in the crypt, only she could make the connection. She was the historian in the group.

Emma began, "**Joseph of Arimathea**, a relative of **Brons**, was the great uncle of Jesus Christ. **Corbenic** is a mysterious and magical castle in the time of King Arthur. The **Holy Thorn of Glastonbury** is a sacred tree, alive since the time of Jesus. It only flowers twice a year, once at Christmas and again at Easter. **Perceval** is a story written by **Chretien**. **Robert de Baron** was a French poet. **Sir Thomas Mallory** of Newbold Revel in Warwickshire was a thirteenth-century English writer. **Galahad** was one of the Knights of the Round Table in the time of King Arthur. **Gradale**..."

Before Emma could finish, Charles interrupted, "But how are they connected?"

Emma explained, "Chretien is one of the first to mention the gradale in his work Perceval. Baron introduces us to Joseph of Arimathea, from whose staff sprung the Holy Thorn of Glastonbury. Joseph used the gradale to catch Christ's blood after he was pierced in the side while on the cross. Thomas Mallory wrote about Sir Galahad and his quest for the gradale, which was protected by Brons at Corbenic Castle."

Charles, like everyone else, was still confused. Yet, one word kept coming up. He asked, "What is gradale?"

Emma explained, "In Latin, it means grail."

To which Fitzroy asked, "As in the Holy Grail?"

"Yes!" she affirmed.

"So," wondered Gilbert, "what is the connection between the Holy Grail and the deluge?"

Fitzroy suggested, "There is a rumor that Samantha Wallace was conducting experiments on the Holy Grail when her sister was killed. Some believe that the *hum* is connected with it. Since we can no longer hear the hum, maybe the Grail is free. Maybe, someone is using it to create all of these earthquakes and tsunamis."

While Charles and Gilbert did not know what he was talking about, Fitzroy scared Emma with his suggestion. Unlike the others, she saw a real danger since their town was downstream from a dam. Emma wondered why Fitzroy would even make such a suggestion. Even if he was not serious, she knew that it was not something to joke about. How he learned of the *hum* in the first place, was a more disturbing matter altogether. There is only one person alive who has ever heard this beautiful noise. He lived next door to Emma. Except for her, he has never told anyone else about it. While Fitzroy may have read about it in history books, how he knew that it could be connected to earthquakes and floods worried Emma. There was only an idea, a theory that it could be. Fitzroy seemed certain that it could.

Of course, no one knew the connection. Not Emma, Charles, Fitzroy, or Gilbert. It would be another three months before Emma would receive another letter. By then, Fitzroy and his family had already left for Australia. While Emma missed him dearly, she knew that he had to go back. After being laid off, Fitzroy's parents could not find work, and moving back to their native Australia was the only answer. The past six months were the happiest time for Charles, if only because Fitzroy was halfway around the world. Though, of course, Emma kept in constant contact with him.

One day, Emma invited Charles to a special place behind their school, next to Old Oak. Old Oak, as it was affectionately known, is the tallest and oldest tree in town. Some claimed that it was alive since the time of Christ. It was so large that there was talk of cutting it down but Mr. Lyell insisted that no such action be taken. Before Emma got there, Charles hid a specially prepared basket at the base of Old Oak. He wanted to impress her, now that Fitzroy was gone.

When Emma arrived, Charles beamed with confidence, even though he was extremely nervous. He had a speech prepared and well-rehearsed. Before he was able to say anything, however, Emma told him that someone in their class liked him. Her name was Catherine. She encouraged him to talk to her.

Charles was completely devastated, but he put on a brave face. After Emma left, he retrieved the basket full of treats and threw it in a nearby garbage bin. Charles knew that Emma was sending him a hint. So, even though he was heartbroken, he played along. His only wish was for her to know what he already knew. However, he knows that he must be patient. What has been revealed to him by Mr. Lyell must be kept a secret, until the time is right.

Chapter 5
The Blue Mustang

During supper, Susannah asked Emma whom the letter was from. She told her mother that she did not know, as there was no return address on the inside or any mention of the sender. However, she reassured her mother that it was not from *Him*.

Susannah was relieved. The second letter that Emma received six months ago caused her much distress. She was worried that this would be a repeat, especially considering that her new microscope set had just arrived.

One year ago, Emma helped to bring down several high-ranking political leaders and police officers during the Aldaine case. Not long after, she solved the case of the missing trophy. Two weeks later, she helped Chief O'Brian with the Photo Murders. Her best work, however, involved a most tragic event.

Emma and Charles are the only ones who are junior constables at the local police station. This was not always the case. Beagle Abbey was once a junior constable, too. He was considered to be the best of the three. Chief O'Brian was very impressed with his knowledge and detective skills. He excelled well beyond what Emma and Charles were capable of. He seemed to have insights into things before anyone else, even the police. No one could figure out how he did it.

Emma was not fooled by his tricks, however. As it turned out, Beagle did not have any special abilities at all. He was simply a cheat. Emma caught him in the act of planting evidence. When the Chief found out, he banned Beagle from the police station. With his badge taken away, and coupled with his humiliation at the quiz tournament, Beagle transferred to another school, on the other side of town. He now attends Bowmore Public School, the same school that Emma will be playing against on Saturday in the football championship game. It is the first time that they will see each other since the quiz tournament. Rumors are circulating that he is planning his revenge by beating Emma's team in the championship game.

After supper, Emma asked her mother if she had bought the flowers.

Susannah replied hesitantly, "It's in the family room, but I can't come with you this evening."

Susannah sounded almost apologetic. She knew that it was not what Emma wanted to hear.

Emma was taken aback for a moment. She did not say anything. Emma knew that this day would come but she was not expecting it to be so soon.

"I'm sorry mom," pleaded Emma for clarification, "what did you say?"

"Robert and I," explained Susannah, "we're going to see a play tonight. I totally forgot that tonight was the night. It was only after I picked up the flowers, that I realized that I had made plans with him. The play is only on for one night. Sorry!"

Susannah turned to walk away. Emma followed her.

"Robert!" exclaimed Emma. "Who's Robert?" She seemed intrigued.

"He is just someone I met recently," replied Susannah, blushing. "You will meet him soon."

"What about Fred?" asked Emma.

Susannah paused in mid-stride. She spun around, looked Emma squarely in the eyes and stated sternly, with her fingers pointed, "The Fred-incident is not going to happen again. Do I make myself clear?"

The football championship game, the microscope and the letter drifted well back into the recesses of Emma's thoughts. She did hear her mother correctly but she could not believe what she was hearing. She asked, "How can you possibly forget?"

Susannah did not respond verbally but with a wink. The argument was over. Emma then realized her mistake. Her mother had pulled the wool over her eyes. The only way Susannah could date anyone is if Emma did not have a say. The microscope was her Waterloo, her Achilles heel. She never saw it coming.

A few months ago, in exchange for a new microscope set, Emma promised to make a sacrifice. She agreed to give up something. Susannah told her that she would know it by a wink.

Although Emma was upset at her mother, she knew that a good promise was a promise kept. She was happy to have her new microscope set. Besides, even though Fred was persistent, he did not last long. How difficult can Robert be?

When Emma was ready, she told her mother goodbye, put on her shoes and left the house quietly with the wrapped bouquet. She went into the garage and got her helmet and bicycle. She placed the flowers in the front basket of the bicycle, as she always does.

The ride was peaceful and contemplative. The soft spring breeze helped to clear her mind, as she rode down the street. Emma wondered how many touchdowns she was going to score on Saturday or whether there were any fingerprints on the envelope and letter. She also thought about what she will say when she sees Robert for the first time. The thought crossed her mind that she may even like him but she brushed it away like the small fly that was buzzing over her head.

Emma rode to the end of her street and then turned left onto Arc Drive. As she did, her friends Mary and John waved to her. They were taking their children, James and Joseph, out for a walk. Emma was very fond of the boys. Although they were born just two minutes apart, they are not twins. Not identical twins or fraternal twins. Most people find this fact hard to believe but Emma knows how this came to be.

After the third stoplight, she made a right turn and rode up the hill towards Angel Bridge. Emma could never quite figure out why it was called Angel Bridge. Some residents say that they felt protected when crossing the bridge as if an angel was looking down on them. Others claimed that the bridge had created many angels. So, protective fences were erected to make sure that no one could go past the railings. From Angel Bridge, it was onward towards her school. The Museum of Natural Science was not far beyond that. Samson's river, one of her favorite fishing spots, was a short distance from her destination.

As Emma rode past the river, she noticed a police car heading towards her. She stopped to look at it. Something seemed odd. While the officer had the siren on, there was no noise and the car was not going very fast. As it passed her, there were several black cars, with tinted windows, following it. None of the other vehicles had a license plate. Emma was unaware of anyone important coming to town. She wondered what was going on. Samantha Wallace's name suddenly came to mind. A lot of strange things have been happening in Silent Hum since her sister's death.

As Emma rode, she noticed a car following her in the rearview mirror. It had been behind her since she turned onto Arc Drive. The driver had kept his distance, especially when Emma stopped to watch the police car. With a long stretch of road ahead and no other cars in sight, the blue Mustang suddenly roared to life. It was the same car that she saw earlier in the day. The scream of the engine gave Emma cause for concern. She began to peddle faster.

Emma shifted her bicycle to the highest gear. She got up from the seat and forced her legs to peddle faster, as her bicycle rocked from side to side. The Mustang gained ground and was on her heels. Up ahead, was the entrance to the trail. Emma peddled as fast as she could. The wheels of the car were next to her back tire. She turned around to glimpse the driver. All she saw were a pair of dark sunglasses.

The trail was not far away. With all her might, Emma grabbed onto the handlebar and jumped her bicycle from the road and onto the sidewalk. The bouquet floated into the air as the bicycle hit the pavement. With one hand on the handlebar, Emma snatched the bouquet and placed it back into the basket. The car drove up next to her, with the pungent odor of gasoline permeating the air. She could lose him if only she could make it to the bicycle trail.

The road ahead separated from the sidewalk, one led to the top of the bridge while the other led down to the trail. The driver sped past Emma up the hill to the top of the bridge. Emma knew that he was trying to get to the pathway to intercept her. The driver got out and raced down the stairs, heading towards the trail's entrance. Emma rode as fast as she could.

Down the stairs the driver raced. A fence separated him and the pathway. He attempted to leap over it but his foot hit the top of the fence. He stumbled onto the pathway and landed on his back. As Emma approached, she summoned all her might and jumped her bicycle over him. The front tire cleared him but the back tire came down pressing against his face, breaking his sunglasses. She did not stop or look back but she could see him wincing in pain in the rearview mirror. She was certain that he was somehow connected with the letters, the Wallace sisters and whoever were in the black tinted cars.

Chapter 6
Mary Smith

When Emma reached her destination, she braced her bicycle outside the entrance. She removed the bouquet and proceeded to the gates. As she stepped through, she felt a sense of loneliness as the cold wind rushed past her. She had never been here by herself before. With caution, she proceeded. When she reached where her father was, she laid the flowers on the ground.

"Hi dad," she whispered. "It's me, Emma, your favorite daughter." She giggled before continuing. "Then again, I'm your only daughter, so I better be your favorite." She smiled, knowing that her father was laughing at her comment.

As she spoke, she removed the fallen leaves from around the flowers that she brought. Mr. Lyell would remind her, "We still need to be taken care of, even after we are gone. This will ensure that we are never forgotten."

Emma always liked to keep her father's site free from leaves and other debris that the wind pushes around. Ever since Emma could remember, she and her mother would visit and make sure that it was kept clean.

Startled, Emma quickly turned around and looked behind her. There was a loud sound not too far from her. She could see someone dressed all in black, kneeling down and crying. This was normal, in such a place, so she turned back around to face her father.

"I guess you're wondering why mom isn't here," she said disappointedly, looking down at the flowers. "Robert! That's all I'm going to say. I mean, in some cultures, it’s customary to wait *forever* before you start seeing other people. Is that too much to ask? Well, at least she didn't forget to pick up the flowers."

Emma could not concentrate on what she was saying. There was too much noise coming from the person a short distance away. She sat down, so her father could hear her better. "As I was saying, we're both doing well since the last time we came to visit." She then remembered her microscope. "Oh, I almost forgot to tell you," she said with excitement, "my new microscope set came in the mail today." Regarding the envelope, she said, "I also got this weird letter. I don't know who sent it or what it means. It's in the form of a poem, but it seems like a riddle or some kind of clue. I'll have to call Charles when I get home and ask him if he can come to school early tomorrow." She informed her father sadly, "There was another earthquake and tsunami earlier today. No one knows what's causing them. Every day this week there has been one. It was reported in the news that a lot of people are missing." She did not say anything about the car that was chasing after her.

There was another loud cry. Emma was surprised because it sounded like a man. She was certain that it was a woman from the way the person was dressed. Emma could no longer stand the crying. She stood up and said, "I'll be right back, dad."

Making sure not to step on any of the flowers on the ground, she made her way over to the other person. She did not want to startle him or her, so she intentionally stepped on the fallen leaves and twigs so that their crunch and snap would give her away. Emma stopped when she was certain that the other person was aware of her presence.

"Was she your wife?" asked Emma quietly.

The person did not raise their head, but sobbed, "She was a stranger, but she was kind."

Her guess was correct. It was a man.

Emma was confused. She asked, "You mean to say that you are not related to her?"

Wiping his eyes on his sleeve, he replied, "She was placed in this world for a purpose. Some would say that she was chosen."

Chosen for what or by whom, Emma was unsure. She did not quite understand what he was saying. He did not raise his head but remained knelt beside a similar bouquet of flowers that Emma had brought with her. When Emma noticed it, she said, "You must have gone to the same florist that my mom went to. They're quite lovely."

"Not compared to her," he answered. He kept his head down, never turning around to look at Emma.

She inquired, "May I ask you a question?"

He nodded, giving her permission.

She said, looking at the headstone, "You are not related to her, but each month for almost seven years now, you have come to visit her and bring a bouquet of flowers."

"It has been thirteen years," he replied in a quiet voice, politely correcting her.

"Oh!" exclaimed Emma. "Has it been that long? I don't remember a single time that my mom and I have come here and not seen you."

The first time Emma remembered seeing him was when she was about six years old. She had not paid any attention to him in the past. They had never spoken to each other before. She was unaware of who he was until now.

He reiterated, "She was a wonderful woman. The two of you could have been mistaken for sisters. She was very young when she died. Some say that a heavy burden was placed upon her, one that she could not bear. In any construction, there are hammers and nails and various other tools and machines. None is more important than the other. The building cannot stand unless each plays its part. Our purpose is to play our part."

Emma was unsure of why he was telling her all this. She searched for clues in what he was saying but could find none. The way he spoke, reminded her of the letter that she received earlier. She began to consider the possibility that he was the sender.

Her train of thought was interrupted when he inquired, "Where is your mother?"

"She is out with Robert," replied Emma disappointedly.

He added, "The living has the living, but the deceased has no one."

Emma agreed with him, saying, "That's what I've been trying to tell her. But she insists that it has been long enough. She hasn't even let me see who he is yet. I guess that's because of what happened to Fred." The memories of Fred played in her mind. With a smile on her face, she whispered to herself, "No, I don't think we'll be forgetting Fred anytime soon."

"Now," said the stranger, wiping away his tears, "I'm intrigued. I must know what happened."

"I mean," began Emma, "how was I supposed to know that Fred didn't like spicy food? Well, actually, my mom did mention it to me. I guess I just forgot. But, the funny part was when he began coughing and ran into the family room."

"What happened there?" he asked.

She said, bursting out laughing, "He drank all the water in my fishbowl, including my goldfish."

"Now that is funny," agreed the stranger, chuckling.

"Well," she said, "the good thing about my mom is that I get to choose who she goes out with." However, because she promised to give up something, she did not get a chance to choose this time.

"You must have a wonderful mother," said the stranger. Without saying another word, he got to his feet and began to walk towards the entrance. Within a few seconds, he disappeared behind a few large trees. Before Emma could react, he was gone.

It was not polite the way he left, thought Emma. She was happy, however, as his tears were gone. Her story about Fred cheered him up, as she had anticipated. However, it was not an exact retelling of the Fred-incident because Emma never had a goldfish.

Emma remembered the day when her mother told her that her father had died. The clock in her room stopped on the exact second when she was told about it and has not worked since, even after the batteries were changed. Emma was too young to remember exactly what she felt, but it made her very sad.

Emma was born on the night that her father was shot and killed. He was a young police detective. While responding to a call, he was accidentally shot by his partner as they tried to apprehend the suspect. Emma, however, never accepted this explanation. The evidence just did not add up. While Emma did not know her father, she always wanted to follow in his footsteps. Everything about police work fascinated her. She was especially interested in finger-printing and identification.

In her room, Emma keeps fingerprint samples of everyone that she has met in the past year. She usually asks them to hold or touch something. Then, later on, she would carefully extract their fingerprint and make a copy of it. She had spent many hours looking at them under her old microscope. In total, she had over one hundred prints, mostly of friends and classmates.

A few months ago, Emma and Charles became celebrities at the local police station. Someone had stolen a trophy from her school. They followed a few officers around while they conducted their investigation. Emma's keen eyes noticed what appeared to be a stain on the trophy-window casing. She took a piece of clear tape and lifted a fingerprint off the window. Surprisingly, it matched one of the prints that she had on file. When she told Chief O'Brian whom she suspected stole the trophy, he conducted an investigation and was able to recover it. Emma and Charles were made honorary junior constables and each received a plaque for their efforts.

The Photo Murder case haunted Chief O'Brian until he discussed it with Emma. Two men had rented a private island from Alfred Huxley. When he returned one week later, he found both of them shot to death by the same gun in an apparent murder-suicide. Mr. Huxley told the police that the two men had an argument when they first arrived.

When Emma and Chief O'Brian visited the island, she noticed a photo of the two men in Alfred's cabin. As Emma looked at the photo, she was baffled because the men looked happy. The men were from her church. She also knew that they could not afford to rent a private island as they did not have jobs. Emma asked the Chief to arrest Mr. Huxley on suspicion of murder. Detectives later found eight bodies buried on the island. They were all of men who had gone missing.

When the Chief asked Emma how she knew that Alfred Huxley committed the murders, she said that it was because of the photo. She explained that the photo was taken using an old instant camera shot about twenty feet away from the subjects. Emma knew that these cameras required a photographer to operate them. A third person must have taken the picture. The men were not alone on the island. But what was the motive for killing all ten men? Faced with the evidence against him, Mr. Huxley later admitted that he was homophobic. He invited homeless gay men to the island and murdered them because he knew that no one would be looking for them. Emma could only imagine what Huxley would think of Tessship, being a transgendered student. Alfred Huxley is currently serving ten consecutive life sentences in prison with no chance of parole.

A third case that Emma helped to solve, involved a young couple and their two-month-old son. The father had unexpectedly taken his life on Angel Bridge. His wife was so distraught by the incident, that she called the police before taking her own life. When the officers arrived, they found a crying infant next to his mother's lifeless body. No one could figure out why the young couple did this, especially with all of the support that they had.

During her investigation, Emma found out that the couple was inseparable since they were about ten years old and had never spent a day apart. They were always seen hand-in-hand and very much happy and in love. That is why she was so intrigued by the case.

Emma learned that the baby's father had visited a clinic only a few days before taking his life. She asked Chief O'Brian to find out why he was there. The Chief learned that the father had a DNA test done. Emma then suggested to the Chief to have a DNA test done on the mother. It was only after the Chief visited the clinic to get the results, that it all became clear. Everyone was surprised and shocked by what he learned.

Unknown to the mother, the father found out that the baby's DNA did not match his. Emma could only imagine the father's heartbreak when he got the results. She began to understand why he made the decision that he did. Not knowing why her husband took his own life, the baby's mother could not go on living without him. So, she made the same decision. What the Chief found out, and what the father did not know, is that his wife's DNA did not match the baby's either. *The couple had left the hospital with the wrong baby!* Emma's only satisfaction was in reuniting the baby with his rightful parents. The couple chose to keep both babies and raise them as their own. The names of the children were James and Joseph. Emma is one of very few in Silent Hum who knows why the boys, born just two minutes apart, are not twins.

Over the next few months, Emma was given greater access to the police station. She spent most of her weekends there. She did her homework at the station and she was safe there. So, her mother *hesitantly* approved of it. Chief O'Brian, a close friend of Susannah, assured her that Emma would be safe.

Susannah was conflicted about letting Emma visit the police station. The more time she spent there, the more she would want to become a police officer. She feared that Emma would one day try to find her father's killer and she was very fearful of what may happen.

Maybe it was just a phase, thought Susannah. This was something that would only last a little while and then Emma would find another interest. Quite the opposite had occurred. Emma's interest in police work increased exponentially.

Six months ago, Susannah's worst fears were realized. While following a set of clues, Charles fell and injured himself. He spent two days in a hospital and several weeks recovering at home. Both Emma and Charles had their honorary junior constable badges taken away. Emma's mother took her microscope set away and Charles's father took his telescope set away. They were both barred from the police station for six months. Part of their probation stipulated that they did not get into any trouble during that time. They both heeded the warning and kept their promise. As a reward for their commitment, they were both given new instruments to mark the end of their probation.

Chapter 7
The Second Letter

Emma remembered well why she and Charles lost their microscope and telescope. It happened six months ago. Emma received a second ominous, unmarked white envelope, similar to the one that she opened earlier. It was an invitation that the newly appointed special junior constables could not pass up.

The letter contained the following:

e21g14o20d **5n15c** 19d1e8b **15w20a** 14o26a13a26 **e8t25**
s20e5m24 **e12i14w** 5h20v **5r5h23u** 19n9g5b20 **e19a3s**
18u15y18 m16e5r8t17 **t1p** 25a4r21t1s15 **n15n** 13u5s21m13
y18o20s9h12 l1r21t1n11 e8t10 **o20i** 5m15c8
s5v9t3e20e4g 5u18t6 **e2e** 15t4 t14a23c **21o25b** 6i1

There were no instructions provided. However, Emma knew that Gilbert could crack the code. In his mind, Gilbert isolated the letters and the numbers in the crypt. He instantly recognized that the numbers ranged from 1 to 26. Since there are 26 letters in the alphabet, he knew that he had to substitute the numbers for letters. This is exactly what he proceeded to do.

eugnotd **enoc** sdaehb **owta** nozamaz **ehty**
steemx **elinw** ehtv **erehwu** snigebt **esacs** ruoyr
mpeerhtq **tap** yadrutaso **non** muesumm **yrotsihl**
larutank **ehtj** oti **emoch** sevitcetedg **eurtf**
ebe **otd** tnawc **uoyb** fia

After examining what they had uncovered, Gilbert recognized that the end of all of the letter-groupings contained a letter from the alphabet in descending order.

eugnot**d** eno**c** sdaeh**b** owt**a** nozama**z** eht**y**
steem**x** elin**w** eht**v** erehw**u** snigeb**t** esac**s** ruoy**r**
mpeerht**q** ta**p** yadrutas**o** no**n** muesum**m** yrotsih**l**
laruta**nk** eht**j** ot**i** emoc**h** sevitcete**dg** eurt**f**
eb**e** ot**d** tnaw**c** uoy**b** fi**a**

He theorized that since they were *all* in descending order, they were only there as a distraction. So, he removed all of them. Often in a crypt, there are extra clues added to delay the solver from decoding the message.

eugnot eno sdaeh owt nozama eht
steem elin eht erehw snigeb esac ruoy
mpeerht ta yadrutas no **muesum** yrotsih
larutan eht ot emoc sevitceted eurt eb ot tnaw uoy fi

They were one step closer to solving the crypt. While most of the words were unrecognizable, some seemed obvious, like **muesum**, or as Charles figured **museum**. It was simply spelled backward. They then realized that all of the words were spelled backward. After rearranging all of the letter-groupings, they found words that they recognized.

tongue one heads two amazon the
meets nile the were begins case your
threepm at saturday on museum history
natural the to come detectives true be to want you if

The crypt did not give up its secrets easily. All of the words were there, but the message was still incomprehensible. Charles wanted to try and rearrange the words but Gilbert knew that it was not necessary. The clue to unscrambling the message, he surmised, was in the original crypt. The clue was in the extra letters that he removed.

eugnot**d** enoc sdaehb owta nozamaz ehty
steemx elinw ehtv erehwu snigebt esacs ruoyr
mpeerhtq tap yadrutaso non muesumm yrotsihl
larutank ehtj oti emoch sevitcetedg
eurtf ebe otd tnawc uoyb fi**a**

Gilbert had solved it. He said, "Since 'a' starts the alphabet, 'a' must start the crypt. All we have to do is read the words backward, starting with **if** and ending with **tongue**."

Emma could not believe it was so simple. She read the message for everyone to hear,

"If you want to be true detectives, come to the Natural History Museum on Saturday at three pm. Your case begins where the Nile meets the Amazon. Two heads, one tongue."

They had uncovered the crypt with one day to spare. It was an intriguing invitation, one that Charles and Gilbert accepted. They did not know what to expect when they got to the museum or what the last two statements referred to. However, they knew that if they arrived at the museum at the specified time, they may find some clues. They were both eager to learn who was sending them the letters. If they did not accept the case, they may never know.

Charles volunteered at the museum and he knew every square inch of it. He encouraged Emma to accept the invitation. She was not so certain. Even Gilbert, as timid as he was, was excited to see what they would find. Finally, Emma agreed.

The next day, Susannah drove them to the museum, knowing nothing of the crypt. They arrived a few minutes early. While the three of them wandered off in one direction, Susannah went in the opposite direction. They all agreed to meet up in the cafeteria in a few hours.

Their first task was to figure out where to start. The clue said that their case begins where the Nile and Amazon meet. They all knew that it was not possible for the Nile River and the Amazon River to meet, but there must be a connection. The only place that they could start, figured Charles, was at the South American exhibit, where the Amazon River would be. The African exhibit was closed for renovations, so he ruled out the Nile River. At the entrance of the exhibit, they all held hands and repeated: "Together, for each other!"

The moment they entered the museum, Snevyl, a 13-year-old volunteer guard, noticed them on the security monitor. He was competing with Charles for the volunteer-of-the-month award. He wanted to see what they were up to. If Charles does anything out of the ordinary, he could issue a ticket and disqualify him for the award.

There were two distinct differences between Charles and Snevyl. One, Snevyl was not as athletic as Charles due to his asthma. He gets winded quite easily. Two, Snevyl followed every code of law, down to the smallest detail. He always carried his notepads around his waist, along with an ample supply of sharp pencils. He used them to write down every indiscretion of the museum's patrons, from littering to running. Charles, on the other hand, was less strict.

Peering from behind statues and artifacts, Snevyl followed them closely. When Emma and her friends stopped, he stopped. When they moved, so did he, often covering his face with his notepad so they could not see him.

At exactly 3 pm, the codebreakers walked into the South American exhibit. They diligently searched for clues that connected the Nile and Amazon. It took less than a minute before Charles recognized that an Amazon milk frog and a Nile delta frog were staring at each other, one with its tongue sticking out. This seemed the most likely place to start, as it matched the second part of the clue: "**Two heads, one tongue**."

Upon closer inspection, Charles noticed that a rolled-up piece of paper was on the frog's tongue. He nudged Emma to take the piece of paper and see what it said. They made sure that no one was looking before proceeding.

Snevyl was absolutely appalled when Emma touched the exhibit. He began to write her a ticket immediately. His furrowed brow and pouted lips expressed his displeasure as he wrote.

Emma took the piece of paper, unrolled it and read,

"Congratulations, you have made it. Choose the frog on the left or right to continue your mission.

Oprah Winfrey
Leonardo da Vinci
Aristotle
Sir Garfield Sobers
Barack Obama

You have 20 minutes to find all eight clues, one in each exhibit. The missing exhibit is your final destination. After 20 minutes, the fire alarm will sound."

"We better hurry," instructed Emma. "We only have 20 minutes to find and uncover all of the clues."

"We should go to the right," immediately suggested Charles.

"No," corrected Emma. "We have to go to the left because the only thing these people have in common is that they are all left-handed."

"Good enough for me," stated Gilbert.

They all ran to the next exhibit on the left, the Canadian exhibit. Gilbert kept track of time on his watch. They had 18 minutes left. As they enter, Emma notices a nanulak and a wolverine. The nanulak was standing on its hind legs, while the wolverine was standing on all four legs. Similar to the two frogs, the nanulak's mouth was closed while the wolverine had its mouth open and tongue visible. Emma noticed a similar rolled-up piece of paper in its mouth. It was the second clue:

Angel
Tugela
Utigord
Yosemite
Kaieteur

"We have to go to the right," said Emma. "These are among the highest waterfalls in the world. The nanulak is taller than the wolverine and it's on the right."

Snevyl had caught up to them just in time to see Emma taking the piece of paper. Though he was breathing heavily and hunched over, he began to write her another ticket. As he wrote, he noticed that they were on the move again.

They all ran to the right and into the Arctic exhibit with 15 minutes to go. Charles quickly pointed to an arctic fox and a snowy owl that were facing each other. In the fox's mouth was another clue:

Vatican City
Monaco
Nauru
Tuvalu
San Marino

"They're getting easier," informed Gilbert. He pointed to the left, saying, "These are among the smallest countries in the world. With its wingspan, the snowy owl is much larger than the fox."

Just as Snevyl entered, the others were leaving. He could only imagine what acts of desecration they may have performed. He began writing his third ticket, including one to all of them for running. He labored to keep up with them.

The next exhibit was the Australian. They entered exhausted and out of breath, but they knew that they only had 12 minutes to go. A Tasmanian tiger and a kangaroo stood facing each other.

In the kangaroo's mouth was another clue:

Irish Deer
Caspian Tiger
Cave Lion
Dodo Bird
Aurochs

"This is easy," said Charles. "We have to go to the left. Just like the Tasmanian tiger, these are all extinct animals."

There was no way to turn, however, as the Australian exhibit was the last one on the floor. They would have to continue on a different floor of the museum.

"Should we go upstairs or downstairs?" asked Gilbert impatiently, knowing that time was against them.

"The Tasmanian tiger is lower than the kangaroo," pointed out Charles.

"Let's go downstairs then," instructed Emma.

Down the staircase they raced, rushing past other visitors. Time was ticking away. Their pursuer followed. He had already written his fifth ticket.

The first exhibit on the left was the ocean exhibit. They entered with only nine minutes remaining, according to Gilbert. They quickly found a blue whale and a dolphin staring at each other, with a clue in the dolphin's mouth:

Jeanne Calment
Sarah Knauss
Emma Morano
Violet Brown
Kane Tanaka

Charles grabbed Emma's hand and ran to the right. He announced, "These are among the oldest people to have ever lived. The blue whale can live much longer than a dolphin."

They entered the European exhibit with only five minutes remaining. Gilbert found Sir Winston Churchill and a little girl looking at each other. She was sticking out her tongue at him. On the note in her mouth, were the following names:

Eugenia Charles
Mary Robinson
Ruth Perry
Mary McAleese
Kim Campbell

"These are all names of women," identified Emma. She pointed in the direction of the little girl, saying, "To the left!"

"No!" said Charles. "What they have in common is the fact that they were all political leaders, like presidents or prime ministers, as was Sir Winston Churchill. To the right!" he instructed.

The precious seconds that they used to deliberate the clues allowed Snevyl to catch up. He did not look like he could go any further, as he crawled into the exhibit. He was still writing tickets, however.

Time was almost up. Though each was tired and could go no further, they struggled to continue. They were unaware that Snevyl was not far behind. They entered the Asian exhibit, with just under 3 minutes remaining. There, they found a cheetah and an Asian buffalo. In the buffalo's mouth was the next clue:

Sailfish
Marlin
Wahoo
Tunny
Bluefin tuna

"To the left," pointed Emma. "These are among the fastest fishes in the world. The cheetah is much faster than the buffalo."

Snevyl staggered into the exhibit and rolled onto his back, giving some patrons cause for concern. He kept saying, between each breath, "I'm ok! I'm ok!" He wondered how much longer he could keep this up. Yet, his hands were as lively as ever, churning out one ticket after another. When one notepad was full, he pulled out another one from around his waist.

There were less than 2 minutes to go. In the Antarctic exhibit, they found a leopard seal and a penguin staring at each other. The note had the following names written on it:

Sahara
Australian
Arabian
Gobi
Kalahari

"These are among the largest deserts in the world," informed Gilbert. They all ran to the right, in the direction of the leopard seal, the bigger animal.

They hurried with less than one minute to go. In the American exhibit, they found a large rattlesnake and a possum. It was the eighth and final clue:

Nile
Amazon
Mekong
Mississippi-Missouri
Congo

They all shouted in unison: "These are among the longest rivers in the world. To the left!"

The final exhibit was to the left, but not on that floor. They headed for the stairs that led to the basement. Charles wailed and gestured for everyone to clear a path. The other museum patrons scrambled to get out of their way.

Lying on his back, Snevyl radioed for help. He could go no further. So, he relayed his location to security and asked for backup, stressing, "The museum is under attack!"

"Only thirty seconds to go!" announced Gilbert.

The final exhibit was a wide selection of gold artifacts. There were pieces from all around the world on display. Most were ancient pieces. Some were over two thousand years old. While some were plain and simple, others were jewel-encrusted and elaborate.

From a distance, Charles noticed a small rolled-up piece of paper. It was close to the gold exhibit but high up on a post. Charles immediately ran towards it. He jumped as high as he could but he could not reach it. There were only 10 seconds remaining. They scanned the room but there was nothing for him to stand on.

Emma had an idea. She and Gilbert both got down on their knees. They grabbed onto each other's arms and formed a bridge. With one foot on their arms, Charles jumped as high as he could. His index finger nipped the piece of paper before he fell back down. He landed awkwardly on one foot and fell backward. Trying to break his fall, he pushed out his left hand. The force of the impact buckled his hand and twisted it backward, dislocating his shoulder.

Time had run out.

The fire alarm did not sound.

With Charles screaming in pain, everyone around him stopped to look. Several people tried to help. Susannah heard the screams and commotion. She rushed to his location. By the time she got there, someone had already called for an ambulance.

Three security guards arrived upon the scene, carrying Snevyl. One held his feet, one his midsection and one his upper body. He was still writing tickets when they found Charles. The guards dropped their passenger to the ground as they attended to Charles. Snevyl quickly sprang to his feet and approached the museum's curator, who had just arrived. In the junior guard's hands were three books of tickets.

He spoke at the top of his lungs for everyone to hear, as he waved the tickets. "These three should be banned from the museum for life! Unlike the rest of us, they have no respect for our facility and its loyal patrons."

As he spoke, Snevyl leaned against a post, thinking that it was secured to the ground. It was not. It fell to the ground and rolled under the security barrier, heading towards the ten-foot-high house-of-cards exhibit nearby. Everyone held their breath when the post hit the glass casing. Snevyl shielded his eyes with the tickets. Peeking through his fingers, he noticed that the exhibit was still intact. He was relieved. As he said, "Thank God," the cards began to fall, one by one. Within seconds, there were thousands of cards spread out all over the floor.

Everyone watched as the last card fluttered gently to the ground, heading for the domino exhibit, housed within the same glass case. Snevyl cringed in fear. He pressed his hands together and prayed that it stayed away. His knees began to tremble and sweat poured from his forehead. He gazed upward, seeking divine intervention.

The card landed on a domino. It teetered back and forth, as everyone looked on. Then, the card fell, knocking down the domino. Snevyl glanced at the placard indicating that the exhibit contained two million dominos. The crowd followed the dominos as the lines went up and down, side to side, through twists and turns, and all around until every last domino fell.

All eyes swiftly focused on Snevyl. He lumbered over to the nearby recycling bin and dropped the tickets into it. Taking out his notepad, he proceeded to write himself a ticket. Snevyl placed the ticket in his shirt pocket. He then approached the museum's curator and handed in his badge. He kissed his notebook, twice, before handing it over. He held his head low as he excused himself. Snevyl could not stand to look anyone in the eye.

Suddenly, the fire alarm sounded. Everyone began to exit the museum. In the commotion, Emma forgot all about the rolled-up piece of paper on the wall. Later that night, thieves broke into the museum and stole most of the gold from the exhibit and removed the rolled-up piece of paper. When Chief O'Brian found out what had happened to Charles, he took away their badges and barred them from the police station. Emma's mother took her microscope away and Charles's father took away his telescope. They never found out what was written on the last piece of paper, nor did they ever find out who had sent them the letters. They did not hear from him again, until now.

Chapter 8
Angel Bridge

As it was getting dark, Emma went to say goodbye to her father. She then got on her bicycle and began to ride home. As she approached Angel Bridge, she noticed a man standing on one of the protruding bridge supports. He had somehow managed to scale the barbed wire fence.

Emma feared the worst. From where he was to the shallow river below, was a ten-story drop. Emma had heard stories of people who had climbed onto the bridge supports. On three separate occasions, no one had survived. After that, the town agreed to put up a fence, so that it would not happen again. It was successful, until now.

Emma did not recognize him. He did not look like anyone whom she knew, and she knew everyone in town. She watched as he moved to the edge and peered over. He tried hard to steady himself as the wind began to blow harder. The calm night had suddenly turned violent.

Emma yelled out to him not to jump, but he could not hear her in the deafening wind. She hoped that someone would pass by or drive by, but the usually busy bridge was surprisingly deserted. To her amazement, he turned around and walked away from the edge. Her racing heart began to slow down. Yet, she could not believe what she was witnessing.

The wind began to blow even stronger and the tree branches all around her started to shake violently. The clouds dissipated and the light of the full moon bathed everything that it touched in pure, white light. She could almost feel the moonlight in her open palm. It was as though the moon had been pulled closer to the Earth, for its light was immensely bright.

Although the man had walked away from the edge, he did not climb back over the fence. Emma wondered what he was waiting for. She figured, at least, the worst was over. As she turned to get her bicycle, she caught him at the corner of her eye. He pushed himself off the fence, took two steps and leaped off the bridge support. Emma spun around with her hands over her mouth and her eyes wide opened. Her heart skipped a beat.

He fell.

Emma whispered, as quickly as she could, "And the Lord charged his angel to save him, lest he strike his foot on the rock below."

No sooner did his unconscious body approach the river, he laid suspended over the water. Emma watched in amazement as two hands wrapped around him, cradling him like a child in his mother's arms. Two wings emerged, fully extended, gently flapping over the river. The moonlight revealed the rest of the shimmering body, covered in pure, white light.

The tiny hairs on her arms and the back of her neck began to pulsate. Emma's heart raced and tears of joy filled her eyes. She saw the body, floating in protective arms, carried to the top of the bridge. While the man was still unconscious, Emma saw his body being placed on the bridge.

Emma became scared and excited when the angel focused its attention on her. She could not turn from his gaze. In awe, she stood, as he descended before her; his wings gently flapping, keeping him just above the ground. Sweat began to drip from her forehead and fingertips. Emma could feel her heart pounding inside her chest.

The features of his face were distinctly human, yet more than human. The light emanating from his body was intense, yet soft. Emma could not look directly at him for too long. Yet, she was compelled to stare.

"You gave me charge *Master*," he said, in a deep, yet childlike voice.

"Am I your *Master*?" she asked nervously.

"Come with me," he said, reaching for her hand. He began to vanish as the clouds covered the moon. Emma stretched forth her right hand to touch his. She reached out to pull him back but he disappeared into thin air. The clouds completely covered the moon. The winds ceased and the trees calmed.

Immediately, Emma collapsed to the ground, her face covered in sweat. It took a moment before she opened her eyes. She was lying on the cold ground. When she remembered the stranger on the bridge, she rode as quickly as she could to be by his side. When she got there, she could not find him. He was nowhere to be found. Emma searched and called out for him but there was no one there. She looked for signs of disturbance in the sand on the ground, but found none, even where the angel had laid the body.

In the distance, in both directions, Emma could see cars speeding towards her. She quickly made her way off the road and onto the pedestrian pathway. She stood there for a moment contemplating just what she had witnessed.

The moon must be playing tricks with her mind, she thought. There was no other explanation that made sense to her. Many have claimed to see angels on or around the bridge, but they could offer no proof, nor could she.

Emma believed in angels but did not think that she would ever see one. She could not tell anyone about it because they would accuse her of having a wild imagination. After all, there is no evidence that she could offer. Even the man, who was saved, is nowhere to be found. Emma came to the conclusion that the whole episode was a hallucination. There were too many things going on in her life and Silent Hum recently. She must have imagined the whole thing.

Suddenly, her head snapped skyward and she stood motionless. Her fingers pointed to the ground, like a compass needle. She had no power to move her hands. She stood on the tips of her toes, as though a force was pulling her skyward. Her eyes were forced open, as though to be a witness to something.

A steady beam of bluish-white light shot out of the clouds and enveloped her, while a beam of purple light bounced back into outer space. It levitated her off the ground. She could not move, even though she fought to free herself. Even her eyes, she had no power over. Her breathing hastened and her heart raced. Beads of sweat rolled from her forehead and the tips of her fingers, as she struggled to free herself. She labored with each breath until she began to hear every beat of her heart, as though she was watching it in her hands. Then she understood what she had to do. She began to let go, realizing that she need not fight it. This was something that she needed to see. She then heard the angel proclaim:

"Over the rolling hills of green and through the forested trees of red;
Beyond the stone sentinels ever watchful of the sea;
Enter the Black Gates.

Through the mountain of gold and around the sacred spider's web;
Cross the Bridge of Mist guarded by the restless demons;
Stay clear of the Cave of Forgotten Memories.

Tread lightly over the honeycombs;
Hasten through the tunnels;
The Beast you encounter is your own fear.

The Tower of Light shall be a beacon onto you;
Follow it southward, it shall reveal your path;
Step through the waterfalls.

Forge an alliance with the armies of the four corners of the Earth;
Fear them not;
For they will bow to you.

Find hope where you least expect it;
Seek help from the least likely source;
Do not trust your senses, for they will lead you astray.

My people, the people of the wastelands await their savior;
Reveal yourself to them, for they will follow you;
I choose you to lead them."

Then, as suddenly as it began, it ended. As Emma opened her eyes, she noticed that she was lying on the side of the road. Her bicycle was beside her. She felt as though she was dreaming in a dream. Emma did not understand what was going on. She had never fainted in her life before. Yet, it just happened. Twice. It could not have been a hallucination. It was just too real. Emma did not want to wait for it to happen again. Just in case, she thought, there was someone whom she could talk to. She jumped onto her bicycle and rode as quickly as she could, never looking back.

Chapter 9
The Grail

Emma flew past her house and almost crashed into her garage. After putting away her helmet and bicycle, she ran over to see Mr. Lyell. He was still sitting outside on his porch. She carefully made her way up the steps. They were rapidly deteriorating and unsafe to walk on. Mr. Lyell was like a prisoner in his own home. He had not attended church for many Sundays. He could not even tend to his front lawn.

Emma was visibly shaken when she reached the porch. Her skin and clothing were covered in sweat and dirt. She was completely out of breath from the ride home. When Mr. Lyell saw her, he asked in a concerned tone, "What happened?"

Emma said nothing as she simply tried to catch her breath. Eventually, she managed to blurt out, in between breaths, "I'm not sure."

He reassured her, "You are safe now."

He reached for a towel and handed it to her. She put the towel over both of her hands before sinking her face into it.

Mr. Lyell looked outside his porch to see what Emma was trying to avoid. He was very concerned about her. He had never seen her like this before. He thought, maybe, that someone was following her. He could not see anyone.

After a few deep breaths, Emma was ready to talk.

Mr. Lyell asked, "Would you like to tell me what happened?" He braced himself for the worst possible news, as he leaned forward to hear what she had to say.

Getting right to the point, she said, "I just saw an angel on Angel Bridge." She did not know what he would think or say.

"Is that all?" he replied immediately, chuckling. It did not take him much time to consider what she had revealed. He was relieved that it was nothing serious. He then sat back in his chair with a smile on his face.

"What do you mean?" asked Emma, confused by his reaction.

"I see them all the time," he confessed.

Although she thought of Mr. Lyell as a close friend or even a grandfather, she did not expect that he would believe her so easily or make such a personal confession.

"I was three years old," he began, recounting his experience. "I saw something floating on the water. I told my mother that I saw an angel. She told me that I was blessed."

"What do you think it means?" asked Emma.

He replied, "Some people say that they are there to protect us. Some say otherwise. Yet, some say that we are seeing things, that the water and moon are playing tricks with our minds."

Emma said, "I don't want to know what others think, I want to know what *you* think it means."

He replied, as honestly and truthfully as he could, "Angels are a sign. They only appear when important events are about to happen."

Emma asked, "What's the difference between an angel and an ordinary person?"

Mr. Lyell replied, "In heaven, angels are perfect, but on Earth, every imperfect human being is an angel."

Suddenly, Emma did not feel so alone. However, Mr. Lyell was unlike anyone she has ever met before. He was a contradiction. He loved to talk to children and to be around them, yet he had none who were alive. He spoke of the virtues of marriage, yet he has been single for over sixty years. She could not understand him sometimes. Actually, Emma liked that about him.

Emma was happy that she could share her experience with someone and not be judged. Throughout her life, Mr. Lyell has always been that way with her. She could be completely honest with him and he knew just how to make her feel good about herself. She felt more comfortable talking to him about certain things than she did with her mother, Charles or anyone else.

Leaning forward, Mr. Lyell announced, "I think it's time you know the history of our town."

Emma asked, "The history of Silent Hum?" She always thought that it was a strange name for a town. She was curious as to how it got its name. There were many stories but only one person knew the truth.

Emma's interest in history comes directly from her conversations with Mr. Lyell. Ever since she was a little girl, he has been teaching her and telling her stories of things that happened long ago.

He began, "A long time ago, in southern Europe, there lived a mysterious people. They lived close to the sea. They were masters of the sea. They pillaged and plundered everywhere they went. They constantly and relentlessly pursued material wealth. Women and children were treated like slaves. Seeing this, God became angry and turned away from them. A great flood came and destroyed all of the wicked. Only the righteous remained. From then on, they became a peaceful people. You see, they were the ancestors of Noah, children of the great flood. They understood the wrath of God.

"As time passed, while other human tribes were still warring with each other, they sought only to know God better. Every year, they would send out three ships to explore faraway places and to teach others and bring back whatever knowledge they gained. On one such expedition, someone found a goblet and brought it back to the village. Magically, everyone who touched it became possessed with the knowledge of science, astronomy and mathematics, the likes never seen before or since. Some claimed that they could even see the future.

"They became like God. Their cities were completely transformed. They built magnificent structures, which could rival even modern ones. They created machines that were thousands of years ahead of their time. They discovered things that we are only now finding out. They were like no other people before. Yet, they never felt safe.

"With their newfound knowledge, they decided to take to the sea. It was the one place that they truly felt safe. In all, they crafted fifty vessels to carry all ten thousand inhabitants. For weeks and months, they planned their journey. With their enemies closing in on all sides, they hastened to complete the ships.

"Faith was not on their side, however. The day they disembarked, a great earthquake and a mighty wave came and took the fleet. It was all gone in a day and a night, save the one ship carrying the goblet and five hundred souls. Those onboard saw the goblet as a sign. Its powers made the trees on the ship bear fruits and vegetables and turned the salty seawater into freshwater. Their fishing nets were always full of fish. No matter the weather, the water around them was always calm. They sailed until no one could remember how the earth felt beneath their feet.

"Over the next one hundred years, they sailed around the globe. Everywhere they went, they passed on their knowledge. They told their stories and shared their skills with every tribe they met, both friendly and hostile. No matter where they sailed, however, they never left the vessel."

Emma agreed, "There are, for instance, pyramids in Africa and Central and South America. Almost every culture has stories of floods, even land-locked ones. All around the world, there are similar things, even though there is no evidence that different cultures could communicate with each other." Emma asked, "What does this have to do with our town?"

Mr. Lyell continued, "After three generations at sea, those on the ship began to view the goblet with disdain. All of them were born on the ship and never set foot on land. They simply wanted to find a place to call their home. When they had all decided on a place to settle, the waters around them were troubled. A mighty wave overtook the ship and sank it. On a floating fragment of the ship, hundreds of years later, the goblet was found outside the ancient city of Alexandria. Eventually, it came to be possessed by Joseph of Arimathea. He filled it with the blood of Christ when he was crucified on the cross.

"The goblet then made its way to Perfidious Albion. It was later taken to Scotland, Spain, Jerusalem, and Tibet. There it was entrusted to Thondup for its safekeeping. Shortly after Jacques De Molay became grand master of the Knights Templar, he secretly formed the Magdalene Brotherhood. In 1294, several of its members traveled to Tibet to recover the Grail. But they were attacked by Kublai Khan himself. He wanted to possess the Grail to prolong his life. During the battle, the Grail was lost. A month later, Kublai Khan died. Years later, the Grail found its way to China, but it did not stay there long. Soon, it was on a ship headed for North America. After months at sea, it arrived in the year 1319 AD."

"1319 AD?" questioned Emma. "How is that possible? Columbus wasn't here until 1492."

Emma had accepted that Columbus discovered America. However, Mr. Lyell told her that many explorers had visited North America long before Columbus.

He insisted, "Silent Hum was founded in 1319 AD. From China, a group of monks sailed to Africa, crossed the Atlantic Ocean and sighted what is now North America. They brought the goblet with them."

Emma interrupted, "Are you saying that the Chinese discovered America?"

He simply winked at her before continuing, saying, "As it turns out, they were trying to rid themselves of the goblet. So, they buried it deep into the ground under Old Oak. The goblet began to give off a low-pitch hum. It could only be heard if you are perfectly still and quiet. In 1908, our town was officially named Silent Hum. We cannot hear the hum anymore because there is too much noise."

To which Emma inquisitively asked, "Is it possible that we can no longer hear the *hum* because the goblet is no longer buried?"

"Could be," reasoned Mr. Lyell. This possibility came as a surprise to him. He never thought of it before. He simply assumed that since it was buried so far beneath the earth, that no one would be able to get to it.

"Why do you ask?" he inquired.

Emma revealed, "A few months ago, I received a letter in the mail. It was a crypt. It said that a deluge is coming and that it would be connected with a Grail. The Grail could be the same goblet."

Mr. Lyell sat motionless and speechless. Emma looked to him for some reassurance that everything would be alright. His muted state assured her that everything was definitely not alright. Emma remembered him once saying, "Any creation that can rival its creator, is destined to be destroyed by its own hands."

He explained to her that every ecosystem has a keystone species that keeps everything in check. The starfish determines who lives in a tide pool, wildebeests keep the savannah healthy and wolves keep all prey animals in Yellowstone moving. Humans can keep all of them in check. But who keeps humans in check? No one. So, unknowingly and knowingly we have created wars and diseases to keep ourselves in check. We have become a species that has stopped moving. The key to health is movement. We are doomed by our own hands, he would say.

Mr. Lyell knew that she was scared. So, he tried to alleviate her fears. He reassured her, "From the beginning of time, we humans have always feared water. Nostradamus and da Vinci wrote and painted about it. Just look at the quatrains and the Mona Lisa. In the future, people will still be writing about the same things. It's nothing to worry about."

The fear lifted from her face. She knew why she could talk to him. He always knew just what to say. Yet, deep inside, she suspected that even he did not believe what he was saying.

"The one thing I don't understand," she confessed, "is why the angel referred to me as his *Master*."

He said, "From all of the stories that I have heard about angels at Angel Bridge, only one other person has ever been called *Master*. It is because you have so much faith in the angels. You believed with all your heart that you could save that man. Your heart and your mind are pure and true, my child. There is nothing that the Good Lord cannot do, if only you surrender your trust and faith."

Emma sat quietly as he spoke. She listened carefully to everything that he was saying. There was something that caught her attention. How is it possible that Mr. Lyell knew that she may have helped save a *man* on Angel Bridge?

Mr. Lyell interrupted her train of thought. He inquired, "Did the angel say anything else to you?"

"No," she answered. "He vanished before I could ask any questions."

Emma became very quiet. She was troubled by something. Mr. Lyell waited to hear what was bothering her. He dare not ask.

After a moment, she said, in a whisper, "I saw something."

"What was it?" asked Mr. Lyell without hesitation. He leaned closer to hear what she was about to say.

She whispered, "I think I had a vision. I saw the Black Gates. Once I entered, I saw twelve very large domes. There were only a few people inside each of them. Everyone else was in the wastelands. It was raining outside the domes. It never stopped raining. The Earth was paved. Everywhere I looked, I could only see concrete. There were no trees, no oceans and no deserts. There were no cities, no countries and no continents. Then I stepped back and I saw the entire Earth. Except for concrete, the only other thing I saw was a blue spot."

Mr. Lyell sat quietly. He was unsure of what to say. He seemed perplexed. What he knew and what Emma was telling him seemed to conflict. He wanted to believe her but how could he?

A little confused, Emma asked, "Who am I?" She knew that Mr. Lyell, of all people, should know the answer. He has guided her from the day she was born. He knew everything about her. Surely, he could answer even this simple question.

Mr. Lyell knows that all is not written. He said to her, trying to answer her question, "There are two kinds of people in the world: those who try to destroy it and those who try to build it up."

Emma was satisfied with his answer. She whispered, "I think I know which one I am. In my vision, I saw myself falling towards the ocean. I sacrificed myself to save my friends."

"That's quite a vision," said Mr. Lyell.

"What does it mean?" she asked.

The smile disappeared from his face. He told her, as truthfully as he could, "Some say that a war is coming!"

Emma was not scared. She knew that there was a strong possibility of a war. However, Mr. Lyell spoke as though it was imminent. All around the world, it was reported in the news, that people are freeing themselves from the bondage that is daily life. There is not enough work, food or clean water. It was reported in the news that people were losing faith. Many were suffering from the recent spate of earthquakes and tsunamis. They wanted answers. But no one knew for sure what was causing them, or when or where the next one would be.

Mr. Lyell warned Emma, "In the final days of humanity, the God-fearing believers will not perish but will be saved, just as it is written. But the vast majority will fall. The Devil and the Christ will battle for the souls of every human. Visions are the first sign that the final war is upon us. I believe that *He* is already here."

"Who?" asked Emma, with a slight pause before saying, "Christ?" She was beginning to get scared.

"No," replied Mr. Lyell, "the Devil!"

Emma jumped. A chill went down her spine. She said nothing. She stared blankly at him.

He continued, very animated, "Before the end, the Devil will come and try to corrupt humanity. He has been here for some time, not knowing his true identity. But he will and soon."

Emma asked, "What about people who do not believe?"

He answered, "They will find God when they are in need of a God."

"Do you think that there is hope for any of us?" asked Emma.

"There is always hope," he reassured her, resting his hand gently on her shoulder. "As long as people like you believe, there will always be hope." With that, he began to smile again.

Mr. Lyell is a local legend. He is the oldest resident in town. He was born there and has lived there all of his life. For the past two decades, he has traveled all over the world, sometimes leaving for months at a time, including when Malthus was on trial. However, he always returned. The first time he left was to fight in the war. He was the only one out of three hundred soldiers from Silent Hum to return. Many considered him a miracle. Most people revered him but some despised him.

Some say that the Lord was by his side during the war and some say that he made a deal with the Devil. No one knows what transpired on the day his platoon was decimated or how he managed to escape. The only thing that he has told Emma is that there are things that he is not proud of. He would say, "I've stopped trying to understand what the Good Lord has in store for me a long time ago. I simply try to give thanks."

For as long as Emma has known Mr. Lyell, he has always lived his life giving thanks to God. There have been so many tragic events in his life, yet his belief never ceases. In fact, it only grows stronger. His father left when he was two months old. He spent ten years in an orphanage, where he was abused and punished after his mother suddenly passed away. He lived on the streets and in hostels for many years. He witnessed the demise of his entire platoon during the war. His wife passed away after battling cancer and he was unable to save his only child.

Emma remembered the story well. When his daughter was conceived, the doctor said that it was a miracle. His wife had been gravely ill and could not have a child. Mr. Lyell prayed every day for a chance to be a father. He would say, "Just give me a chance to know what it feels like. You can take it back whenever you want. Just give me a chance."

No one thought that the baby would develop to term. Again, they were all proven wrong. Even the delivery was natural. Mr. Lyell got his wish. For six years he cherished his wife and daughter, knowing that they could both be taken at any moment.

When his daughter was six years old, he and his wife took her fishing in a small boat. It was her first fishing trip. The sun was shining bright on that beautiful, sunny, summer morning. They paddled the small boat a short distance from the shore and began to fish. Without warning, a large wave suddenly hit the boat. They were all thrown into the water. No one was wearing a life jacket.

They were all separated in the water. Mr. Lyell was the only one who could swim. To his left was his wife and to his right was his daughter. He frantically swam to save his daughter. With his daughter secured by his side, he turned around to go back for his wife. As he did, she began to go under. He told his daughter to spread her hands out over the water and kick as hard as she could to stay afloat. She bravely did as she was instructed.

He dove under the water to save his wife. A few seconds later, he emerged with her in his arms. But as they surfaced, he could not see his daughter. She had slipped under the water. He immediately swam towards the capsized boat for his wife to hold onto. He spent what seemed like an eternity searching for his daughter, diving and rising for air continuously, but to no avail. There were several times that he did not want to come up for air, but thought of his wife and swam to the surface. Each time he did, he could hear her screaming in agony, unable to do anything to save her child.

Their daughter has never been found. A month later, his wife succumbed to the cancer that she had been battling and passed away. Mr. Lyell claimed that she did not die of cancer, but of a broken heart. All this before he was even 27 years old. He has spent many lonely nights crying and praying and thinking of his wife and daughter. Oh, how he loved them. He did not remarry. He never once blamed God for his misfortunes. He only tries to understand why.

While most people would consider him cursed, Mr. Lyell did not. He said that he is blessed. He said that the Good Lord has been kind to him. Emma remembered him saying, "Do not judge God's love by the things he gives you, but by your perseverance in him." He is often heard saying, "There is nothing more precious than the life you have." But he would warn, "We each owe a debt."

Chapter 10
The First Clue

The next day, Emma arrived early at school. She waited by the swings in the playground. In the distance, she could see Charles heading towards her. He was on time, as she glanced at her watch. In his hands, he carried an extra bag. Whatever was in it must be light, as he had no trouble carrying it.

Emma arrived at school before Charles because the highlight of each morning is to see what he is wearing. It never ceases to put a smile on her face. While Charles's blue and green jeans did not match his red and orange sweater, Emma was accustomed to his unusual choice of uniform, at least for the past month. His white handkerchief, however, was still white. He always kept one in his pants pocket, with a small piece of it visible. He never uses it, but he always carries one with him.

"Good morning," said Charles, as he approached Emma. The crackle of his voice indicated his 13 years, though his sandy brown hair made him appear older.

"Good morning to you, too," replied Emma. She inquired with interest and enthusiasm, "So...so how is your telescope?"

"It's great!" replied Charles excitedly. "It would have been better if the skies had been a little clearer last night. That was some kind of weather we had. One minute it was bright and the next it was dark. I've never seen the wind blow so hard before."

Even after speaking with Mr. Lyell, Emma was still convinced that she simply fainted the night before. She wanted to tell him about her experience but decided not to. She did not even tell Susannah about it.

Charles then remembered Emma's microscope and asked, "What about your microscope?"

Emma exaggerated, "You would not *BELIEVE* the things that you can see with this one!" Giggling, Emma said, "I heard about what happened yesterday between you and Catherine."

Charles knew exactly what she was talking about. He could not hide his embarrassment.

Emma laughed. She then explained to him, "Charles, when they say that a boy should give a girl a huge rock, they don't actually mean a huge piece of rock. They mean a ring with a diamond in it. I can't believe you gave Catherine a big piece of rock." Emma burst out laughing.

"Yeah," he said disappointedly, with his head facing the ground, "she thought it was pretty funny, too." He added, "I also found out that carats are not an orange vegetable."

Emma reminded him, "It was like the time your dad gave you ten dollars and he told you to give me half. I still can't believe you tore it in two and gave half to me; or the time we went to the farm and you tried to milk the male cow; or when you thought that resistance training was refusing to go to the gym; or in dance class when you reached for the scissors when the instructor asked you to cut-a-rug; or the time you picked Mr. Copley's apples without permission. He said, "Thou shalt not steal." You thought it was great because you got free apples and Bible verses quoted to you; or when you asked, why does it take the Earth all day to rotate around itself?"

Emma could not stop laughing. Charles was completely embarrassed that Emma remembered all of those incidents. Emma offered him some advice, saying, "The next time you come up with a brilliant idea, run it by me first, ok." Charles agreed.

Emma began to swing. She pointed with her feet for Charles to look in the direction from whence he came. Down the pathway that led to the swings, she could see Gilbert. They were the only ones he ever spoke to at school. No one else understood him or treated him with respect. He was a little different than most of the other students. He also walked with a noticeable limp. As Emma would say, "Being different is what makes us all special." To which he would reply, smiling, "I know, Miss Emma. I know."

Emma's swing came to a screeching halt, as indicated by the large cloud of dust that formed when she plowed her feet into the soft sand. After clearing the dust with the wave of her hands, she walked over to her school bag and took out a piece of paper. Charles got off the swing. Standing beside Charles, Emma waited patiently for Gilbert.

As Gilbert approached, a student, Max, followed him from behind. He acted crippled to mimic him. He also made fun of Gilbert's Indigenous heritage by doing a pow wow dance. Some of the other students laughed upon witnessing it. Gilbert was unaware of what was happening. Emma and Charles simply shook their heads in disbelief.

Emma later found out that one of the students had reported Max for his behavior to Principal Grant. As part of his discipline, Max would have to recite the Land Acknowledgement and perform a traditional pow wow dance, in a homemade costume, before the entire school during the school dance.

"Do you have one for me today, Miss Emma?" inquisitively asked Gilbert, as he approached them. Emma simply smiled. He knew that she did because she was holding a piece of paper and looking directly at him.

Emma read the instructions without stopping. "Put the following letters, from A to J, in order:
No two letters are in alphabetical order except G and H, neither are end-letters;
Only 3 letters are to the right of A, one is E;
Only one letter is between D and J;
J is not an end letter;
I is directly after B and I is one of the end letters;
F is not the first letter;
D is not beside G, but is after the letter following G."

As Emma finished reading the last clue, she looked up at Gilbert. The instant she did, he said, "C is the first letter, followed by G, H, D, F, J, A, E, B, and I."

Emma smiled and said, "You are correct."

The only word Charles uttered was, "Amazing!"

"What it is!" replied Gilbert, shrugging his shoulders.

Charles marveled at his speed and accuracy. It was simply incomprehensible. Emma, too, was amazed. Then again, this was Gilbert and she expected nothing less from him.

The smile disappeared from Gilbert's face. He reached out his hand and shook theirs. He then said to them, sadly, "I'm going to miss you guys the most." He then ran as fast as he could towards the entrance and disappeared inside the school.

"What was that all about?" wondered Charles.

Emma said, "Don't worry, I'll talk to him later."

"So," asked Charles, seemingly weary and suspicious from the moment he put down his bags, "why did you ask me to come to school so early? You're not planning another water balloon attack on me, are you? If you are, I should warn you, I have an extra bag of clothes."

"No," reassured Emma. "Catherine said that your behavior has been exceptional over the past few weeks. Well, except for the *rock* thing." Charles wished that she would stop bringing it up.

Emma walked over to her bag. In a concerned tone, she said, "No, actually, I wanted to show you a letter that I received in the mail yesterday." She handed him the envelope. Charles took out the letter and read to himself:

"A treasure in a tomb,
The casket unlocked;
To the right of that figure, don't assume.
Here is his head,
Etched in wood;
Much too late to have been wed.
Unless you see him by day,
Stay away.
Enter with your fears,
Usually, an ironic figure appears.
My whereabouts will be revealed if my name is Acrostic."

Emma asked, "What do you make of it?" She could see that he was puzzled.

He replied, "Were there any prints at all on it?"

She informed him, "The only ones that I found matched my mother and the letter carrier."

Charles pointed out, "Three letters so far and no clue as to who is sending them."

Emma added, "Mr. Lyell was on his porch for most of the day. Around ten o'clock in the morning, he went inside to put away his groceries. Someone was watching him. They made their move when he went inside."

Looking at the letter, Charles said, "Everything rhymes except the last line. It's the only one that seems out of place."

Emma confessed, "I have never heard of someone named Acrostic before."

With a revelation, Charles said excitedly, "If **Acrostic** is not a name, maybe it is an important clue word."

Emma quickly hunted through her bag, took out a small dictionary and flipped through the pages. She summarized, "An acrostic is a word or phrase, in which the first, last, or certain other letters in each line, form a word or phrase."

"What is the first letter in each line?" asked Emma. Charles looked at the letter.

A treasure in a tomb,
The casket unlocked;
To the right of that figure, don't assume.
Here is his head,
Etched in wood;
Much too late to have been wed.
Unless you see him by day,
Stay away.
Enter with your fears,
Usually, an ironic figure appears.
My whereabouts will be revealed if my name is Acrostic.

He called out the letters, one at a time, "**A.T.T.H.E.M.U.S.E.U.M.** AT THE MUSEUM," he repeated out loud. "That's it! It makes sense," shouted Charles as he leaped into the air with joy.

"What's AT THE MUSEUM?" asked Emma.

"Whatever he is after," stated Charles excitedly, "must be *at the museum.*"

"Yes," agreed Emma, "but which museum?" She reminded him, "There are three museums that we know about. Each one has something different from the other. He has to tell us which museum he's going to steal from, what he's after and when he's going to do it. I'm pretty sure if he wants us to catch him, we will hear from him again."

The first school bell rang.

"By the way," asked Charles, "you didn't tell anyone else about the letter, did you?"

"Charles, Charles," pleaded Emma, "a true detective is always careful to protect every clue."

"You're thirteen years old," he reminded her. "You are not a detective."

"Good," replied Emma, "because Fitzroy knows."

"What?" screamed Charles. While Charles and Fitzroy are friends, he did not like the fact that Emma still had a crush on Fitzroy, who was halfway around the world.

"Well," said Emma, trying to calm him down, "he doesn't know what the letter is about."

The second bell rang.

They both picked up their bags and began to walk towards the entrance. Suddenly, they heard the screeching sound of a car speeding away. Emma recognized the sound of the blue Mustang's engine.

Charles asked nervously, "You don't think we were being watched, do you?"

"If we were being watched," said Emma, "then he knows that we have figured out the clue."

"How?" asked Charles.

She reminded him, "You jumping in the air like that would be a pretty good indication."

"Sorry," stated Charles. He was a little disappointed with himself. He was just so happy to have another case, he could not help himself.

"No!" reassured Emma. She explained, "As long as he knows that we have figured out the first set of clues, he's surely going to send us another."

As everyone else began to run to their classes, so, too, did Emma and Charles

CHAPTER 11
Gilbert's Last Stand

Emma, Charles and Gilbert shared English as their first class. As the class was about to begin, there was a knock on the door. Their teacher, Mr. Mayr, said, "Please continue with our exercise and then take out your book and read quietly." He then excused himself and closed the door behind him.

From his instructions to the students, he anticipated being away for a while. Both Emma and Charles sensed that something was not right. However, the rest of the class did as instructed. Several students lined up at the right-hand side of the room. One by one, they approached the front of the class and spoke.

The first student came forward and announced, "You should never trust atoms because they make up everything. Did you know that your body produces about 9 kilometers of hair each year?"

There were some "ewes" that could be heard from the front, back and every corner of the room.

Another student came forward and announced, "My math teacher said that I am average. That's mean! Did you know that tiny plant-like organisms, known as phytoplankton, produce more oxygen than all the plant life on earth? They live in the upper part of the ocean and most of them can only be seen through a microscope."

She was followed by another student who informed everyone, "I read a good book about anti-gravity. It was really hard to put it down. Did you know that in ancient times, people used moldy bread to cure illnesses?"

Another student informed her classmates, "There are three kinds of people in the world: those who can count and those you can't. If you put Mount Everest into the deepest part of the Mariana Trench, its peak would still be two kilometers below water."

Most of the students were surprised to learn that the ocean was deeper than the tallest mountain peak. There was also non-stop giggling throughout the classroom.

Another student claimed, "I am very proud of myself. The book that I read said 4 to 5 years, but I finished it in 24 months. If the Earth was not tilted on its axis, we would not have different seasons like spring and fall."

The parade continued. The next student stated, "I got 50 cents every time I failed a math test. Now I have $2.25. You may know that there are more than seven billion people on the Earth, but did you know that there are more bacteria on each of us than there are humans on the planet? But don't worry, most of them are helpful and harmless."

Most of his classmates were surprised to hear that and relieved at the same time. Some just didn't get it.

Charles came forward. He announced, "My dog can do math. When I asked her what is one minus one, she said nothing. Did you know that if you take all of the empty space out of the CN Tower in Toronto, what is left would fit in your hand? However, it would weigh so much, you would not be able to lift it." The other students were surprised to learn that most things are made up of empty space.

Another student came forward and announced, "Seven is an odd number. To make it **even** just take out the **s**. Did you know that by blowing out a birthday cake, you are adding 1400 percent more bacteria to it?"

A lot of students were disappointed when they heard that.

The last student to come forward, pointed out, "A honeycomb is not something bees use to brush their hair. Did you know that if you dig a hole through the Earth and jumped in, it will take you about forty minutes to appear on the other side?"

There were a few eyebrows raised when they heard that one.

This was an exercise that Mr. Mayr did every morning. As part of independent learning, a handful of students would find creative and interesting facts to share with the class. Mr. Mayr insisted, "The student is capable if the student is willing."

The students applauded all of the presenters. Following their teacher's instructions, everyone went back to their seat, sat down and began to read quietly. Everyone that is, except for Emma, Charles and Gilbert. They wondered what was going on outside. After a few minutes, there was a larger gathering outside of the classroom. It was no longer Mr. Mayr and one individual, but at least four.

Emma glanced over at Gilbert. He was not reading. He kept his head down and climbed an invisible ladder with his two thumbs and index fingers. He climbed up the ladder and then down. He repeated the process several times before pausing. He seemed unsure of which direction he was going in. Emma feared that they were going to transfer him to another school because his grades were poor.

What Gilbert was good at, was coming up with new ideas. He often talked about things that moved faster than the speed of light; finding only single-celled fossilized life deep beneath the ground on Mars because it lost its magnetic field early on; the common cold being the next Black Death; the creation of the outernet to parallel the internet; giving Nature its own rights and freedom; giving A.I. robots citizenship; having a world-wide Good News Day each month; space planes and the everyday astronaut; the shakers on the West Coast; the global citizen; how the universe was *really* created. He also wanted an Apology Day each year to ask for forgiveness. For everyone to be truly equal, he predicted that one day there will be one president for the entire population of the Earth. He was concerned that scientists were not warning us about the South Atlantic Anomaly.

He also talked about the ***what-if*** world. He would ask, "What if Hitler and the Nazis had won World War 2? What if Martin Luther King Jr. had not been assassinated? Are there parallel worlds that exist alongside ours, in which all of the ***what-ifs*** still lived?"

The only way that Emma knew how to answer him, was to say, "There does not exist a world in which we are free from our disabilities, but there can exist a world where everyone is treated equally."

While Emma did not see the complete destruction of the human race in her vision, she did see other things that will come to pass. She saw a future when entire countries will go bankrupt and richer nations will again become colonizers. She witnessed the exodus of more than two billion people in Asia due to climate change. She saw the racial turbulence in North America.

She saw a future with no machines. The world she saw had regressed five thousand years. There was no evidence that an intelligent species ever existed on the planet. Mr. Lyell warned her that when we are done, we will not have the resources to even build a pyramid.

While Gilbert was generally the one who came up with new ideas, Emma told him that Methuselah could have lived longer than 969 years old if he did not die in the same year as Noah's flood. When Gilbert looked at the evidence, he came to the same conclusion. Mr. Sedgwick had suspected that Beagle was cheating and asked this clue at the quiz tournament to reveal him. Emma had told her teacher of her findings, so Beagle could not have known the answer. Emma was happy that Gilbert chose not to buzz in, even though he also knew the answer to the final clue.

Although Emma found it hard at times to match wits with Gilbert, she always found him to be interesting, just like Mr. Lyell. They would sit and argue and laugh and discuss things that no one in their school even thought about. Emma sensed that these times were nearing an end.

After about twenty minutes, Mr. Mayr opened the door and came inside. He was followed by the principal and several others, including Gilbert's father.

Mr. Mayr called Gilbert to the front of the class. Gilbert picked up his bag and reluctantly came forward. His teacher quietly whispered to him that he is to go with his father.

Gilbert began to cry immediately. Everyone stopped reading in time to hear him cry out loud, "I don't want to go!"

He threw himself to the floor, as he wailed. Gilbert's father and the other gentleman tried to put him to his feet.

Emma stood up from her chair. She did not say anything, though she was very concerned.

Gilbert refused to remain standing, as he fussed and complained, "I want to stay! I want to stay!"

Everyone in the class stood up, even those who had bullied him. Principal Grant nodded her head and Gilbert was led outside. Gilbert still refused to go quietly, begging and pleading to stay, but to no avail.

No sooner did they disappear outside the classroom, the rest of the students emerged, led by Emma and Charles. Mr. Mayr could not stop them from following Gilbert, even though he demanded that they returned to their seats.

When Gilbert saw Emma, he screamed, "Miss Emma, don't let them take me. Help me! Help me!"

Tears streamed from Gilbert's eyes, his voice getting hoarse and weak from yelling and screaming.

Emma clenched her fist, powerless to do anything. She wanted to do something but she could not. Her heart raced. She felt a power raging throughout her, as though she could reach out her hand, touch him and make him whole. Emma felt helpless, knowing that he needed her and she could not do anything.

The commotion caused all of the other classrooms to empty into the hallway. Students from the entire upper floor of the school witnessed the incident.

It was Max, of all students, who did the unthinkable, who made the noblest of gestures. He, who had tormented Gilbert the most, stood up for him in his moment of need. In a weak and quiet voice that grew stronger and stronger, he began to chant, "Gilbert! Gilbert! Gilbert!"

Soon, some of the other students joined in and began to chant: "Gilbert! Gilbert! Gilbert!"

Then all of the students began to chant his name: "Gilbert! Gilbert! Gilbert!"

The chorus rose in strength over Gilbert's cry until it reached his ears. When he heard his name, he stopped kicking and screaming. The tears stopped flowing and a smile came over his tear-filled face. He stood up by himself. They had accepted him, he now understood, as he wiped away the tears. He didn't need to try and fit in anymore. He was one of them now. The emotion was too much for him. The tears he now shed were those of joy. Even his father admired their respect and acceptance. They continued to chant his name. Everyone watched as a happy, but tearful, Gilbert walked through the double doors and out of sight. It would be the last time that most of them would ever see him.

There was a moment of silence throughout the hallway. Most of the students suddenly felt guilty and some were even ashamed of themselves for bullying him. Most of them had tears in their eyes, especially Emma. In his plight, they saw who he really was. He was one of them. They finally saw him as someone who just wanted to fit in, to be just like them. At that moment, most of them wished that they were more like him, brave and determined, instead of cowards and bullies.

Chapter 12
Visiting Ms. Coraline

At Emma's school, for one week each school year, students volunteered their time at a charity or at a home-for-the-aged, or as in Charles's case, at the museum. It was a way for students to gain hands-on experience in the real world.

After school was over, Emma told Charles that she was going to visit Ms. Coraline. Charles asked if he could go with her. Emma said yes.

It was a short bus ride to Ms. Coraline's. Along the way, they talked about the earthquakes and tsunamis. They also talked about what had happened to Gilbert. Emma knows that his education is very important. She, like Gilbert's parents, only wanted what was best for him. Charles knew that Emma would miss him most of all.

Emma told Charles about Ms. Coraline. She met her two years ago. Charles found out that Ms. Coraline was once married but that her husband had passed away. His death was sudden and unexpected. She never remarried and she did not have any children. She spent the remainder of her working life as a school teacher. Susannah was one of her students.

As the bus pulled up to the stop, Emma and Charles could see protesters holding up signs and waving them. As they approached the gathering, the shouts became louder and louder. The crowd was shouting, over and over again, "Life is a choice, let us choose!" Some were saying, "End the needless suffering!" While others yelled, "Let us choose how and when we die." Someone then announced, "Ladies and gentlemen, please welcome Thomas to the stage."

The crowd rushed to the makeshift stage and surrounded the speaker, so Emma and Charles could not see him. They proceeded to the building's entrance. After they signed in, they took the elevator up to Ms. Coraline's room. It was the first time that Charles had ever been in a home-for-the-aged. He could hardly believe his eyes when he saw just how many elderly people there were.

"What are they all doing here?" he asked with childlike innocence.

Emma explained to him everything that he needed to know on the elevator ride up to Ms. Coraline's room. Charles promised Emma that he would never smoke a cigarette when he saw Mr. Abbey. He was a relative of Beagle Abbey. His voice was barely audible and he was in critical care, living with lung cancer.

They arrived at Ms. Coraline's room on the tenth floor. When they walked in, she was sitting on the bed. The radio was on and she was reading the newspaper. The window was closed because of the noise from the protesters outside. She was enjoying the sunlight that scattered through the flickering blinds. The fan, oscillating from side to side, gently separated the blind with each pass, allowing the sun to quickly beam in and out.

As they entered the room, a big smile came upon Ms. Coraline's face. She is always happy to see Emma. It is the first time that she has seen Charles. Emma had told her that Charles came from the United States when he was three years old. She also told Ms. Coraline that Charles's mother had returned home to care for his grandmother. He lived with his father.

"Well," said Ms. Coraline with an inviting smile, "you must be Charles. It's nice to finally meet you."

Charles smiled.

A news bulletin came over the radio.

Emma asked, "What are you listening to?"

Ms. Coraline responded, "They're giving an update on the tsunamis in the Philippines and Japan. The casualties may number in the millions."

Ms. Coraline reached over and turned off the radio. She did not want them to hear all of the grim details of the report. Emma remembered the warning of a deluge and wondered if they were all somehow connected.

Emma went over to the dresser, took out a small box and placed it on the bed. Ms. Coraline opened it. Charles was expecting to see family photos or some kind of keepsake, but he was surprised when she took out a pack of cards.

Utilizing her best Texan accent, Ms. Coraline inquired, "How good are *ya* at Texas Hold'em?" She sounded like a veteran poker player.

Charles was happy that he did not have any money with him. Before he could respond, there was a small tremor throughout the Home.

"Earthquake!" yelled Ms. Coraline.

The fire alarm sounded. The tremors began to increase in frequency and intensity. Then, the Home began to sway back and forth, knocking Charles and everything that was not secured to the ground. An announcement over the PA system informed everyone to evacuate immediately.

Emma became worried when she thought about the letter and the warning of a deluge. She hoped that the tremors were not felt at the dam upstream.

The building continued to sway back and forth, as the tremors intensified. Each tremor was more powerful than the one before. Ceiling tiles began to fall and cracks appeared in the walls. A portion of the floor under Ms. Coraline's bed disappeared and the bed slipped partially into the void. Ms. Coraline held onto the bedpost as her body dangled through the floor below. Charles and Emma rushed over to Ms. Coraline. Charles held onto the bed to prevent it from slipping further. Emma grabbed onto Ms. Coraline's hand and gently guided her off the bed.

Emma led Ms. Coraline to the door. Charles followed behind. As he headed for the door, ceiling tiles continued to fall and one knocked him to the ground.

Larger cracks began to appear in the walls. Ms. Coraline's room ran down the center of the Home. As Charles stood up, half of the building with Ms. Coraline's room began to separate from the rest of the Home. Emma yelled for Charles to jump. He jumped just as half of the building completely separated and crashed to the ground below. Emma caught Charles as he held onto the door with no ground under his feet. She pulled Charles to safety only to find that they were surrounded by flames and water spraying from the sprinklers. Screams and crying filled every hallway and corridor. Emma could see no one though, as the thick smoke made it hard to see.

They stayed low to the ground and covered their faces, as they made their way through the exit doors and down the stairs. Emma led the way as other patients joined them in a long line. They could not go beyond the seventh floor, however, as the staircase had broken off, leaving a large gap. Everyone was trapped as the tremors continued to shake the unstable building.

From the floor below, Emma could hear firefighters yelling instructions. They spanned the gap with a ladder and instructed everyone to keep moving. There was not much time to spare as the remainder of the building could collapse. One by one, patients, nurses and visitors made their way down the ladder until Emma and Charles were the only ones left. Before they could get on the ladder, a piece of the stair that they stood on separated and crashed to the floor below, taking the ladder with it. The gap grew wider and wider with each piece of falling debris.

A firefighter tied a piece of rope to a rock and threw it up. Emma secured it to the stairs. She told Charles to hold onto it and climb down. He did so hesitantly, as he did not want to leave Emma. As Charles reached the firefighters below, Emma reached for the rope. The stair became more unstable with each tremor until it completely collapsed.

Emma was all alone. She told the firefighters that she would go back and look for another way out. She went back through the door and into the hallway. Even with fires burning and sprinklers gushing, there was an eerie silence.

She knew her best chance of getting out would be if she could get to the elevators. Jumping over burning towels in the hallways and ducking under burning beams, she slowly made her way to the elevators. As she attempted to pry the elevator doors open, she could hear a faint noise, like two pieces of metal clanging together.

Emma could not open the elevator doors. She continued to hear the noise and wondered where it was coming from. She made her way towards the noise. As she walked, it became louder and louder. She forced a door open and found a nurse in a pool of blood on the ground, unresponsive. In the bed was Mr. Abbey, hitting his cane onto the metal bed rails.

Mr. Abbey uttered, "Oh, thank God," when he saw Emma. She rushed over to him and tried to get him up but he refused. There were warning and beeping sounds coming from the display monitors next to his bed. All of the tubes attached to his body had been removed.

"I am not going anywhere," he said in an inaudible voice. "This is my time and this is how I choose to go."

"So why were you hitting the bed rails?" asked Emma.

He cried, "I just wanted someone to pray for me. Can you do that?"

Emma nodded and began to pray the Lord's Prayer as the tremors continued. Mr. Abbey simply closed his eyes before Emma could finish. She wiped the tears from her eyes as she left the room. She picked up a towel and returned to the elevator. To her surprise, the elevator doors were open. She could see all the way down to the ground, as there were no walls beyond the elevator cables. She could see the fire trucks, police cars, ambulances, and Charles.

There was no way for them to get to her. Emma took the towel and wrapped it around an elevator cable. She took a deep breath before straddling the cable with her legs and descended to the ground. Charles was the first one to greet her, saying that he was sorry for leaving her behind and how happy he was to see her again. He told her that Susannah and his father were aware of what was happening.

Ms. Coraline and most of the residents from the Home had already been transported to a hospital. Emma was surprised to learn that the Home was the only building to suffer damage. It seemed that the tremors specifically targeted only the Home. It was like the other earthquakes that were happening around the world. There were no patterns and they were not specific to areas with fault lines. She knew that Malthus, Samantha, the goblet, the angel, the earthquakes, the tsunamis, and the letters were all connected somehow.

Thomas was not dissuaded by what was happening. He was still speaking when Emma reached the ground. Emma was hoping that by visiting Ms. Coraline, Charles would begin to change his way of thinking. While she did not reveal her true motive for inviting him to the Home, she was not counting on the protesters and Thomas being there. While she was inside the building, Charles was listening and absorbing everything that Thomas was saying. Everything that happens from now on was inspired by what he heard from the protesters, especially Thomas. It set off a storm of ideas in his head.

There was nothing that Emma could do to stop it. Everything that Mr. Lyell had said to her was beginning to make sense. Her only wish was for Charles to know what she already knew. However, she knows that she must be patient. She cannot reveal anything to him before its time.

CHAPTER 13
The Dinner

After seeing Charles home safely, Emma rushed to get home. When she checked the mailbox, another white envelope, with her name on it, was sitting inside. She now realized that they were being watched at school.

Hoping that Mr. Lyell may have seen who delivered it, Emma went over to see him. As she walked across her driveway, she noticed that the "For Sale" sign on Gilbert's front lawn had a red "SOLD" sticker across it.

As usual, he was sitting on his porch, when Emma walked up the old wooden steps. It was impossible to sneak up on him. The creaking sounds could be heard from some distance away. The endless winters and countless carpenter ants have taken their toll over the years. Emma loved to listen to Mr. Lyell's stories of how his daughter used to play on the steps that he built with his own two hands.

"Heaven-o, Mr. Lyell," Emma gleefully greeted the gray-haired, white-bearded man when she stepped onto the porch.

He replied with an affectionate smile.

Emma was known in town as the "Heaven-o" girl. She never liked the way "hell-o" sounded. There was even a "Heaven-o" chant at her football games.

"They're gone," Mr. Lyell sadly informed her, looking over at Gilbert's house. "Four men came with two trucks and took everything away. They didn't say where they were going."

"He never said goodbye," whispered Emma sadly.

She already missed him. Emma remembered the first time she met Gilbert. He was extremely shy and did not say a word to anyone, except her. The first time she met him at school, she knew that they would be good friends. Their friendship grew stronger when his parents purchased the house across the street. Now, he is gone.

Emma was happy that Gilbert finally saw that not everyone is a bully and that he has friends. She did not know where they had gone, though. She wondered if she would ever see him again.

Emma asked Mr. Lyell if he saw anyone come by her house earlier in the day.

"Most of the day," he replied, "I was outside. Except for the mailman, no one came to your house."

Emma said nothing. She looked at the envelope in her hand. It looked just like the first one that was delivered.

"Is something wrong?" asked Mr. Lyell. He had never seen her so puzzled.

"I'm not sure," said Emma. "You see, I received a letter yesterday, but I don't know who sent it. This morning, Charles and I looked at it. It was some kind of puzzle, a clue."

"Why don't you go to the police?" asked Mr. Lyell. He reminded her, "Chief O'Brian is your friend."

Not knowing any other neighbors whom she could ask, she went home. When she opened the door, her mother dropped the vacuum and ran to her. She hugged her and made sure that she was not hurt. Emma reassured her that she was doing well.

Emma could see that her mother was busily cooking while vacuuming at the same time. The placemats on the dining room table lined up perfectly with the chairs. Emma could not remember the last time she saw such a lovely decoration of flowers, in the middle of the dining table. Even Fred did not get flowers.

"Emma," shouted Susannah, over the sound of the vacuum, "please go and put on your red dress after you've showered." Susannah turned off the vacuum. She reminded Emma, "Robert is going to be here soon."

Emma reminded her mother, "I don't have a red dress."

"It's on your bed," said Susannah, running past her to get to the kitchen.

Emma was not very happy but went upstairs like her mother asked. She tried her very best to follow Mr. Lyell's rules and did not argue with her mother. Besides, she wanted to see her new dress. While Emma played football and ran track and field, she still loved to wear dresses. Charles would call her Doctor Jekyll and Miss Hyde because of her dual personalities.

Emma realized that it was the second clue when she opened the envelope. After reading the letter, she analyzed it for fingerprints, using her new microscope and a few tricks that she had picked up at the police station. There was none. She then called Charles. She read the letter to him but it was not like the first one. They agreed to meet at their school's library early the next morning. She also reminded him that the Chief had just returned from his trip to Australia and that he wanted to meet with them.

Emma did not go back downstairs until her mother came up and got her. She was quite content with her family and was not interested in adding anyone else to it.

"You are going to love him," said Susannah, as they walked to the living room. As they entered, the doorbell rang.

Susannah nervously squeaked, "That's him. Now, I want you to be on your best behavior."

"Am I not always, mother?" asked Emma sarcastically.

Susannah opened the door and said, "Robert, I would like you to meet my daughter, Emma."

"It is a pleasure to finally meet you," sincerely greeted Robert.

Emma glanced at him but hesitated to look above his shoulders. She was impressed with the flowers that he gave her mother. She looked at his attire and thought that it was a carefully chosen three-button black suit with fine grey stripes. His tie was done in a Windsor knot and neatly attached to his shirt with a gold-colored clip. His black dress shoes were recently polished, as she could still smell the finish. However, she could not bring herself to look at his face.

"Nice to meet you," said Emma robotically, her eyes glued to the floor.

Robert added, "May I say, that is a very pretty dress."

Emma did not respond to him. She refused to look him in the eyes. She turned around and walked over to the dining table. Seeing Emma's reaction to him, Robert sensed that something was wrong. Susannah's smile reassured him that everything was alright.

Dinner began promptly. Emma did not answer any of the questions that Robert asked her. She simply nodded or shook her head. Susannah had told him what her favorite subject was, so Robert said, "I bet that your favorite subject is history."

"Well," replied Emma in a monotonous tone, "you wouldn't know the things that I know."

Finally, he got her to talk to him. Robert felt more at ease. Susannah felt quite uneasy. She knew what was going to happen next and could not prevent it, even with offerings of garlic mashed potato and baked lamb.

"Go ahead," Robert insisted, "test me."

Emma thought of something that he wouldn't know and asked, "What do Galilei, Shakespeare and Simoni have in common? Hint: Simoni would wish that they didn't share it."

Robert thought for a second and said, "I know Galilei is Galileo's last name and I know who William Shakespeare is, but who is Simoni?" He was embarrassed. Not only was he unable to answer the question, but he also did not even understand it.

Emma asked teasingly, "Give up?"

He scratched his head and nodded up and down. Emma was beginning to like him. This may turn out to be a good night, after all, she thought. Her composure and demeanor had completely changed towards Robert. Susannah was worried.

"Simoni," informed Emma, "is the last name of the Italian sculptor/painter Michelangelo. Maybe you've heard of the Sistine Chapel? He painted most of it. From 1508 to 1512, Michelangelo painted almost 12 000 square feet of the Chapel."

Focusing back to Robert, Emma pressed him for an answer. "Well, what do they have in common?"

She stared him down like a lioness stalking its prey. Emma did not look away from him. She knew that he was nervous when she saw a bead of sweat rolling down his forehead. He tried very hard but could not think of anything to say. Susannah could offer no help, as he glanced over at her.

Finally, he admitted defeat and nervously said, "Actually, you've caught me off guard with that one. Why don't you enlighten us with the answer."

Emma was more than happy to oblige. She explained, "It was the year that science, literature and art all came together. What they share is the year 1564. Galileo and Shakespeare were born in 1564 and Michelangelo died in that year. That's why Michelangelo would wish that he did not share it with them."

"That's quite impressive," congratulated Robert.

"Actually," informed Emma, "that was pretty basic stuff."

Susannah interjected, "But that would be a bit hard for someone to get. Why don't we talk about something else?"

Susannah could not deter Robert. He tried his best to interact with Emma. Even if he was not able to answer her questions, at least she was talking to him.

He asked Emma, "Could I have a pinch of salt, please?"

Susannah closed her eyes and clenched her teeth and fist. She squeezed the fork so hard that it bent in her grasp. With a cleansing breath, she opened her eyes, knowing what was about to come. After putting down her fork, she placed her elbows on the dining table. She brought her hands together, rested her chin on them and watched the spectacle unfold. This was nothing new to her. She had witnessed it before with Fred.

Emma picked up the salt shaker and dropped a few grains on the table. She then picked up one grain and pinched it before handing it to Robert. He finally realized what Susannah knew all along. While he was not amused, he did realize his mistake. After all, he did ask for a *pinch* of salt.

Emma then asked, with a smile, "Would you like me to toss your salad?"

"No, no," he replied, leaning forward and placing his hands over his salad bowl.

After he composed himself, Robert asked Emma, "Why don't you ask me another question?"

Susannah tried to change the subject. She knew what would happen if Emma asked any more questions. Robert seemingly refused to take a hint. She thought about throwing something at him so he could get a clue. However, he was a guest and she did like him.

Robert encouraged Emma to ask him another question, saying, "Go ahead. I'm ready."

It was the last thing Susannah wanted to hear. Her eyes rolled in the back of her head.

Emma accepted, saying, "Elizabeth was born in what would eventually be called Rainbow City, Alabama on Wednesday, September 2, 1752. On Thursday, September 14, 1752, she was two days old. How is this possible?"

Robert did not know where to begin. How could 11 days go by and someone does not age? He was beyond stumped. This was worse than the first question.

Emma could see that he was thinking really hard. However, he could not come up with an answer. He asked Emma to explain.

Emma was having a great time at dinner. She was the only one. She said, "The United States switched from the Julian calendar to the Gregorian calendar and it was necessary to take out 11 days in September of 1752. So, they went directly from Wednesday, September 2nd to Thursday, September 14th."

Both Susannah and Robert were in awe.

Robert begged Emma, "One more please."

Susannah looked dumbfounded at Robert.

Emma could do this all night. She said, "This one is really easy. Imagine that you are flying a plane. At fifteen thousand feet, you experience turbulence. So, you climb five thousand inches higher. You encounter a gaggle of geese and climb two thousand meters more. The radio tower informed you that you are on a collision course with another plane and that you should descend by five kilometers. Instead, you only descend by 2 miles. How old is the pilot?"

Robert looked like a deer in a headlight. Before he could even attempt to answer, Susannah got up from her chair. She admitted defeat.

Robert looked at his half-eaten food and again to Susannah. He then realized just how serious she was.

He simply got up from his chair. Susannah walked to the front door. He followed her. She opened the door. He looked at her. She looked at the door. Though he was not the smartest person at the table tonight, he managed to figure out what to do. After putting on his shoes and jacket, he excused himself.

Emma ran over to her mother and gave her a big hug. Susannah knew how much Emma appreciated the sacrifice that she just made.

Emma said sincerely, "You're the best mother a daughter can ever have." She knew that her mother had made a great sacrifice. Susannah knew that she had made the right decision. Though, she was still a little sad to see him go.

Emma held her mother's hand. They slowly walked back to the dining table. Emma began to sing a song that she had been practicing for her church:

"There's a place I've heard of,
There's a place I've dreamed of;
Jesus Christ, you're my Lord, take me home.

I was born by your grace,
I was born to serve you always;
Jesus Christ, you're my Lord, take me home.

When I cannot see the light,
My path you will make bright;
Jesus Christ, you're my Lord, take me home.

You gave me sight to see,
You gave your life for me;
Jesus Christ, you're my Lord, take me home.

When I am scared and wanting,
You relieve my haunting;
Jesus Christ, you're my Lord, take me home.

I don't know where I'm going,
But I know who is guiding;
Jesus Christ, you're my Lord, take me home.

Now I am old and failing,
And my time is nearing;
Jesus Christ, you're my Lord, take me home."

Chapter 14
The Acrostic

Charles arrived at school early the next morning. He was wearing blue jeans and a purple and orange sweater. These were not the original colors of the sweater. It was, in fact, light blue. Emma smiled upon seeing his outfit. She was waiting for him outside the library.

A little embarrassed, Charles explained, "My dad did the laundry last night."

"He'll learn," reassured Emma, smiling.

"I sure hope so," he replied. He then added, "Well at least my Aunt Bessie is coming over tomorrow."

"I thought she was coming over on the weekend," said Emma.

"Oh, no," replied Charles. "I spoke with her last night and told her what my dad did. She insisted that she be here early."

As they spoke, they walked through the entrance to the library. Except for the librarian, they were the only ones there.

Charles dearly missed his mother, not only for her laundry and culinary skills but because they spent so much time together, especially when his father was away on military duties. Sometimes, it was just the two of them for months at a time.

As they made their way to a desk at the back of the library, Charles asked, "So, how did dinner go last night?"

"It was perfect!" replied Emma, without hesitation.

He knew exactly what she meant. Charles knew how much Emma wanted things to remain the same between her and her mother, especially considering that she did not have a father.

"After Robert left," informed Emma, "we saw a television report saying that a tsunami warning was issued for Bangladesh and Sri Lanka. There are so many earthquakes occurring. Every day this week there has been an earthquake and a tsunami warning somewhere around the world. It just doesn't make any sense." Emma could not stop thinking about the warning of a deluge in the letter.

They both sat down. Emma reached into her bag and took out the envelope. She opened it and handed the letter to Charles. He read it aloud,

"What do these figures have in common?

Christopher Columbus
John Adams
Joe Louis
Ivan the Great
Sigmund Freud
Robert Owen
Reu
Nahor
Jean Ingres
Adam

Add us up and you will find a number,
an event and my name."

"Last night," said Emma, "I tried to see if the names spelled out an acrostic. You can see for yourself that C.J.J.I.S.R.R.N.J.A does not spell a particular word, words or phrase. I've tried using the first letter, last letter and middle letter, but something is still missing. I wish Gilbert was here."

"Let's see," said Charles, as he leaned over and glanced at the list of names. He asked, "Why did he give us these names and why do some of them only have one name?"

Emma said excitedly, "I can't believe I didn't see it before."

"See what?" asked Charles.

Emma explained, "Whenever you identify a person, you always ask for them by their last name."

Charles placed the letter on the table and Emma called out the last names of the people who were listed in the letter.

"Good," said Charles, who had been circling each letter as Emma called them out. After the last letter was identified, Charles called out the circled letters: "C.A.L.I.F.O.R.N.I.A."

"CALIFORNIA," announced Emma. "That's definitely a word." She asked, "Besides the word CALIFORNIA, what else could **What do these figures have in common?** mean?"

Charles informed her, "If you look at the first clue again, you will realize that one word doesn't belong there."

Emma looked at the letter and said, "You mean *figure*?"

"Exactly," said Charles. "For someone to be called a *figure*, they would have to be important."

Emma suggested, "Well then, we need to know a little about each of them. What we need is a dictionary."

They both got up from the desk and went in opposite directions. Within seconds they both returned. Charles had two large dictionaries in his hands and Emma had a Bible.

Charles could not resist teasing her, "You know, praying will not help us solve this case."

"That's not what the Bible is for," insisted Emma, scuffing at his sarcasm.

Emma took one dictionary from Charles. They both decided to alternate looking for the names on the list.

It didn't take long for Charles to find the first name. He summarized, "It says that Christopher Columbus lived from 1451 to 1506. He was a navigator and an explorer. He is credited with discovering the Americas for Spain in 1492."

Emma added, "According to Mr. Lyell, it was the Chinese who discovered North America. They were here even before Leif Erikson. But when you really think about it, people were in North America about 15 000 years ago, before the last ice age started, so they were the first ones here." She informed Charles, "It says here that John Adams was the second President of the United States."

Charles paraphrased, "Joe Louis is considered the greatest heavyweight and the most influential boxer ever."

Emma found the next name on the list. She said, "Ivan the Great laid the foundations of what would be Russia."

Charles stated, "Sigmund Freud is one of the most controversial figures in psychology."

Emma added, "Owen was a social reformer and one of the founding fathers of socialism and the cooperative movement."

Charles admitted, "I can't find Reu in this dictionary."

Emma pointed out, "That's because he is not in the dictionary. Reu is the son of Peleg and the father of Serug. He is found in the Holy Bible."

"What about Nahor?" inquired Charles.

"He, too, is in the Bible," said Emma. "Nahor is the father of Terah and grandfather of Abraham."

"I know Ingres," announced Charles. "Although he considered himself a painter of history, his portraits are his lasting legacy."

Emma added, "Adam was the first person created by God."

"How did you know about Reu, Nahor and Adam?" asked Charles.

Emma knew that Charles and his parents did not attend church. She handed Charles the Bible. She said, "You will learn about them if you read the Bible."

Charles took the Bible with uncertainty. He had never held the Bible before or read from it. He admired the cover for a little while before opening it. To Emma, he seemed undecided. It was a big decision for him, almost like taking the training wheels off a tricycle.

Before Emma could say anything, he flipped the cover over. Several pages magically turned with the force of opening the book. The first word he saw was Genesis. He began to read. Charles found the word of God to be simple, straightforward and easy to understand. It was not what he expected, but it was just as Emma had explained to him. He did not catch on fire, nor found himself in the depths of the underworld, as he had recently been warned in the news. Nothing bad happened to him from reading the Bible.

After they had researched all of the names, Emma could see no commonality among the individuals. She whispered her displeasure, as they were in the library. "We've gotten nowhere. We have an explorer, a president, a boxer, a ruler, a psycho-analysis, a reformer, three people from the Bible and a painter. There is absolutely nothing in common among all of them."

Charles kept reading the Bible. He did not pay any attention to Emma, even after she asked if he was listening.

"Are you listening to me?" she asked Charles again, in a whispering scream.

Suddenly, he looked up and asked, "Did you know that Reu lived to be 239 years old?"

"What?" asked Emma, as she drew herself closer to the Bible.

Charles said, "It says here that Reu was thirty-two years old when he became a father and lived for two hundred and seven years after that."

"That's it," said Emma excitedly. "You've figured it out."

"That's great!" he said congratulating himself. Although he was pleased with himself, Emma could see that he was uneasy.

She asked, "You haven't figured it out, have you?"

"Not a clue," he responded, shaking his head.

Emma showed him the letter. She explained, "He gave us a random list of names because regardless of what list he could have generated, they would still only have one thing in common."

Charles interrupted, "You mean that everyone is born and they die."

"More specifically," stated Emma, "we all have an age. With the names in the Bible, we don't have specific birthdays, but we know how old they were when they died. If you look at the letter, the clue said to *add them up*. The only thing we can *add up* is their age."

Emma asked Charles to find the age of Adam and Nahor, while she looked for the others. She quickly flipped through the dictionary and found the individuals on the list. She wrote down when each of them was born and when they died. Charles had already figured out how old two of the people in the Bible were. By the time he had figured out how old Nahor was, Emma was almost finished.

Emma read aloud what she wrote down. Charles subtracted the two numbers and entered it into the calculator that he took out of his bag.

Emma began, "Columbus 1451 to 1506."

Charles entered 55 into his calculator.

Emma called out each of the other names. Charles entered their age into the calculator. He announced, "Reu was 239 years old, Nahor was 148 and Adam, a remarkable 930 years old."

"What did you get?" asked Emma excitedly.

"Well," said Charles, "they have a combined age of eighteen hundred and forty-nine years."

Emma asked, "What else do we need to figure out?"

Looking at the letter, Charles said, "We know that each of the *figures* has one letter in the word CALIFORNIA. We also know what they have in common is their age and we have the *number*. The only thing remaining is the *event*."

"CALIFORNIA and 1849," repeated Emma to herself. "Where have I heard that combination before?" She searched her memories for clues.

Charles already knew what she was looking for. He asked, "Isn't there a museum on 1849 California Street?"

Emma stated confidently, "Whatever he's looking for must be in that museum."

"But what does he mean by the *event*?" wondered Charles.

"So far," reminded Emma, "he has told us that he's going to steal from a museum. Now he has told us which museum he's going to steal from. He still has to tell us what he's going to steal and when."

"But what *event* happened on 1849 California Street?" asked Charles.

Emma stopped him with the signal of her hand. She said, "It's not what happened on 1849 California Street that's important, but what happened in California in the year 1849."

"Hello, Charles," said someone walking by. They both jumped. They thought that they were the only ones in the library. Charles looked up. It was his history teacher, Mr. Sedgwick.

"Good morning, Mr. Sedgwick," greeted Charles.

Mr. Sedgwick complimented them, saying, "It's nice to see you two studying so hard."

"Mr. Sedgwick," asked Emma, "can you think of an important event that happened in California in 1849?"

"Well," he said, scratching his chin, "The most important thing that happened was the California gold rush of 1849. It was so important, the San Francisco 49ers football team was named in recognition of it."

Emma's eyes lit up when she heard the word *gold*.

"Well," he said before leaving, "now I know who to direct my questions to in class today. Goodbye."

It took a few seconds before Charles realized what Mr. Sedgwick had said. He would have screamed had he not been in the library.

"Oh, great," sighed Charles. "Now look at what you've done." He then asked Emma, "So, when do we go to the police?"

"The police?" asked Emma.

"Yes," insisted Charles. "When do we tell the police that someone is going to steal the gold from the museum?"

"Unfortunately," reminded Emma, "you don't seem to remember our last case and why we lost my microscope and your telescope."

"We have to tell them," insisted Charles. "We just have to show them the letters."

"They won't believe that the letters are real," stated Emma. "Besides, it's nothing two detectives can't handle."

"We are not detectives," he reminded her. "We are two thirteen-year-old, eighth-graders."

"Listen," reassured Emma, "we have lots of time. Besides, I'm 25 percent confident, that I'm 50 percent certain, that I am 75 percent sure, that I'm 100 percent positive that I know what I am doing."

"What?" screamed Charles in a whisper.

Emma pointed out, "He knows that no one will believe us. So, he's going to give us all the information we need to catch him. He has told us where he is going to steal from, what he is going to steal, but he didn't say when. He is going to send us one more letter. But I have a surprise for him. Mr. Lyell will be inside his house all day. When he shows up, Mr. Lyell will get a good look at him."

Chapter 15
The Stair

After school was over, Emma and Charles walked to the bus stop. They had less than thirty minutes to get to the police station. They were both nervous to be going back. Neither one knew what to expect when they got there. What they were sure of, is that they did not want to keep the Chief waiting. Chief O'Brian was not entirely clear about what he wanted to talk to them about. Emma and Charles stayed outside the police station until it was time to see him. They were invited into his office and asked to sit down and wait.

Emma admired the Chief. He was a tall man, standing 6 feet, 1 inch. At 64 years old, he had been a police officer for 29 years and police chief for 13 years. He was promoted two weeks before Emma was born. He was looking forward to his retirement in less than a year. He was a devoted family man. His office was decorated with pictures of his children and grandchildren. Emma and Charles loved to listen to him talk about his family, especially his grandchildren. In every conversation that they have had in his office, he always managed to include them.

Emma also liked to talk to the Chief because he was there on the night that her father was killed. She found out a lot about her father from the Chief. He told her that her father was a very dedicated detective. He was well-liked and well-respected by his fellow officers and members of the community.

On the subject of her father's death, however, he was less forthcoming with details. She knew that it happened late in the evening, around 10 pm. It had been raining that night. The Chief arrived on the scene just after her father was shot. He held him in his arms until his final breath. "Her name must be Emma Herschel Keeling," the Chief remembered her father saying. "Tell her that I will always love her." These were her father's final words, according to the Chief.

Emma was born on the night that her father was killed. The Chief arrived at the hospital just after three in the morning to tell her mother what to name the baby. Susannah was absolutely devastated when she found out that her husband was killed, based on the Chief's recollection.

Chief O'Brian has been like a father figure to Emma since she was born. Although he had five children of his own, none of them followed in his footsteps. He told everyone at the station that Emma was his sixth child. He was very proud of her. The first opportunity he had to make Emma a junior constable, he took it. He has guided her in the procedures of police work from the beginning. She always wanted to follow in her father's footsteps.

However, the Chief was very disappointed with her following Charles's accident at the museum. He reminded her that police work was serious business. It was not something that should be taken lightly. In the past six months, he had not visited her and Susannah. He used to drop by every week before Charles's accident.

After they had sat in the office for a few minutes, the Chief walked in. They both stood up to greet him. Emma did not look directly at him. She still felt some guilt about her judgments in the past.

"I'm going to make this very short," the Chief stated sternly, as he sat down. He spoke in an even and serious tone. "I am going to give you your badges back today. You will not get an opportunity like this again. You will follow all of the rules and regulations set forth in this book." He handed each of them a copy. "Under no circumstances will you ever practice what you have learned outside these doors. Do I make myself clear?"

They both responded with, "Yes, sir!"

The Chief then stood up and presented each of them with their own badge. They were both very happy to have their badges back and wore them proudly. The meeting ended abruptly as sirens began to sound in the station. Whatever it was, it required the attention of all the officers. The Chief quickly ushered Emma and Charles out of the station. He told them to go directly home.

Emma was happy and sad at the same time. She was happy to get her badge back but sensed that the Chief was still disappointed with her. It was the first time that she has had a conversation with him and he did not talk about his grandchildren. The haste with which he gave them their badges bothered Emma. She vowed that she would make him proud of her again.

When they exited the station, Susannah was outside waiting for them. Emma asked her mother if she had picked up the supplies.

"They're in the trunk," pointed out Susannah. She was very happy for both of them when she saw their badges.

It was just after 5 pm when Susannah pulled into the driveway. Emma told Charles that she needed his help with something that she had been working on. He agreed to help but was unsure of what she needed him to do. Emma knew that Charles could not keep a secret, so she did not tell him what she needed his help with.

From inside his house, Mr. Lyell could hear a lot of noise coming from outside. It seemed as if it was coming from his front lawn. He couldn't concentrate on his painting, so he went to see where all the noise was coming from. When he looked through his window blinds, he saw Emma and Charles at the bottom of the steps.

Immediately, he went to see what they were doing. In her hand, Emma had a hammer. As he stepped onto the porch, she hammered in the final nail. Mr. Lyell was wide-eyed and surprised to see that Emma and Charles had cut his lawn and built him a new stair. He was so excited that he almost leaped into the air as Emma and Charles yelled, "Surprise!"

Back and forth he went up and down the steps, with a big smile on his face. He wasn't even using his cane, as he was accustomed to. After walking up and down the steps a few times, Mr. Lyell stopped to wipe his forehead.

Emma asked excitedly, "Well, how do you like it?"

"This is quite a surprise," said Mr. Lyell, almost out of breath. He could not stop smiling. "Thank you too, Charles."

"You're welcome," replied Charles. "But Emma deserves all the thanks. After all, she paid for the wood and tools."

"I almost feel young again," Mr. Lyell exclaimed excitedly. "This is the first time, in many years, that I'm not afraid of these steps. I don't know how to thank you."

"I believe you just did," said Emma, smiling. "The only thanks we need is to see the smile on your face."

"Well," he said sincerely, "I think you two are the greatest."

They both received his comment with a smile on their faces. For his years of invaluable education and friendship, Emma felt that it was a small token of her sincere appreciation.

Emma showed Mr. Lyell her badge. He was very excited for her. For the past six months, he listened to Emma talk about getting her badge back. Although he never told her, he prayed every night that she would have the courage and strength to successfully complete her probation. He knew that his prayers were answered when she showed him the badge.

"Actually," Mr. Lyell said, "there is a way that I can thank you. Please, come inside."

Emma quickly replied, "You don't have to give us anything. We did this because we wanted to."

"Well spoken," commented Mr. Lyell, heading up the stairs to the front door.

They both followed him into the house. According to Charles's expression, it was a well-kept home, even though Mr. Lyell lived alone. Charles was overcome by the portraits that hung in the hallway. He admired the brush strokes and choice of colors. The details were flawless.

He asked, "These are not originals, are they?"

Mr. Lyell responded, "After Norma was gone, I spent a few years wandering. The results are on these walls."

Emma detected a change in his voice as he spoke with Charles. It was quite the opposite of the one that he had a moment earlier when he was outside. Mr. Lyell went upstairs while Emma and Charles went into the living room.

Suddenly, there was a loud sound upstairs. Charles and Emma looked concerned. Charles quickly ran up the stairs. He found Mr. Lyell on the floor in his bedroom. Charles looked absolutely mesmerized. Mr. Lyell pointed to the door. Charles locked the door behind him before attending to Mr. Lyell.

Emma banged on the door for Charles to open it.

"Just a minute!" yelled Charles.

Emma demanded, "What is going on in there?" She could hear Charles panicking and mumbling to himself.

"Just a minute!" repeated Charles.

Emma pressed her ear to the door but could hear nothing. There was complete silence. Then she heard a very quiet humming noise.

Charles opened the door and closed it again after stepping outside. He prevented Emma from seeing inside. He pointed Emma to the stairs without saying a word. Charles closed the front door as they left the house.

Emma asked him what happened. Charles was unsure. He said nothing other than, "Mr. Lyell said that no one came by today."

When Emma opened her mailbox, there was lots of mail, but no white, unmarked envelope. She was sure that it would be delivered.

"What happened in there?" asked Emma again.

Charles simply stared towards the heavens, looking far into the distance. Eventually, without saying anything else, he said goodbye to her and went home. When Charles reached home, he called her. She was surprised when he told her that he had received a white, unmarked envelope.

Emma was baffled. How did the sender know that Mr. Lyell was on the lookout? That must be the reason why the letter was sent to Charles's house. They agreed to meet at their school early the next morning.

Chapter 16
The Final Clue

The next morning, Charles arrived early at school. Emma was already there. She waited for him by the swings. While she could not figure out why Charles received the letter, she was excited to see the final clue and the colors of the clothes that he was wearing. This morning's colors were wilder than anything that she had ever seen before. Actually, Emma was confused when she saw Charles's clothes because he had mentioned that his Aunt Bessie was at his house. She thought nothing of it.

Without hesitation, Charles showed the letter to Emma. It was simply a list of names. There were no instructions or indication of what the list was for. It contained the following:

Great Pyramid of Giza Sir Flinders Tyldesley Tutankhamun Imp
Temple of Artemis Uruk Natural History Ephesus Egeria
Mausoleum of Halicarnassus Newton Idrieus Malta Mausolus
Lighthouse of Alexandria Dinocrates Neptune Earthquakes
Hanging Gardens of Babylon Al Hillah Ezekiel Rassam
Statue of Zeus at Olympia Yosemite Altis Iliad
Colossus of Rhodes Aphrodite Nymph Delphi

"Clearly," said Charles, "we need a history lesson on the Wonders."

"Let me help you get caught up," said Emma.

Charles knew how much Emma loved to talk about history. She had spent many hours reading about ancient times and listening to Mr. Lyell's stories. When Mr. Lyell told her that she needed to know the past to understand the present and the future, she took him literally.

Charles looked at the list as Emma went through each of the names. He was interested to see how the clue words were connected to each of the Seven Wonders of the Ancient World.

Great Pyramid of Giza Sir Flinders Tyldesley Tutankhamun Imp

Emma began, "**Sir Flinders Petrie** conducted the first precision measurements on the pyramids around 1880. **Tyldesley** was sure that the pyramids were robbed of their treasure even before al-Mamun entered and tried to steal their riches around 820 AD. **Tutankhamun,** or King Tut, was a ruler during the New Kingdom era in Egypt when Memphis was its capital. Likewise, it was the capital when Hemiunu built the Great Pyramid, which was a tomb for Pharaoh Khufu. An **imp** is a minor deity of nature. There is a stone carving in the Lincoln Cathedral which is known as the Lincoln Imp. The Great Pyramid was the tallest human-made structure until the Lincoln Cathedral was completed around 1311 AD."

Temple of Artemis Uruk Natural History Ephesus Egeria

"The Bronze Age began around 2900 BC, in the late **Uruk** period. On the site where the Temple of Artemis was erected, there is evidence that sanctuaries were built dating back to the Bronze Age. **Natural History** was an encyclopedia published by Pliny the Elder, around 77-79 AD. It is one of the primary sources for the Temple of Artemis. **Ephesus** is where the Temple of Artemis, also known as the Temple of Diana, was built."

Mausoleum of Halicarnassus Newton Idrieus Malta Mausolus

"In 1852, archaeologist Charles **Newton** was sent by the British Museum to search for the remains of the Mausoleum of Halicarnassus. **Idrieus** was the brother of Artemisia and Mausolus. In the 15th century, the Knights of St. John of **Malta** invaded the region and built a massive castle called Bodrum Castle. By the 1520s, most of the Mausoleum's stones were used to fortify the castle's walls. The Mausoleum of Halicarnassus was built around 350 BC. The tomb was built by Artemisia for her husband **Mausolus**. The word mausoleum is derived from the name Mausolus."

Lighthouse of Alexandria Dinocrates Neptune Earthquakes

"Dinocrates was the chief architect used by Alexander the Great to build the city of Alexandria around 330 BC. He was also involved in rebuilding the Temple of Artemis. **Neptune** is the Roman equivalent of the Greek god Poseidon. There was a statue of Poseidon on top of the Lighthouse of Alexandria. Two

earthquakes in 1303 and 1323 damaged the lighthouse beyond use."

Hanging Gardens of Babylon Al Hillah Ezekiel Rassam

"**Al Hillah** is in Iraq. It is the present-day site of Babylon, of which Nebuchadnezzar II was a ruler. He is credited with constructing the Hanging Gardens of Babylon for his homesick wife. **Ezekiel** was part of the Jewish population that was exiled when Nebuchadnezzar II pillaged Jerusalem and Judea. **Rassam** discovered the stone tablet which contained the Epic of Gilgamesh, the world's oldest known example of written literature."

Statue of Zeus at Olympia Yosemite Altis Iliad

"**Yosemite** National Park contains giant sequoias in the Mariposa Grove. A grove is a small group of trees. A sacred grove is an enclosure that contains trees of great importance to a particular culture. The **Altis** was such an enclosure. It was a sacred location in Greece. It included the Temple of Zeus, which contained the Statue of Zeus. The **Iliad** is an epic poem written by Homer. In it, Homer writes about the Gods, including Zeus. According to legend, the Athenian sculptor Phidias claimed that his portrayal of Zeus was based on Homer's description in the Iliad."

Colossus of Rhodes Aphrodite Nymph Delphi

"**Aphrodite** is the Greek goddess of love and beauty. When Aphrodite and Ares were caught together by Helios, he told on them and they were punished. Helios is the Sun god. The Statue of Rhodes was of Helios. **Nymphs** were minor deities. The Temple of Nymphs at Mieza was given to Aristotle by Philip as a classroom where he would tutor the young Alexander the Great. The only person Alexander considered worthy of portraying himself was Lysippos. Chares of Lindos was a student of Lysippos. Chares was a Greek sculptor who constructed the Statue of Rhodes. He probably never saw it completed though because he committed suicide. **Delphi** is a town in Greece. The

Oracles of Delphi were famous for their prophecies. After the Statue of Rhodes was destroyed by the 226 BC earthquake, they warned against its rebuilding. It was never rebuilt. Incidentally, the only time the Seven Wonders of the Ancient World could be seen together is during the approximately 60 years that the Statue of Rhodes was standing."

Charles was quite impressed with how Emma connected all of the keywords to the Seven Wonders of the Ancient World. However, he could not see the meaning behind it. "So," he asked, "what does all of this tell us?"

"Well," explained Emma, "the only thing we don't know is when the thief is going to steal the gold." She pointed to the letter, insisting, "There must be a clue in here."

Charles suggested, "Well, we know how much he loves acrostics. There has to be a way to arrange these clues to form one."

Emma and Charles figured that the clue words were the key to solving the crypt. They both agreed that the Wonders were not part of the answer, just there to organize the clue words.

Great Pyramid of Giza Sir Flinders Tyldesley Tutankhamun Imp
Temple of Artemis Uruk Natural History Ephesus Egeria
Mausoleum of Halicarnassus Newton Idrieus Malta Mausolus
Lighthouse of Alexandria Dinocrates Neptune Earthquakes
Hanging Gardens of Babylon Al Hillah Ezekiel Rassam
Statue of Zeus at Olympia Yosemite Altis Iliad
Colossus of Rhodes Aphrodite Nymph Delphi

So, Charles removed them.

Sir Flinders Tyldesley Tutankhamun Imp
Uruk Natural History Ephesus Egeria
Newton Idrieus Malta Mausolus
Dinocrates Neptune Earthquakes
Al Hillah Ezekiel Rassam
Yosemite Altis Iliad
Aphrodite Nymph Delphi

Charles then showed Emma a piece of paper which he had prepared the night before with the remaining words in the form of a list:

Sir Flinders
Tyldesley
Tutankhamun
Imp
Uruk
Natural History
Ephesus
Egeria
Newton
Idrieus
Malta
Mausolus
Dinocrates
Neptune
Earthquakes
Al Hillah
Ezekiel
Rassam
Yosemite
Altis
Iliad
Aphrodite
Nymph
Delphi

Both Emma and Charles examined the list. They were unable to come up with any clues to solving the puzzle. They could not form an acrostic. They tried using the first letter, the last letter and all other combinations, but they could not come up with an acrostic.

When they had just about given up, Emma made a suggestion. She said, "The only thing I don't agree with is the order that he listed the Seven Wonders."

"What about it?" asked Charles.

"Well," said Emma, pointing to the letter, "they are not in their proper order."

Emma reached into her bag and took out a pair of scissors. She cut each of the Wonders and corresponding words that followed into strips and laid them out according to the original letter. She said, "Here is how he listed them."

Great Pyramid of Giza Sir Flinders Tyldesley Tutankhamun Imp
Temple of Artemis Uruk Natural History Ephesus Egeria
Mausoleum of Halicarnassus Newton Idrieus Malta Mausolus
Lighthouse of Alexandria Dinocrates Neptune Earthquakes
Hanging Gardens of Babylon Al Hillah Ezekiel Rassam
Statue of Zeus at Olympia Yosemite Altis Iliad
Colossus of Rhodes Aphrodite Nymph Delphi

Charles watched carefully. She then began to rearrange the strips that she had cut. She said to Charles, "The order should be like this."

Great Pyramid of Giza Sir Flinders Tyldesley Tutankhamun Imp
Hanging Gardens of Babylon Al Hillah Ezekiel Rassam
Temple of Artemis Uruk Natural History Ephesus Egeria
Statue of Zeus at Olympia Yosemite Altis Iliad
Mausoleum of Halicarnassus Newton Idrieus Malta Mausolus
Colossus of Rhodes Aphrodite Nymph Delphi
Lighthouse of Alexandria Dinocrates Neptune Earthquakes

Emma further explained, "In the list he gave us, he didn't go in order from oldest to youngest or 1 to 7, he went 1, 3, 5, 7, 2, 4, 6. He is skipping each Wonder once."

Charles suggested, "Why don't we rearrange the clue words according to the new pattern."

Emma agreed. She cut the strips further, separating the name of each of the Wonder from the clue words following it. Emma placed the name of the Seven Wonders in order from oldest to youngest on the ground. She then cut each of the clue words into individual pieces and laid them out on the ground. The first clue word was **Sir Flinders**, followed by **Uruk** and ending with **Mausolus.**

Sir Flinders	Tyldesley	Tutankhamun	Imp
Uruk	Natural History	Ephesus	Egeria
Newton	Idrieus	Malta	**Mausolus**
Dinocrates	Neptune	Earthquakes	
Al Hillah	Ezekiel	Rassam	
Yosemite	Altis	Iliad	
Aphrodite	Nymph	Delphi	

When she was done, they both looked at the list again. In all of the previous crypts, the first letter always formed an acrostic.

Sir Flinders
Uruk
Newton
Dinocrates
Al Hillah
Yosemite
Aphrodite
Tyldesley
Natural History
Idrieus
Neptune
Ezekiel
Altis
Nymph
Tutankhamun
Ephesus
Malta
Earthquakes
Rassam
Iliad
Delphi
Imp
Egeria
Mausolus

Charles called out the first letter of each clue word,

"S.U.N.D.A.Y.A.T.N.I.N.E.A.N.T.E.M.E.R.I.D.I.E.M."

The acrostic was clear. Charles was happy to say it again, "SUNDAY AT NINE ANTE MERIDIEM."

They both knew that **ante meridiem** was the long version of 'AM', just as **post meridiem** stood for 'PM'.

Emma said, "The exhibition starts on Sunday. He will be there at 9 am." Then, remembering what she knew about the exhibit, she added, "This will also be the first of many viewings. Since everyone wants to see the exhibit first, the biggest crowd will be there early in the morning, where it will be easier to steal the gold and disappear."

"I think we're ready then," said Charles, amazed with their effort. He was both exhausted and relieved that they had uncovered the last clue. He summarized, "We know that he's going to try and steal the gold from the Egyptian exhibit on Sunday at 9 am, at the museum on 1849 California Street. We're going to catch this thief for sure." The fire and passion that he had for detective work, had been rekindled. Emma was surprised by his exuberance.

"Unfortunately," stated Emma, "it's only called stealing if you get caught."

"Meaning?" asked Charles.

"We still haven't figured out everything yet," said Emma. She reminded him, "We did not uncover all of the clues from the first letter." She took out the letter and showed it to Charles.

A treasure in a tomb,
The casket unlocked;
To the right of that figure, don't assume.
Here is his head,
Etched in wood;
Much too late to have been wed.
Unless you see it by day,
Stay away.
Enter with your fears,
Usually, an ironic figure appears.
My whereabouts will be revealed if my name is Acrostic.

"Fortunately," beamed Emma, "I've been working on what they could mean. They are all clues to the museum. The first part of the clue, **A treasure in a tomb, the casket unlocked**, must refer directly to the open-casket exhibit. From the layout of the museum, the casket is going to be placed to the left of the giant chameleon statue. We know that chameleons change their colors, so we should never *assume* anything when it comes to them. This could refer to the second part of the clue: **To the right of that figure, don't assume**."

"So," asked Charles, "what does **Here is his head, etched in wood, much too late to have been wed**, supposed to mean?"

"Well," confessed Emma, "I didn't get that one."

"Good," said Charles excitedly, "because I did."

Emma listened patiently.

He began, "When I went home, I looked up how old the oldest people were when they got married. I found out that Harry Stevens was 103 years old when he married Thelma Lucan at a retirement home. The oldest bride in history was 102 years old when she married Dudley Reid in Australia. But I don't think this is what he is referring to. Besides, these records will be broken one day.

"Yesterday, I borrowed the Bible from the library. There were lots of facts in the Book of Genesis. When I came to Noah, it said that he was 500 years old when he became a father. There are some who believe that a couple is married only when they have a child. So, I'm sure that is **much too late to have been wed**."

"It does make sense," agreed Emma. "Just a few weeks ago, the museum acquired a piece of wood which they claimed came from Noah's Ark. **Here is his head, etched in wood** could refer directly to Noah."

Charles agreed, "That's exactly what I was thinking."

Emma continued, "**Unless you see him by day, stay away**. This could only refer to a vampire, being a creature of the night. The museum has an exhibit containing things to do with vampires and vampire bats."

"Unfortunately," said Emma scratching her head, "the next two lines give no mention of the museum directly."

Charles confessed, "I can't think of anything that it could mean."

"Well," said Emma, "at least we have two days to try and figure it out."

"Now," said Charles, "what we have to do is to figure out a way to catch the thief."

"With this capture," reminded Emma, "we're going to get some recognition at last."

Charles insisted, "But we still have to find a way of notifying the police."

"We have lots of time," said Emma, although she had no intentions of going to the police. Emma was convinced that she and Charles were capable of capturing the thief themselves.

Emma said to Charles, "To be a good detective, you must possess three important skills. First, you must be able to follow clues."

"I can follow clues," responded Charles.

"Second, you must have patience."

"I have patience."

"Third, you must be fearless."

Charles responded hesitantly, "I have patience."

Charles was not like Emma. Fearless, he was not. He would rather look danger in the rearview mirror than face it head-on. Emma, however, knows that she can still count on him to be by her side when it really matters.

Charles wondered out loud, "Even though we've solved all of the puzzles, do you think there may be more hidden clues in these letters?"

Emma suggested, "I wouldn't be surprised."

Looking at his watch he told her, "C'mon, we still have about twenty minutes remaining."

"Where are we going?" asked Emma, running behind Charles. She then remembered that Charles had told her that Mr. Sedgwick was not impressed with his knowledge of the California gold rush.

Charles announced, "To the library! Today, Mr. Sedgwick is going to lecture on the Canadian Confederation. I don't have an excuse for him."

Chapter 17
The Big Game

Early in the morning, the next day, Emma called Charles. They agreed to meet at his home. When she got there, Charles was already on his bicycle. After ensuring that they had everything that they needed, they began to ride to the museum. Along the way, Emma pointed Charles in the direction of a caravan of black cars with tinted windows. They watched as a police cruiser escorted them. While they were both curious, neither one knew who or what was inside.

One of the many privileges of being a junior constable is the free passes that you get. Emma and Charles were allowed to enter the zoo, museums and galleries in town for free. Upon walking through the turnstiles, someone accidentally bumped into Charles. It was Snevyl. When he recognized Emma and Charles, he dropped his pencil and notepad as he screamed and ran out of the museum. Emma and Charles simply stared at each other in bewilderment.

Emma did not want to waste any time. She headed straight for the location where the treasures will be on display. While the treasures were not set up yet, the casket was being constructed. Charles was surprised to see the size of the chameleon beside which the display will be.

After surveying the layout of the exhibit's location, Emma told Charles that the best place to spot the thief would be from a high place. The museum will be crowded with patrons, so they needed an unobstructed view.

They took the spiraling stairs to the second floor of the museum. Emma and Charles looked for places where they could hide. Emma decided that the railing next to the stairs, which led to the main floor, would be the best possible location. There wasn't much room next to the railings but it was the perfect place to hide. Charles tried to get comfortable next to the railings, close to the corner of the wall. No one would notice him there, especially when he stooped down beside the armored suit of a knight.

At the other end, and opposite of Charles, was Emma. She found a similar setting. The only thing that they could do is to try and identify who the thief is. They had no plan for actually capturing him.

When they were satisfied with their plans, they ended their visit by testing their walkie-talkies. They could hear each other clearly. Of note and importance, Charles reminded Emma of the clue from the first letter which they had not figured out. Neither one of them could come up with a suitable explanation for the last piece of the clue: **Enter with your fears, usually an ironic figure appears.**

They could not stay too long at the museum because, in just a few hours, there was the football championship game. Before heading home to get his aunt and father, Charles wished Emma good luck. Emma headed directly for her school.

It was just after 11:30 am when the referee blew the whistle and signaled the start of the championship game. Emma's Monarch Park Kings were the underdogs as they played the defending champions, the Bowmore Lions. The game was being played at Emma's school.

Every student, teacher, parent, and resident of Silent Hum was in the stands. All of the stores in town were closed. For someone visiting, it would appear like a ghost town. Charles, Susannah, Mr. Lyell, and Ms. Coraline were in the front row.

There was one notable difference about the opposing team from last year. Their new quarterback was Beagle Abbey. For the past few weeks, rumors were circulating that he was looking to get back at Emma. He was still angry that she turned him over to the police for planting evidence and for what transpired at the quiz tournament.

The game began with a short ten-yard return after the opening kick-off. The cheering from the stands was lively and energetic. From the coin toss to the opening kick return, no one sat down. Everyone was confident that their team was going to win the championship game this year.

Their cheers and support were rewarded by two quick first-down passes thrown by Emma. On the very next play, Emma chose to keep the football and completed a 40-yard run to the opponent's one-yard line, eluding four defenders in the process. Two plays later, the crowd erupted in cheers. The game was not two minutes old when Emma scored the first touchdown on a trick play.

It was a play that Emma had designed. As she yelled, "Six, six," two wide receivers ran towards her. She took the ball, turned around and extended her hands. Half of the defense went to the right and half went to the left. They were going to stop both receivers, as they did not know which one had the football. Emma was left all alone in the middle. Without turning around, she took two steps backward and crossed the goal line with the football held high for all to see. Beagle screamed in frustration, but it was drowned out by the cheering from the crowd.

Suddenly, the Kings were up by six points against a stunned Lions team. Beagle was not very happy, as he slammed his helmet to the ground. However, the Kings gained nothing as the extra point kick sailed wide. Yet, the crowd exploded in celebration. The home team held an early lead. Unlike the game last year, Emma's team never had the lead. The fans were hoping that this was a sign of things to come.

The Kings' defense was absolutely dominating on their opponent's first drive. On the first three plays, they got three quarterback sacks. The opposing team was completely frustrated and disorganized. Beagle kept yelling instructions to his teammates but the cheering from the stands was overwhelming.

The first quarter ended on a 6-play, 70-yard drive. It led to a 20-yard field goal and a 9-0 lead. The fans were as confident as Emma and her teammates. On the very next drive, their lead was cut to 9-7, as the ball was tipped and intercepted early in the second quarter. It was a huge letdown, considering how well they were playing. They handed the Lions seven points: six points on the touchdown and one on the extra point kick. Emma encouraged her teammates to focus on the goal ahead. Her guidance and leadership paid dividends, as her team scored a field goal on its next possession.

At the end of the first half, their opponent scored another touchdown and led 14-12. Emma suspected that they would try something underhanded. A wide receiver pretended that he was hurt by falling to the ground and holding his ankle. His defender left him alone to double-cover another receiver. Once there was enough separation between them, he got to his feet and Beagle threw the ball into the end zone.

After they scored, Beagle walked past Emma and gave her a big smile. Emma knew that Beagle would do whatever it takes to win the game. For the first time since the opening whistle, there was silence in the stands. Everyone sat on the edge of their seats. Their team was down by two points but they had seen this before. In many of their regular-season games, they had given up the lead early, only to reclaim it later in the game. The crowd seemed nervous but optimistic.

Things did not start off well in the third quarter for the Kings. The opening drive netted their opponent 3 more points on a field goal. Their lead was now 17 to 12.

The next drive was more akin to expectations, as Emma split the defense and scrambled for a 50-yard touchdown on a run-pass option. Practically, the entire opposing team followed her into the end zone. However, once again, they missed the extra point, giving the Kings a slight 18-17 lead. Throughout the entire season, their kicker had not missed a single extra point conversion. It was uncharacteristic for him to do so. So far, he has missed two in a row.

Most importantly, however, they had home-field advantage and the crowd let them know how they were doing. They repeated the wave, over and over again. Not since the beginning of the game did they cheer so loudly. The atmosphere was absolutely electric. Everyone could sense victory.

The third quarter ended with each team scoring a field goal. Emma's team was ahead 21-20. There was still one quarter left to play. A one-point lead against the defending champions was not safe. Although the Kings had the best defense in the league, anything could happen, especially in a championship game.

Precisely as Emma had feared, they quickly found themselves down by 6 points after only one minute in the fourth quarter. No one had bothered to cover an open receiver downfield and it led to a quick 60-yard score. Emma reminded herself of the team's motto: 'It can be overcome!'

The Kings 21-20 lead quickly became a 27-21 deficit. Emma knew that she needed to come up with a new play on the next drive. She called a timeout. Everyone huddled together and she quickly explained what she came up with. On the next play, Emma played running back. The quarterback yelled, "Six, six," and the ball was tossed to him. He tucked it into Emma's arms as she ran past him. But instead of barreling forward through the defense, she changed direction, dropped back, and launched a

Hail Mary pass. It spiraled 35 yards downfield to a waiting receiver.

However, the ball stayed in the air too long and the opposition picked it off and dashed across the gridiron, dodging several tacklers, including Emma, to score a touchdown. With the extra point, the deficit grew to 34-21, with only 6 minutes to play.

"It can be overcome," she encouraged everyone. They looked to her for leadership and inspiration. The next drive only took one minute off the clock and resulted in 3 points on the ensuing field goal, cutting the deficit to 34-24. After an impressive and much-needed stop on the defensive end, the offense took over on the opponent's 40-yard line. After 3 successful first downs, they managed to kick another field goal, bringing them a little closer. They were only down by seven points.

With less than four minutes to go, Emma called another timeout. She wanted to discuss a new play. They were seven points behind: one touchdown and an extra point kick away from tying up the game and sending it into overtime.

There was renewed optimism on and off the field. Everyone stood up and cheered as loudly as they could. They sounded like 20 000 people, even though there were less than a quarter of that.

The referee blew the whistle and the ball was punted. However, it did not travel very far. Emma and the coach had called for an onside kick. Their opponent was caught off guard. Everyone, on both teams, piled onto the ball at the fifty-yard line. No one in the crowd knew who had the ball. One by one, the referees cleared the pile-up. Everyone in the stands held their breath until only one player emerged with the football. The ball was in the hands of one of Emma's teammates. The crowd cheered them on. They were down by seven points and they had the ball back with only a few minutes to play.

Chants of "Heaven-o, Heaven-o" began to be heard from a few people in the crowd. Soon, the entire crowd joined in and everyone lent their support to their beloved Kings. The players soaked up every emotion and passion from their fans. The entire team surveyed the stands. Everyone was cheering and dancing. They began to feed off the energy of the crowd.

On their first drive, Emma threw a short 5-yard pass and the receiver scrambled to their opponent's 40-yard line. The clock was still running. They had 3 minutes and 34 seconds to play.

Their momentum was temporarily slowed down as Emma was sacked on the next play. Emma seemed hurt, as she laid on the ground. There was complete silence in the stands. Everyone held their breath. Unwilling to let them down, Emma forced herself to get back to her feet. The crowd showed their appreciation by cheering, upon seeing her getting up. Beagle slammed his helmet to the ground in disgust for a second time. He was hoping that she would stay down.

After a 7-yard run on second and 18, Emma threw a 17-yard pass on the next play. They were on a roll again. In the stands, the crowd was as loud as ever. They were now on the 24-yard line with one minute and 56 seconds remaining to play. On 4 consecutive rushes, they gained 3, 6, 7, and 2 yards. The plays ate up one minute and 29 seconds off the game clock. They found themselves on the 6-yard line with 27 seconds remaining in the game.

The next play was not successful, as they opted to throw the football. The ball was batted away by a defender. They were very close to tying the game; even the crowd could feel it. On 2nd and goal, Emma was rushed by the defense and ended up throwing the ball away. Their chances were slipping away. They were not being patient. Emma tried to settle everyone down. On 3rd and goal, the wide receiver began to run before he caught the ball and so dropped the pass, even though he was wide open. Emma stressed to everyone to be patient. There were only 10 seconds remaining. A tough decision lay ahead. There wasn't enough time to kick a field goal and then try to get a touchdown. They had to go for it on fourth down.

Surprisingly, the Lions called a timeout. This gave Emma's team a chance to contemplate their options. Again, Emma reminded everyone to be patient and to not rush the play. "It can be overcome," she reminded everyone. Soon, the crowd got wind of it and began to chant: "It can be overcome! It can be overcome!"

The decision was made. Emma would play running back. After the snap, the football was tossed to Emma by the quarterback. She dropped back to pass rather than run it in for the score. There were two receivers in the end zone. With all her might, she launched a rocket, before getting knocked to the ground. She watched from her knees as the ball was caught. The referee immediately put both hands up to signal a touchdown. The crowd erupted in cheers.

They were still down by one point with 4 seconds remaining. The game was not over. The jubilation and excitement of the touchdown sent the crowd into a frenzy. However, as the field goal unit lined up to kick the extra point to tie the game, everyone held their breath. With only 4 seconds remaining, Emma called the last timeout. The field goal unit had missed the extra point kick all day. If they had not, they would have the lead.

After the timeout, they took to the field, trying to tie the game. Surprisingly, Emma was on the field to kick the extra point. She was the only one who could perform under that much pressure. But everyone knew that she had never kicked a field goal before, including the opposition. So, Beagle came onto the field as a defender. William, the kicker, was now to receive the snap so Emma could attempt the field goal.

The ball was snapped to William, who immediately spun the laces out. Emma stepped in for the kick but stopped at the last second. William picked up the ball and ran backward, as the entire defense collapsed on the goal line, attempting to stop the kick. Emma scampered into the end zone with Beagle behind her.

Seeing Emma open, William lobbed an 18-yard pass into the back of the end zone. Emma leaped into the air and tipped the ball straight up. It was thrown too high. As she fell to the ground, she did not take her eyes off the ball. She reached out her hands to secure the ball as she was being pushed from behind by Beagle. With both feet inbounds, she corralled the ball, having possession of it, before falling to her knees.

Everyone looked at the referee. Without hesitation, he immediately raised both hands in the air.

The crowd erupted in cheers. The two-point conversion was successful. The Kings had won their first championship trophy, 35-34 with no time left on the clock.

Led by Charles, everyone ran onto the field to congratulate their champions, who were already hi-fiving and hugging each other. Emma could see Mr. Lyell and Ms. Coraline in the stands.

They were both giving her a thumbs up for a job well done. Emma was overjoyed as she pumped her fist in the air.

Even their bitter rivals admitted that they were beaten by a better team. Everyone stood and applauded the Kings' performance from the sidelines, except a very frustrated Beagle.

Once the celebrations settled down, Principal Grant came onto the field to present Emma with her first championship trophy. However, Beagle stepped in front of her. No one knew what he was going to do when he picked up the trophy. He admired it for a few seconds. Several teachers came forward to see what he was doing. They decided to let him take the trophy. He approached Emma. Standing before her, he reached out his right hand to shake hers before he handed over the trophy, saying, "Congratulations!"

The crowd cheered as Emma thrust it into the air for all to see. Emma's stats were impressive. She ran the football ten times for 131 yards and threw 29 passes for 325 yards. With three touchdowns, including the game-winning catch, she was named the game's MVP. At last, her trophy mantle was complete.

Chapter 18
The Fishing Trip

Susannah had promised Emma and Charles that she would take them fishing after the big game. As Mr. Lyell and Ms. Coraline were in no rush to go home, Emma asked her mother if they could go with them. Susannah thought that it was a great idea. Mr. Lyell and Ms. Coraline were happy to join them.

The sun was shining bright and hot when they arrived at the picnic area by the river. Charles wanted to go fishing right away but Susannah needed some help unpacking. Ms. Coraline, too, wanted to go fishing. Emma and Mr. Lyell volunteered to stay behind.

Ms. Coraline picked up the tackle box and Charles carried his rod and bait. They hastily walked down a narrow path to the water's edge. Charles was having a hard time keeping up with Ms. Coraline. When they got there, they saw a boat in the water, just a short distance from the shore. Onto the larger boat was tied a small rubber raft. There were five men in the larger boat.

When Charles and Ms. Coraline saw the men in the boat, they waved to them. One of the men replied, mockingly, "You're not going to catch much from shore."

"Don't listen to him," advised Ms. Coraline.

Charles did as Ms. Coraline instructed and paid no attention to them. He was about to cast his line when Ms. Coraline pointed to the water, saying, "Look out for those rocks when you cast."

There were several large pieces of rocks jutting out of the water. Before casting, Charles took out a float from his tackle box and attached it to the line. Ms. Coraline looked on.

She told him, "I think you have it a little too high. If your bait drags on the ground, the fish won't bite it."

"I didn't know you knew about fishing," said Charles, as he adjusted the float a little lower.

She told him, "My father used to bring me here to fish when I was a little girl. I think fishing is a metaphor for life."

"How so?" asked Charles. He made his first cast. The float landed only a few feet away from where the raft was in the water.

Ms. Coraline said, "The fish in the water represents all of the opportunities that you will get in your lifetime. Your fishing rod and reel are your strengths or your weaknesses. Those who are best prepared are better able to meet life's challenges."

Charles listened to every word that she said but paid attention to the float as he reeled in the line. She said, "The bait that you use is your knowledge. Using the right kind of bait will help you catch more fish. As for the weights on your line, they represent how much desire you have to succeed. If the weight is too heavy, it will sink fast and you will miss out on some of your opportunities. If it's too light, it sinks too slowly and others will get ahead of you."

"What about the hook?" asked Charles, as he reeled in the line and cast out near the boats again.

"The hook represents your confidence," said Ms. Coraline. "The sharper the hook, the more confident you are. The more confident you are, the more fish you will catch."

While Charles listened to Ms. Coraline, the float quickly sank below the surface and came back up. Seeing this, Ms. Coraline said, "If you are too slow to react, you will miss out on some of your opportunities."

The float quickly disappeared under the water again but Charles set the hook too hard and the float rose back to the surface. While this happened, Ms. Coraline was in the middle of saying, "If you react too quickly, your knowledge may go unnoticed and others may think that you are impatient."

Charles and Ms. Coraline paid close attention to the float in the water. When it sank below the level of the water, Charles set the hook and saw the rod bending.

"It's on for sure this time!" he announced excitedly. The fish ran towards deeper water as Charles reeled it in. He held onto the rod as tightly as he could. All of the men stopped what they were doing to watch him.

"It's *huge*!" exclaimed Charles.

Ms. Coraline looked disappointed, knowing from experience that something was not right.

"I'm telling you," disagreed Charles, as he seemed to be in the fight of his life, "it's a GREAT BIG ONE!"

Then, all of a sudden, the fish stopped moving. Charles looked at Ms. Coraline before he reeled in the line. Something was definitely wrong. The rod was bending over in a great arc but the fish was not moving.

"What...is...it?" asked a puzzled Charles.

When the fish got to the edge of the water, they both looked on in amazement. It was a small fish, but it had run between a branch in the water and Charles reeled both of them in. Ms. Coraline said nothing, but Charles was very disappointed, especially after the men in the boat saw what he had caught.

"Thanks for cleaning out the river," one of them teased. They all laughed at him from the boat.

Ms. Coraline encouraged him not to pay attention to them. Charles let the fish go and tossed the branch to the side. He cast out again but this time the hook landed in the rubber raft. He tried to pull it out but the hook fastened itself even more. Ms. Coraline held her breath. Charles pulled harder and the hook slipped through the rubber raft and fell into the water.

"Thank goodness nothing happened," whispered Ms. Coraline. Charles reeled the line away from the raft. The men in the boat had finally decided who should go into the rubber raft. Two of them carefully maneuvered themselves into it. The engine from the larger boat roared to life and took off for the other side of the river.

"Maybe you'll catch something bigger next time," shouted one of the men in the rubber raft.

"Don't listen to them," said Ms. Coraline. "Just keep your line in the water. You'll catch a big one."

Charles appreciated her words of encouragement.

The men in the rubber raft paddled out into deeper water. They stopped paddling and seemed to be in some distress. Ms. Coraline noticed them. She immediately informed Charles of what was happening. The inflated rubber raft suddenly appeared deflated. The men began to panic as they sank into the water.

Charles looked at Ms. Coraline, just as she turned to him with a vacant expression on her face. She finished her lesson by stressing, "But it's also important to know when to call it a day!"

Charles agreed.

Emma had just arrived with her fishing rod. Charles quickly picked up the tackle box and bait and began to run back to the picnic site. Ms. Coraline followed.

"Where are you guys going?" asked Emma.

"I think it's time we find another spot," suggested Ms. Coraline, running past her.

They did not turn back, as they raced up the hill and back to the picnic site. Neither Charles nor Ms. Coraline said anything regarding why they returned so soon. Ms. Coraline stayed behind, while Emma and Charles went to find another place to fish.

It was a short walk from the picnic site to Emma's favorite fishing spot. It was just beyond a few small trees and down a narrow path. Emma's feet stepped lively, as she led the way. Charles paced himself to keep up. When they got there, they were both surprised at what they found. The water and the surrounding area were completely littered with garbage.

"What in the world!" exclaimed Emma, with a look of disgust on her face.

"Are those tires in the water?" asked Charles, peering over the narrow cliff to get a better look at the water. He saw old car tires throughout the river. The water ran stagnant.

"Who could have done this?" wondered Emma, as she put down her fishing rod.

"Well," said Charles, "I'm pretty sure it wasn't the smallmouth bass."

Emma replied, "I agree with Gilbert when he said that we should give equal rights to Nature."

Emma picked up one of the open garbage bags and began to put the boxes, cans, paper plates, and paper wrappers into it. Charles did the same, though he would rather be fishing. He said, "We can learn a lesson from the people on Easter Island. When they had basically destroyed the island and depleted all of the resources, they wanted to leave. But they couldn't because they had no wood to build boats. When we are forced to leave the Earth, we will not have enough resources to do so." He then proclaimed, "There is a way to solve all this."

"How?" she asked hesitantly.

He replied with one word, "Sacrifices!"

Emma asked, "What would you do?"

"Well," explained Charles, "I would clear out all prisons and similar institutions. I would sacrifice all abusers of any likeness, anyone who suffers, any adult who could not provide for their own basic needs, and limit life to 75 years or sooner. I agree with those people protesting at the retirement home. I would also allow anyone who did not want to live to end it."

"How would you justify this?" asked Emma. "I mean, this is basically twenty percent of the people on the planet."

He answered, "In the natural world, the weak and sick are not allowed to survive. Why do humans allow it? We will have a healthier human population. If you think about it, hundreds of millions of people live in poverty and will never get out of it. There are about ten people that die every minute just due to hunger. Most people exist, but they don't live."

"Isn't there another way?" asked Emma.

Charles responded, "If I was the ruler of the world, I would give everyone a million dollars at birth. You can do whatever you want with your money. You can save it or spend it. You can use it now or use it later. You can have as much fun as you want or be as miserable as you wish. Everyone will be equal at birth. Everyone will have the same opportunity to succeed. However, no one will be allowed to be a burden on the system. Which means, when your money runs out, so does your time on Earth."

How this all came about, Emma only glimpsed in her vision. Following the third major recession in 10 years, were three years of prosperity. The human population swelled to nine billion people. Wealth was abundant. Everyone was happy. It would not last, however. Soon, all of the wealth was gone.

It began suddenly. Some suggested that it was due to the Earth's magnetic field temporarily weakening as it flipped its polarity. The oceans turned red, killing all of the fish. All of the birds of the air fell out of the sky. Food supplies everywhere began to dry up. Clean drinking water became scarce. Diseases, earthquakes and volcanic eruptions preceded drought, famine and starvation.

The savior did not take long to come. Among all people, Charles came forward. His ideas of how to end the crisis and food shortages gave everyone hope. His ideas were simple. He had a way to provide work, food and water for all. In their desperation, the whole of the Earth listened to him.

Charles was then responsible for the *Stop the Machine* movement. With so many people out of work, he realized that we needed to replace machines with people. Within one week, all non-essential machines were turned off. Everyone who could work had a job, all across the Earth. He also realized that food production was not the main problem, but that storage and distribution were. He solved these problems, too.

Then, the *Age of Building* began. Following the population explosion, Charles realized that the only fertile land left was the land that houses were built on. He reasoned that since the oceans could not provide food anymore, they could be used to house people. So, one-third of the world's population was employed to move the mountains and high places, to fill in the oceans. Three billion were employed in relocating all housing to the new land. The water from the oceans was purified and ran in tubes high above all dwellings.

A third of the population was employed in food production and water sanitation. Charles knew of a storage facility in northern Europe that contained a warehouse full of seeds that could be used to grow food. A team ventured to Svalbard and returned with millions of seeds. The remaining people were employed in the construction of the Twelve Mighty Domes.

When their work was done, two years later, all of the oceans were paved, save a blue spot - a small piece of ocean preserved to remind us of the world of old. It was like a watery modern-day Eden.

When two years had passed, food was abundant and everyone was equal. There were no wars for the first time and there was peace throughout the earth. Equality was the norm. "Existence is subsistence," Charles would preach to everyone. He reminded them that one day we will be someone's ancestors. We needed to save some of our resources for them. Without countries and continents, all people were governed as one. Everyone was equal. Charles ensured that their basic needs were met.

Some were not pleased, however. They demanded more. They saw Charles as putting himself before all others. So, they schemed to destroy him. They arrested him on his wedding day and imprisoned him. In the chaos, his bride was killed. The peace that was forged was broken. There was no order over the Earth or over the people. Chaos reigned when food and clean water became scarce again.

With the world in chaos, some realized the mistake of imprisoning Charles. So, he was released from prison and given back his post. However, he was hardened against his fellow humans. All that he had accomplished was undone in just two months. There was not enough food or clean water for all.

For their betrayal, he set the people against each other, spreading lies and falsehoods. He did not see it fit that all humans should be spared. He set the people against each other. In one week, more than half of all the people returned to the dust. Within a month, half of all those that remained succumbed to their injuries. Immediately, Charles and his newly formed army enacted new laws. Among them, that life expectancy would be set at 50 years old, save himself and his inner circle. A further two billion suffered under his other atrocities.

When it was all done, only twenty million people remained. Charles was still not pleased. There were still too many people. Each of the Twelve Mighty Domes was designed for only 12 000 people each, just as it is written in the Bible in the Book of Revelation. So, he and his army began to hand-select the most capable citizens to enter the Twelve Mighty Domes. To unite the people and to give them a common purpose, everyone was employed to find intelligent life in the Milky Way and beyond.

All of those who were not chosen languished in the wastelands, waiting for their turn to enter the Twelve Mighty Domes. No one inside the Domes was allowed to have relationships or children. If anyone dies, reaches age 50 or if they choose to leave, they would be replaced by one of the Wastelanders. In this way, Charles was able to keep order over both groups. The Wastelanders worked and provided food and other services to the Domelites in exchange for the hope of one day joining them in the Domes. In the meanwhile, they awaited their savior in the wastelands.

"If I had my way," said Charles, picking up a few discarded plastic bags, "everyone would live under giant domes. We would live and work and play when the sun is out and sleep when night falls, just the way nature intended. People would not need to suffer the effects of old age. They would only live as long as they were fruitful. We need to make these decisions now while we still can."

Emma contended, "I still believe in something more. I still believe that Jesus will save us."

"Well," said Charles, "my family and I don't believe it."

"What do you mean?" asked Emma.

He said, "I don't believe that Judas betrayed Jesus."

"Who did?" she asked. She had never heard him talk like this before. He was beginning to scare her.

He said, "It was Jesus all along."

The litter dropped from Emma's hand. It missed the garbage bag and fell to the ground. She had never before heard that Jesus was implicated in his own death.

Charles explained, "Jesus foretold everything that was going to happen to him, including the people involved. He foretold the future because he wrote it. Jesus used Judas to make himself a martyr."

"A true Christian accepts the words of the Bible," confessed Emma.

He countered, "The lost years of Christ were spent wandering and learning in the far reaches of Asia, even beyond India. Some of his later teachings reflect Buddhism and other religions. He also learned deep meditation, where you can slow your breathing down to the point where people think that you are dead.

"He did not die upon the cross. The time in the tomb was enough for him to recover from his injuries. The Bible further gave accounts in the Gospels that following the resurrection, Jesus was seen by many people. These were not apparitions, it was actually him. After he recovered from his injuries and got married, Jesus lived out the rest of his life in secrecy with Mary Magdalene and their children."

"Charles," said Emma, "Christianity is grounded in the belief that Christ died on the cross and rose from the dead three days later. You are questioning the foundations of Christianity itself." Emma did not want to pursue the matter further.

Suddenly, the men who were in the rubber raft approached them.

"How was the fishing?" asked Charles, trying to hide the smile on his face.

The man, who had spoken to Charles before, raised both of his hands in the air, letting the water drip to the ground. He said, "It was so good, we just had to join the fishes."

Emma whispered with a smile on her face, "Today, the fishes won."

Chapter 19
To Catch A Thief

It was just after 8:30 am on Sunday morning when Emma arrived at Charles's house. Charles joined her on his bicycle. Along the way, they talked about Gilbert. No one knew where he and his parents went. He had Emma's phone number but he did not try to contact her. She was very concerned about him.

They also talked about what they saw and heard on the news the night before. There were more tsunamis reported around the world. Emma and Charles did not know what was causing them. With each passing day, more tsunamis and more fatalities were being reported. More than one hundred thousand lives were lost in the past week alone and over ten million since the first report a few months ago.

The oceans were not safe. Governments around the world have closed waterways to any kind of traffic, from oil tankers and fishing vessels to cargo and cruise ships. Even the world's navy was on high alert. More than twenty submarines have been beached so far. No one knows what was causing the earthquakes and tsunamis. The only thing they knew for sure is that they are not natural. Everyone around the world living at or below sea level was being evacuated. The Canadian government took in all of the residents from the Caribbean islands and the Pacific islands. With each news report, Emma is reminded of the crypt that warned of a deluge.

Governments from around the world are blaming each other. Every country is suspicious of each other. The effects of each disaster are beginning to take their toll. Entire countries are running out of food, oil and gas. People are rioting and hoarding supplies. The clashes with authorities are becoming increasingly more violent as people grow desperate.

They reached the museum before it opened. While locking up their bicycles, Emma asked Charles, "Are you afraid?"

To which he responded, "There's absolutely no reason to be afraid."

"Really?" asked Emma. She was encouraged by his positive thinking.

Charles explained, "You should not be afraid of something that has not happened yet. It will only cloud your mind with unwanted thoughts."

"That's pretty good advice," recognized Emma.

"However," mentioned Charles, "I am afraid because we did not solve the last part of the clue."

Emma confessed, "I can't figure it out either. He would not have included it unless it was important."

"Well," said Charles, looking at his watch, "we have exactly two minutes to figure it out."

It was almost 9 o'clock and the lineup was almost two blocks long. The doors were opened and everyone rushed in. Emma and Charles were surprised to see that only two security guards were on duty.

"I need to go to the bathroom," said Charles at the bottom of the stairs, pressing his legs together.

"I thought you weren't afraid?" teased Emma.

"I'm not," he replied.

"Well hurry up," instructed Emma. "I'm going up to my post."

Charles quickly ran towards the washroom and was soon standing beside the knight's armored suit opposite of Emma. No one else was on the second floor of the museum. They both observed the visitors trying to get a glimpse of the treasures.

"Charles," called Emma on the walkie-talkie.

He quickly responded by asking her what was the matter.

"I think I know what the clue was trying to tell us," said Emma excitedly.

"What did you come up with?" he asked.

She said, "Remember what you told me when I asked you if you were afraid?"

"Yeah," he replied.

"Well," said Emma, "that's what the clue is about. The first part of the clue, **Enter with your fears**, is the same as being afraid of the unknown. Most people are fearful because they don't know what to expect. As for the second part, **usually an ironic figure appears**, could only mean one thing."

Charles quickly replied, "You mean that we should be looking for a female thief?"

"Exactly!" said Emma.

"Good work," congratulated Charles. He asked, "What about the woman standing beside the chameleon in the green jacket? She has been standing there ever since she came into the museum."

"Do you think that she's looking for us?" asked Emma.

He replied, "We can't afford to be seen."

Charles got down on his knees and began to crawl backward while keeping an eye on the woman below. He reached his arm back to feel for the armored suit but his hand hit the leg of the suit and knocked it out of position. The rest of the armor came careening towards him. His path to the stairs was blocked. He just managed to jump over the railing and caught the cable that extended from the chandelier, as the armor broke through the railing and fell to the floor below, narrowly missing several visitors.

With all the excitement, everyone looked up to see what was going on. Charles wrapped his hands around the cable. His feet dangled freely. As he tried to get a better hold of the cable, the electrical wires that were attached to it came loose. As he swayed from side to side, he noticed the woman in the green jacket picking up some of the treasures from the open casket. No one else noticed her. They were all focused on him. The security guards were on the stairs, trying to get to him.

He knew that she was going to get away. He released his grip of the cable, held onto the electrical cord and descended quickly over the casket, knocking over the chameleon which fell onto the woman.

"She's got the gold!" screamed Charles. The woman managed to free herself of the hollowed, plastic chameleon and headed for the back exit. Just then, two police officers burst through the back doors and collided with her.

"Stop her!" yelled Emma, who finally got to Charles.

He looked up at her and said, pointing to the officers, "That was my washroom break."

The officers quickly got to their feet and handcuffed the woman. They found some of the gold artifacts in her jacket. As the officers escorted the thief out of the building, the crowd cheered Charles for his heroic efforts in stopping the thief.

Even the museum's curator thanked him. He immediately announced that Charles would be given a lifetime pass to the museum. However, Charles declined. He said that he would only accept it if Emma also got the same. After thinking it over for a second, the curator agreed. Everyone in attendance cheered when it was announced that they would both receive lifetime passes.

Snevyl could only stare at the ground in disbelief as he threw away his book of tickets. He seemed dejected. He could not catch a break.

Emma and Charles waved to everyone as they left the museum in a hurry. They had to get to church. Emma had convinced Charles to attend church with her this morning. He agreed. He told her to go ahead without him because he did not have *church* clothes on. He wanted to go home and change. They said goodbye as they parted ways.

Chapter 20
Charles Goes Missing

It was just after noon when Emma reached home from church. Her mother was on the phone when she walked through the front door. Susannah noticed that something was bothering her.

"Hold on a minute," said Susannah to Charles's father, Philip. She asked Emma, "When did you last see Charles?"

Emma replied, "Around ten this morning. He told me that he was going home to get ready for church but he didn't show up."

"His father is on the line," informed Susannah. "Charles is not home yet." Before she hung up the phone, Susannah said, "Please call me back when he gets in. Bye."

Emma was worried about Charles. Two thoughts clouded her mind. One, Charles was scared to attend church, so he went somewhere else. Two, someone or something prevented him from attending church. The latter thought troubled her greatly, especially after what he said when they went fishing.

Several hours later, there was another call. Susannah grabbed her coat and shoes and told Emma to do the same. When they got outside, Emma was surprised to see hundreds of flashlights on, beaming back and forth. Virtually everyone in town was out looking for Charles. They checked the school, the hospital, the river, the woods, and every backyard. Volunteers knocked on every door. Police cars patrolled the streets.

The search was called off a few hours later. Charles had been found, or so it was reported. Susannah and Emma were summoned to the police station. All they were told was that the Chief needed to see them urgently. Emma feared the worst.

On their way to the station, Emma whispered to her mother, "Charles fell at the museum and hurt himself because something inside the gold exhibit caught his attention. He was so captivated by *it,* that he lost sight of the piece of paper on the wall."

"Well," whispered Susannah, "now that you're allowed back at the station, don't go get yourself into any more trouble."

"Mom," pleaded Emma, "I've heard that there were people here from the Church in Rome. I saw the police escorting them.

Apparently, the CIA, the KGB, the Chinese, and the Germans have all been here in the past nine months."

Susannah asked, "What do you think they are looking for?"

"It's some kind of ancient artifact," whispered Emma. Before continuing, she made sure that the officer driving the car could not hear her. "It must be something religious because the Church has sent representatives. The others are here because it must pose some kind of national security threat. It could have something to do with all of the earthquakes and tsunamis."

"Thank you both for coming," said the Chief, as Emma and Susannah entered his office.

"Where is Charles?" asked Emma immediately.

The Chief said nothing. He simply stared at the envelope in his hand before tossing it onto his desk. It rotated once before stopping in front of Emma. The Chief gestured to her to look inside. It was already open.

Hesitantly, Emma looked inside the envelope before pulling out a piece of paper. Susannah leaned over to see what was written on it.

"You have any ideas, Emma?" asked the Chief impatiently.

Emma examined its contents closely. It was simply a list of numbers.

								1	5		1	3	2	2		1	3		5	6							
								1	3	7	7		4	3	0		8	3	6	5							
3	3	3	1	1	1	1	1	1	7	8	9	9	1	2	2	2	2	2	2	2	2	2	2	2	2	2	2
1	2	3	0	2	3	5	7	9	7	2	0	1	7	0	0	1	2	4	4	4	4	4	4	4	4	5	5
			9	3	5	6	2	1	1	2	4	1	5	7	8	4	8	1	1	2	2	3	6	8	8	0	0
													3	2	2	1	1	3	4	4	6	7	1	2	3	2	5
																	0										
2	2	2	2	2	2	2	2	2	2	2	2	2	2	2	3	3	3	3	3	3	3	3	3	3	3	6	
5	5	5	5	6	6	6	6	7	8	8	8	8	8	8	1	1	2	2	2	3	3	3	3	4	4	3	
0	0	1	9	5	5	7	9	1	0	1	1	3	3	8	2	4	6	8	8	1	1	9	9	2	3	5	
6	8	3	2	1	3	7	6	2	1	3	4	1	2	9	8	1	2	4	5	4	5	3	4	2	1	1	

The Chief said, "Obviously, the numbers have to be substituted for letters. The problem is that the numbers are not organized in a straight line. You can see, for example, that the number 3 repeats too many times consecutively for it to form words. Since he addressed it to you, he must know that you can solve it."

"The history of cryptology," began Emma, "is more than 2000 years old. Even Julius Caesar used crypts in which he substituted numbers for letters of the alphabet. Likewise, there are people dedicated to breaking these codes. Did you know that the majority of codebreakers during World War Two were women, including 18-year-olds Ruth Bourne, Margaret Bullen and Becky Webb? These were just some of the women of Bletchley Park. A famous Canadian codebreaker, William Thomas Tutte, helped us win World War Two."

No one in the room said anything. Emma had their full attention. She continued, "Over the centuries, people have used many ciphers: reverse the word, code sticks, semaphore, pigpen cipher, block cipher, Morse code, and cryptogram."

Everyone listened as she spoke. They were very impressed with her knowledge. From the moment Emma began to speak, the Chief, Susannah and all of the other officers listened attentively. They all marveled at her. Susannah was especially impressed with how much they admired her. She finally understood why Emma was so captivated by police work.

Emma said, "He is using a famous document, something that doesn't change over time."

"How do you know this?" asked the Chief.

Emma explained, "The reason it's a document is because the first set of vertical numbers is only two numbers long and the codes get progressively longer as you move from beginning to end. The first clue, therefore, is taken from the beginning of the document. The remaining clues follow the document throughout. The clue to the document itself is identified by the first seven sets of numbers at the top."

Emma further explained, "There was a case, a long time ago, where two robbers used the US Declaration of Independence to write down a secret code so that they could find where they hid the treasure. It wasn't that long ago that Charles and I learned about the Declaration of Independence in history class."

Emma's eyes lit up as she examined the numbers more closely. She said, "This could be the same document. From the information at the top of the page, **15** is the number of words in the title. There are approximately **1322** words in the Declaration. The **13** is the number of colonies that declared independence. There were **56** individuals who signed it. They did not all sign it at the same time. It took four months **(4/30**) from when John Hancock first signed it to when Matthew Thornton signed it. The American Revolutionary War lasted eight years **(8/365)** and 137 days **(137/7)**. Believe it or not, even though the US celebrates independence on July 4th, they actually declared their independence on July 2nd. Members of the RR, PB and CU are fighting to reverse this."

Just as Emma had finished speaking, the Chief was on the phone. Within a few seconds, an officer brought in several photocopies of the Declaration.

Everyone looked at Emma. She explained to them how to read the codes. She pointed to the first clue:

3
1

She said, "The first letter in the code is from the third word, first letter."

The officer looked at the document and said, "The third word is **the.** The first letter is **T**."

Emma looked at the next clue.

3
2

She said, "The second letter is from the same word, second letter."

The officer said, "That would be **H**."

Emma called out each of the number sets and the officer identified the corresponding letter. When they were finished, the officer then read, **"The yellow brick road meets the blue suede shoes. Any day, seven dark."**

"Excellent work," congratulated the Chief. "Thank you, Emma."

She smiled knowing that the Chief had approved of her. She was happy, knowing that they had uncovered the crypt.

"Chief," asked one of the officers, "where does the **yellow brick road meet the blue suede shoes**?"

"That's easy," said Emma. "There are two music stores downtown. Elton John sang about the yellow brick road and Elvis sang about blue suede shoes. It must refer to the music stores. **Any day, seven dark** is 7 pm."

"Chief," asked another officer, "why did he send the letter here, if he wanted Emma to solve it?"

"Whoever he is," said the Chief, delighting himself in Emma's presence, "he has a lot of respect for this young lady. He wanted to show us how incompetent we are. He wants her to catch him." The Chief looked at Susannah and said, "With your permission and Emma's, I have a plan to get Charles back and arrest this person."

The Chief explained what his plan was. Although it was a little dangerous, he assured Susannah that Emma would be under constant surveillance and wearing bulletproof clothing. Since the kidnapper is expecting to see Emma alone, the Chief figured that if she was not there, the kidnapper would not show himself. It was their best chance to catch him and rescue Charles. While Susannah was hesitant, Emma was willing to do whatever it takes to get Charles back.

Chapter 21
Emma To The Rescue

It was just before 7 pm, the following night, when Emma got off the bus. The sun was already hidden behind the tall buildings and setting fast. She waited for the stoplight to turn green. Just then, an undercover officer walked past her. Emma recognized her. She saw three other officers. One was perched on a second-floor window sill of the building across the street. One was sitting in the driver's seat of a taxi and another was *sleeping* on the street.

Emma remembered when she and her mother would walk into the record stores and see the long lines. Now, the streets are deserted. When the crowds disappeared, the stores began to close down. The noisy streets calmed. The bright lights dimmed. Many of the buildings were in disrepair.

Emma felt safe as she stood at the entrance of an abandoned building. Chief O'Brian was sure that this is where she should go. On one side was a music store, selling mostly CDs and DVDs. On the other side, was a store specializing in vintage records. Both of them displayed "Closing Soon" signs.

She stood in the empty space where the front door should be. The pungent scent of stagnant water and sewage spread throughout. Emma put her hands over her nose and mouth, as she took slow, shallow breaths. Peering inside the building, she could see the silhouette of someone sitting on a chair. Even though it was dark, she recognized Charles right away. There was something over his mouth and his hands were tied behind his back.

Emma scanned the dimly lit room to see if anyone else was there. Suddenly, a squeaking mouse scurried past her. Charles was by himself. He looked exhausted, hunched forward in the chair. She did not know how long he had been there.

"Charles," whispered Emma. Her voice carried to his ears. His head quickly snapped in her direction. He did not see Emma immediately. He thought he was hearing things, as he frantically looked around in all directions.

"On time!" a crude voice echoed in the darkness. "I was beginning to think that I had made my crypt too difficult for you."

Emma quickly surveyed the room. There was someone behind Charles. He stood up.

"Who are you?" demanded Emma, as she tried to peer into the darkness to get a better look at him.

"Haven't you figured it out yet?" he teased. "I have given you so many clues. Maybe you're not as smart as I think you are." He emerged from behind Charles but still remained in the darkness.

"What do you want?" begged Emma. She did not move from the doorway.

He replied confidently, "Just to show you that I am smarter than you are."

"Well," agreed Emma, "you are smarter than I am. There, I've said it. Now, please let Charles go."

"If I were smarter," he reasoned, "you would not have figured out my puzzle."

Emma's main concern was Charles's safety. She would do anything to protect him from harm, not only because they were close friends, but because she cared about him. So much so, that she wished that he would ask her to the school dance, instead of Catherine.

"Are you the one sending me the letters?" asked Emma, trying to gain his attention.

He was silent.

"What do you want from me?" she asked.

Again, there was silence.

Emma tried to assess whether he was armed. The Chief wanted her to identify if he had any weapons and report it over the microphone attached to her vest. They were listening in on their conversation. She could see no weapons in his hands.

Something just didn't seem right to Emma. First, he knew that she would bring the police. Second, although it was an abandoned building, it was still in a public place. Emma could end it all by simply calling for help. While she kept him distracted, the officers were surrounding the building.

She tested her theory by asking, "How did you put the clue in the nanulak's mouth without anyone seeing you?"

Charles began to move frantically in the chair, shaking it from side to side. He shook it so hard that he managed to knock the chair over. It hit the ground with a thud. Charles groaned in pain.

"I am the smart one here, remember?" he replied, picking Charles up and steadying the chair that he was strapped onto.

Emma's hunch was correct. The clue was not in the nanulak's mouth but in the mouth of the wolverine. He was not the one sending them the letters.

Emma informed him, "I should let you know that the police have this building surrounded."

He had suspected that she would not involve the police, but just in case, he rushed to the stairs that led to the second floor. Several officers came rushing in. Emma pointed towards the stairs. The officers raced after him.

Emma's immediate attention was Charles. The Chief entered just as Emma had loosened the rope from around Charles's hands and feet. His wounds were superficial, as the rope that tied him was not very tight.

Once Charles was on his feet, Emma gave him a tight hug. It was the first time that he noticed how affectionate she was, though he was too tired and thirsty to remain standing. The Chief and several officers escorted them to the hospital across the street where Charles could get proper medical attention. Emma learned from a nurse that Charles suffered from mild dehydration and was being treated for it.

Charles was very quiet the entire time that he and Emma were together. It could have been because of his dehydration why he was quiet. It could have been because of Emma's hug. It could have been because they were listening to the chase on one of the officer's radios.

It was reported that they had cornered him on the roof of the building. As they closed in to make the arrest, the kidnapper leaped off the roof and caught hold of a pipe on an adjacent building. He descended down the pipe in the back alleyway. Officers on the ground pursued after him.

Once he was on the ground, he scrambled to his feet, ran to the convertible, remotely starting it, and jumped inside. He sped off down the street, running a red light and almost careened into oncoming traffic. The officers quickly called for backup and took off after him. Following them were five other police cars, sirens blazing. The chase lasted for several blocks, but in the end, the driver lost control of his car and crashed.

"We have him in custody," they heard an officer report on the radio.

When they arrived at Charles's house, his father was waiting on the front lawn to welcome him home. Philip immediately grabbed him in a bear hug and embraced him. Charles looked embarrassed, seeing that Emma was watching. After waving goodbye to them, Emma and Susannah went home.

Emma immediately went to her room. As much as she tried, she could not make the connection between the letters and who was sending them. There was one hint, however, that she was given during Charles's rescue. The kidnapper said that he gave her many clues in regards to his identity.

Emma started at the beginning. The first letter was a warning of an impending deluge. Only she, Charles, Fitzroy, and Gilbert knew about it. The second letter she received was an invitation to the museum. Besides her, only Charles and Gilbert knew about this one. Of all the museums in town, it occurred in the one where Charles volunteered. The third letter was known only to her, Charles and Fitzroy. All of the remaining clues were known only to her and Charles. Charles was the only one who saw what was in the gold exhibit. Even the person who kidnapped Charles knew little of the second letter when she questioned him.

Charles jumped for joy when he solved the acrostic at their school playground. He was primarily responsible for solving all of the puzzles at the museum, especially when she was stuck. He was the one who identified and caught the thief at the museum. He had recently come up with a lot of theories and ideas that were strange to Emma. The more Emma thought about it, the more she realized that there was only one name: Charles!

It was easy for her to come to this conclusion. The evidence was staring at her. When she thought about it further, she saw other evidence. When she asked the person who kidnapped Charles about the nanulak and the wolverine, he overreacted. He was not trying to free himself. He was trying to stop the other person from responding. He knew that she had asked a trick question.

Emma's head sank when she put it all together. Impossible! It was impossible! It was inconceivable just to think about it. Yet, the evidence was too compelling for her to ignore. It became clear that Charles was more involved than she thought. She sat and cried at the thought that her best friend was capable of such a thing. He had put her life and others at risk.

There must be another explanation. Emma asked for divine help. She had always put her trust in Christ and begged for Charles to be forgiven for his sins. Although Charles did not believe in angels, Emma knew that they were preparing a list for his day of judgment.

Although Emma had always surrounded herself with those who believed in the angels and the messengers, there were no lost sheep in her flock, until now. No one ever did purely evil things, she thought, only things that are contrary to what is good. We only do the things that God has planned out for us, she always thought. At least, that was what Mr. Lyell had taught her.

Emma was saddened. When she looked into the eyes of the angel, she saw more than just a glimpse of the future. She saw a new world created by Charles. She saw the red oceans. She saw the war and its aftermath. She witnessed the fall of towns, cities and countries; morals, conscience and humanity itself. There was only violence, suffering and darkness. She saw the Domes, the paved earth, the perpetual rain, and the Blue Spot.

It was the first true world war, one that involved the entire world. It was brother against sister, father against mother, friend against friend and foe against foe; the rich against the poor, the wicked against the righteous. They fought for food, water and air. Gold, money and possessions are not things of the future. No more can one eat gold, drink money or breathe possessions.

Her death will usher in the final war, which Charles will start. His pursuit of a single world leader cannot be deterred. But, the outcome of the war, she did not see in her vision. Perhaps, her belief is what prevented her from seeing past the wars.

Of all the things revealed to her in her vision, Emma preferred to remember the Blue Spot. The only way she could describe it was to say that it was paradise - the world living in harmony. It was a modern-day Eden, except that there were no humans. She was saddened by the fact that the only way to achieve this seems to be without humans.

Chapter 22
The Confrontation

The next day, Emma's school was closed, as students began their volunteering week. As Ms. Coraline was in the hospital, Emma was volunteering at her local church for one day. She invited Charles. They were going to clean up the church grounds with help from members of the community. Emma met Charles in the Sunday School room before any of the other volunteers arrived. She immediately confronted him.

"What's going on, Charles?" she asked forcefully.

Without looking directly at her, he nervously stammered, "What...what do you mean?"

She pressured him further, "The letters, the puzzles...I know it's you."

"It's not what you think, Emma," he begged. "You don't understand." He did not deny her charges. He looked scared, as he pulled himself away from her.

She demanded, "Tell me what's going on!"

"It's complicated," he said, trying to reason with her. He took a few small steps back.

She cried, "I trusted you, Charles. How could you have done this?"

Charles began to cry. First a sniffle and then tears. Emma moved closer, to within one step of him. Though she was furious at him, she hesitantly put her hand on his shoulder. She pleaded, "Please, just tell me what's going on."

He sobbed as he whispered, "They have my mother."

Emma was confused. She asked, "Who has your mother?"

"Be quiet," he insisted. "We're being watched."

Emma looked around. There was no one there, not even outside, as she looked through the stained glass window. Charles got down on his knees and signaled Emma to sit beside him. She did as he asked.

"Yes," he admitted, "I helped them send the letters. But they made me do it. A few months ago, they kidnapped my mother. She is not with my grandmother. I have no Aunt Bessie. The woman at my house is a spy, keeping an eye on my father to make sure that I do what they say."

This explains why Charles was still wearing multi-colored clothes. Emma said nothing. She listened attentively. She tried to comprehend what he was saying.

Charles took a deep breath. He continued, "If I don't do what they say, I will never see my mother again. They have spies everywhere - the museum, the mall, the police station. The men who walked out of the river are spies. They won't stop until they get what they are looking for. I didn't send the last letter to your mailbox because you told me that Mr. Lyell was on the lookout."

Emma suddenly felt sorry for confronting him. They had been best friends for years and at the first opportunity, she doubted him. Yet, she wondered why he did not come to her earlier. Now, it began to make sense to her. He would never freely say the things that he said when they went fishing. She knew that someone else was behind it. She needed more information.

"Who is making you do this?" asked Emma.

"They call themselves the People of Judas," revealed Charles. "There is a legend that a Christ has been on Earth since the beginning of humanity. In every generation, there is one. Someone who represents all that is good. If the Christ dies before choosing a successor, the **Line** will be broken and the future can be changed. As long as the Christ lives, evil can never triumph. This is why humans have survived for so long. Genghis Khan, Tamerlane, Hitler, and others could have changed the world for the worst but could not because of the Christ."

Emma asked, "So, what does it have to do with you?"

He explained, "They know that I have seen the Grail. It is never far from the Christ. Since the Grail is here, the Christ must also be here. That is why the Church has sent representatives. They want to make sure that they can cover it up if anything bad happens."

Emma asked for clarification, "Are you sure you really saw the Grail?"

"Yes," said Charles.

Emma revealed, "Mr. Lyell told me that it was buried deep into the ground under Old Oak. I have not seen any evidence of someone digging around Old Oak."

Charles answered, "The woman at my house said that it was found tangled in the roots of Old Oak. After seven hundred years, the roots of the tree brought it up to the surface."

Emma asked, "Why do the People of Judas want it?"

Charles explained, "They believe that if the present Christ is killed before the next one is chosen, the Line can be broken and evil can triumph. They believe that they have found the current Christ. They have been watching him for some time now. They will strike him down before he chooses a successor. However, to prove that he is the Christ, they need him to touch the Grail."

Emma asked cautiously, "Did they tell you who *He* is?"

"No," said Charles, shaking his head.

"What is so special about the Grail?" asked Emma.

He whispered, "It is the Holy Grail. The chalice that Jesus held at the Last Supper. It's real Emma. I saw the Grail at the museum six months ago."

There was something even more immediate that Emma wanted to know. She asked, "What about the Chosen One?"

He replied, "They said that the Angel of the Lord will show him a vision of the future. This is how he will know that he has been chosen."

Emma's heart skipped a beat. She was shown a vision of the future by the angel. Emma's heartbeat sped up. If she was the apprentice, then Mr. Lyell was the Christ. He had chosen her. She only now realized that all of her life, he had been preparing her for this.

Although Emma found it hard to believe what Charles was saying about the prophecy, she somehow knew that he was telling the truth. She always trusted in Christ and secretly believed that he would come back to save humanity. However, she could not put into words the idea that she would be given the power to save her fellow humans. Although Emma had suspected and accused Charles, she knew that he needed her help.

"There is something else that you need to know," warned Charles. "I overheard the woman at my house as she spoke with Malthus. Malthus is going to destroy the whole of humankind, save a few. Those that survive are meant for one task: to find life, and possibly intelligent life, beyond the Earth. Every single human being will be tasked with this one purpose."

"Charles," said Emma, looking him straight in the eyes, "we have to protect Mr. Lyell. I don't know how to explain it but he is the Christ. I think that they may be watching him."

"We must warn him," agreed Charles. "We need to get him to safety. I am sorry for not telling you this before. I didn't want anything bad to happen to my mom."

"Don't worry Charles," she said reassuringly, "we will get your mother back safely. But first, we must warn Mr. Lyell."

They both walked out of the Sunday School room and headed for the sanctuary. Emma glanced inside but did not see Mr. Lyell. He had promised to attend the clean-up.

Charles said to Emma, as they headed to the front door, "We must do all we can to protect Mr. Lyell." He suggested, "Why don't you go and see if he is at home. I'll wait here just in case he shows up."

Emma agreed. She ran out of the church and down the street, as fast as she could. As she headed towards Mr. Lyell's house, other volunteers were making their way to the clean-up. As Emma turned the corner, she was only a block away from Mr. Lyell's house. A sickening feeling came over her as yellow police tape was being wrapped around Mr. Lyell's front yard.

Emma knew the officer who was putting up the tape. She walked up to her and asked what happened. She hesitated to answer, knowing the relationship that Emma and Mr. Lyell shared. She said, "Mr. Lyell. He...he has left us. I am so sorry."

"What happened?" asked Emma.

"He had a heart attack," said the officer.

Emma could not believe what she was hearing. She found it even harder to believe that he died of a heart attack. As Emma spoke, there was a message calling for all available officers to head towards Angel Bridge.

"What's going on?" asked Emma.

The officer informed her, "Angel Bridge has been destroyed."

Another officer announced, "It collapsed and fell into the river a few minutes ago. It was kind of strange. The bridge collapsed around the same time that Mr. Lyell died."

Emma could not believe that Mr. Lyell was gone. She had seen his face and heard his voice since the day she was born. There was an instant void in her heart, an unexplained absence.

Emma asked one of the officers for a ride back to the church. As they drove, fire trucks, ambulances, and police cars sped past them heading for Angel Bridge.

Everyone was in complete shock when Emma told them that Mr. Lyell had passed away and that Angel Bridge had collapsed. Charles, though, was more concerned about something else. He told Emma that with Mr. Lyell's passing and the fact that he may not have chosen a successor, the Line was broken and that all of humanity was at risk.

Emma was too grief-stricken to worry about the future. At that moment, she felt as sad as when she first heard of her father's passing. This was the saddest moment of her life. She already missed him - her teacher, her mentor, her friend. She missed his smile, his laughter. She missed his stories. But most of all, she missed him. Though, instead of grieving, she promised that she would honor his life and teachings by living a life that he would be proud of. Besides, she never understood why people cried at funerals, anyways. Mr. Lyell had told her that the deceased will live on if you remember them, through joy or sorrow. Preferably, though joy.

At his closed-casket funeral service the next day, the whole of Silent Hum attended. The Chief insisted on full police escort. Emma prayed that his angels had recorded his many good deeds while he lived and that he could finally find peace and rest with his wife and daughter. The messenger, she was sure, had finally returned home.

After the funeral service was over, Emma and Charles met with Chief O'Brian. They explained to him what had happened to Charles's mother, Helen. He agreed to accompany them to the museum to find what they were looking for. Several officers went along with them.

When they arrived at the museum, the curator met with them in the lobby and escorted them to the dimly lit basement. After the robberies, the remainder of the gold was kept in a locked room at the far end of the museum's basement. As soon as the door opened, Charles announced, "It's here."

The curator put on chain-linked gloves before he opened the first box. He was the only one allowed to touch any of the pieces. Emma, Charles and everyone else looked on. The first four boxes yielded nothing. When he opened the fifth one, Charles noticed a gem-encrusted goblet. He marveled at it before announcing excitedly, "That's the one." The curator picked it up.

"No," said Charles, "the one next to it."

The curator looked again. There was a simple, grey clay cup in the box. He picked it up. "Are you sure?" asked the curator.

Charles shook his head. Everyone stood back, making sure not to touch it or even get close to it. Charles, though, did not believe in superstitions and grabbed it with his bare hands.

"Look," he said, holding it up high for everyone to see, "there is nothing special about it. There is no curse."

The curator grabbed it back from Charles with his gloved-hand and wrapped it carefully in a cloth that he had. He placed it in a box and handed it over to the Chief.

As they drove to Emma's house, the Chief noticed that the driver was going the wrong way. The driver took out his gun and pointed it at Chief O'Brian. The Chief could not see his face as he had a mask on.

He demanded, "Hand over the box." From his accent, he sounded Russian.

The Chief placed the box onto the dashboard of the car and put his hands in the air. The driver stopped in front of Dr. Wallace's vacant institute. He told Emma, Charles and the Chief to get out. As they did, they could see a speeding car heading for the cruiser. The Chief led Emma and Charles into the abandoned building. Picking up speed, the car slammed into the back of the parked car, flipping the cruiser onto its back.

Several other cars drove up in front and behind the cruiser. Masked men with guns got out and ran behind their cars. They were not part of the same group as they pointed guns at each other. They were all looking for the artifact.

"Leave now and no one gets hurt," shouted one of the men.

Another responded, "Germans have no right to what is in the box."

"Neither do Americans," he responded, firing several shots.

They all watched as the bloodied Russian man stumbled out of the cruiser with the box. A German immediately fired at him. He fell to the ground, still clutching the box in his hands.

As the standoff continued, everyone looked down the road as they could hear a whistling sound. Something was heading their way. Everyone, on both sides, scrambled to run away. The missile exploded upon impact with the vehicles that the Americans arrived in. Another missile was fired at the cars that the Germans arrived in. Both the Germans and Americans fired upon the vehicles heading their way. The vehicles surrounded the body of the Russian as they were bombarded with bullets. They returned fire.

The Chief ushered Emma and Charles higher up for safety. On the third floor, Emma could see the remnants of a science experiment. There were several globes half-filled with fluorescent orange and blue liquids. There were also metal boxes filled with something that caused them to vibrate and levitate. They went around the room in a counter-clockwise motion. In the middle of the room, was a central square with a tall four-sided mirror-like structure. Everyone was mesmerized by what they saw.

Emma asked, "What was Samantha working on?"

Suddenly, there was gunfire on the first floor of the building. The Chief pointed Emma to the stairs that led to the next floor. They quickly made their way up the stairs.

They continued to hear gunfire as they entered a room and hid behind a desk. The gunfire was getting louder as several groups made their way up the steps. They were on the third floor as they continued to exchange gunfire. Then, the shooting stopped.

"Just hand over the box and no one gets hurt," shouted someone. "It's three against one."

"You do not know the power in this box," he replied.

Emma knew that the Americans outnumbered the Chinese three to one.

The Chinese man put his gun down but held onto the box. He walked backward with the box towards the structure in the middle of the room. The Americans surrounded him and moved in closer with guns drawn. He put the box on the ground and opened it.

"Do not touch it," ordered one of the Americans. He took the Grail out and stood up. The metal boxes began to vibrate even faster and traveled around the room quicker. The liquids from the globes slowly started to seep out and began to encircle the room and the four individuals. Their guns were ripped out of their hands as they struggled to remain standing. The holder of the Grail kept a tight grip upon it. The entire room began to give off a sound like a jet engine starting up. Then, there was a bright flash of light and a sonic boom.

The Chief, Emma and Charles all fell to the ground due to the shockwave. They could not hear anyone because it was eerily silent. The Chief slowly made his way to the door. He listened but he could not hear anyone. He signaled for Emma and Charles to follow. They made their way out of the room and down the stairs to the third floor. In the middle of the room, they could see the box. There was nothing else in the room. All of the globes and metal boxes were gone, and so was the structure in the middle of the room. There was no sign of any of the men.

The room was completely empty, except for the box. The Chief walked up to the box and opened it. He could see the Grail still wrapped in the cloth. No one said anything. They all just stood there looking at each other. The Chief picked up the box and led Emma and Charles out of the building.

The scale of violence was evident as they stepped outside. No one survived. Burning cars were everywhere. The Chief called for backup. On the ride home, no one said anything. They were all still in awe of what they had witnessed. Chief O'Brian took Emma and Charles back to Emma's house. He did not want to take Charles home, as their presence would alarm the kidnappers.

Charles was instructed not to open the box or touch its content. He was told to go straight home and hand it over. Charles thanked Emma for everything that she had done. He promised to call as soon as he delivered the artifact and his mother was home safely.

Emma went inside and sat by the phone. Her mother could not get her to eat or drink anything. Charles did not call. With each passing hour, Emma became increasingly impatient. Three hours later, the phone rang. It was Philip and he had unsettling news. The kidnappers were satisfied with the artifact and Helen was returned unharmed. However, they took Charles to reassure them that no one was following them. They promised to release him within one day. Philip had called the Chief before he called Emma. Emma was happy to know that the Chief was informed, but she was still concerned for Charles's safety.

Chapter 23
A Band of Protectors

The next day, Emma pleaded with her mother to stay home. She did not want to go to the hospital, knowing that Charles may be in danger. Reluctantly, Emma went to visit Ms. Coraline. As Mr. Lyell was accustomed to saying, "Worrying never solved anything." However, the only thing on her mind, all day, was Mr. Lyell, Charles and Gilbert. She could not stop thinking about them. She wondered what the kidnappers would do to Charles when they found out that the artifact was not real. Mr. Lyell had told her that if anyone, except the Three, touched the artifact with their bare hands, they would instantly vanish.

As soon as her volunteering session was over, she rushed over to Charles's house. His father told her that he had not heard anything from the kidnappers. Helen was still in shock from her ordeal. She was further distraught, as her son had not returned yet.

Emma spent a second agonizing day at the hospital. Nothing that Ms. Coraline said comforted her. She simply stared outside the window all day watching the rain. It was raining from the moment she left her home in the morning.

The news was the same when Emma returned home and called Charles's father. She did not know what to do, so she called Chief O'Brian. He said that he would drop by to visit later in the evening, just over an hour away.

Susannah was sitting in the living room. Emma walked in, holding a piece of paper in her hand. She looked at her mother to gain her attention. When she looked back, Emma announced, "I think I've solved it. Well, sort of."

"Solved what?" asked Susannah.

Emma declared, "I know who killed dad!"

It was not what Susannah was expecting. However, she begged Emma to continue, as it seemed to take her mind off of Charles.

Emma began, "At 9:15 pm, there was a call from the police station. Since dad and his partner were the closest ones to the scene of the robbery in progress, they responded. While dad thought that he could make an easy arrest, a second thief came up from behind him. Instead of two against two, dad soon realized that his partner was not on his side. It was now three against one. They probably tried to convince him to join them. When he refused, they shot and killed him. From the direction that the bullet entered dad's shoulder, the shooter was standing over him. This means that dad was on his knees when he was shot. So, it could not have been an accident. Based on the blood analysis, he could have been shot 45 minutes earlier than what was reported. That would have given them more than enough time to escape with the money. Then, dad's partner called for backup."

Susannah simply marveled at Emma's passion and determination. The flashes of lightning and the rolling of thunder seemed to coincide with each movement that she made.

Emma walked up to her mother. She declared, "But this is not what actually happened. There was no bank robbery. There was no shooter. The whole thing is a cover-up. The bank never reported a robbery on the day that dad died. At the police station, I saw a report saying that a police officer was stabbed outside of a bank. His wife and newborn witnessed it." Emma looked scared. She asked, "Mom, was I the newborn?"

Susannah simply listened. She closed her eyes, reached out and pulled Emma close to her. She sat down next to her mother. Emma put her arms around her. Susannah did not have anything to say. Her tears said more than any amount of words could. Her mother didn't seem too interested in being reminded of what happened. Yet, Emma was puzzled that she did not want to seek justice for her husband, the father she will never know.

Susannah understood what Emma was going through. All of her life, Emma had been in control. She made her own decisions and influenced others. She had become accustomed to life moving at her own pace. That is why she did not want her mother to date anyone. She did not want things to change.

Recently, there were many things that she had no control over - Fitzroy moving away, Gilbert leaving school, Mr. Lyell's death, and Charles's disappearance. There was a feeling of helplessness, something that Emma was not used to.

Mr. Lyell once told Emma that God afflicts tragedy upon those who do not understand their purpose or those who stray from the path, especially the righteous. The meaning of the affliction is only revealed when you dwell and meditate upon it. However, his most important message was this: God will not afflict a person with more burden than they can bear.

It was just before 6 pm when there was a knock on the door. Emma knew that it was Chief O'Brian. He was the only one who knew what was going on with efforts to get Charles back. Emma quickly ran to the door, knowing that it was raining. She had never seen it rain so long and as hard as it was raining today. Emma opened the door to find that the Chief was not alone. As he walked past her, so did three other cloaked individuals.

Emma was a little confused, though Susannah was perfectly comfortable. Emma only saw their faces when they took off their hoods, in unison. There was Mr. Sedgwick, Ms. Coraline and someone whom she did not recognize. They all stood by the door, next to Chief O'Brian, water dripping off their coats.

"Chief," asked a bemused Emma, "what's going on?"

He announced, "It's time, Emma." He looked at Susannah. She nodded in agreement.

Emma tried her best to figure out what was going on. Her mind raced to search for clues. The only thing that she was sure of is that she knew all of the people in her house, except for the lone stranger. What they were all doing here, at the same time, however, made her uneasy. Emma walked over and sat beside her mother.

"What is it time for, mom?" asked Emma, echoing what the Chief had said. She looked to her mother for comfort and reassurance.

After removing their drenched coats, everyone came closer to Emma and Susannah. The only person whom she did not know spoke first.

He introduced himself, saying, "My name is Joseph. It is nice to finally meet you, Emma."

Emma smiled at him. She knew him. He was the one from the cemetery. She recognized his voice immediately. He looked strikingly similar to Susannah's husband. Emma was still confused by his appearance at her home. She was expecting the Chief to be alone.

"Now," said the Chief, "you know all of us. From the day you were born, we have been looking over you. We have all vowed to protect you, especially Susannah."

Emma looked at Susannah and asked, "What's going on, mom?"

Susannah took a quick, shallow breath. "Emma," she said sincerely, holding Emma's hand, "I am not your real mother."

Susannah closed her eyes. She did not know how Emma would react.

"Is this some kind of joke?" questioned Emma, pulling her hand away from Susannah. She was expecting everyone to say, "Surprise!" No one had changed their expression. Emma knew that they were not joking. Now she understood why she did not resemble Susannah.

Emma did not know what to say. After all, what do you say when you learn something like this? She took a few seconds to collect herself. "Who is my mother?" she asked, as she looked at everyone in the room.

"Emma," said the Chief, "thirteen years ago, we were all called to the hospital where you were born. I'm sorry, but your mother died during childbirth. She was only sixteen years old and there were many complications with the pregnancy. We did not know who your father was or any next-of-kin. You were in grave danger. Your heart was weak. We did not think that you would make it. Mr. Lyell asked Dr. Wallace to perform emergency surgery to save your life. Even with the successful surgery, as a baby, you had fainting spells. Can you still feel the scar on your left side?"

Emma looked down and touched her side.

The Chief continued, "We all promised to help raise and protect you."

Emma somehow knew that they were telling the truth regarding her mother. She asked, "Where is she buried?"

Joseph said, "Close to Susannah's husband."

"Smith?" asked Emma in shock.

"Her name was Mary Smith," he told her. "Yes, she was your mother. I have visited her on your behalf ever since she passed away."

"How did your husband die?" asked Emma, looking at Susannah.

Ms. Coraline walked over to Susannah and sat down beside her, holding her hand. Susannah spoke, remembering every detail. "He was a police officer. He died while off duty. He was robbed at knifepoint. The robber was scared and stabbed him even after he handed over his wallet. He died protecting the two of us. Yes, you were the newborn." She broke down in tears in Ms. Coraline's arms.

"I am sorry, Emma," said Chief O'Brian. "It's up to you to judge us for not telling you the truth."

Emma saw the Lord's calling in everyone. Mr. Lyell, Ms. Coraline and Susannah each suffered terrible losses. Mr. Sedgwick had lost his wife and son to an unfortunate car accident. They had each endured much to protect her. She wondered what losses Joseph may have experienced in order to be here.

"How did I end up here?" asked Emma.

Everyone was surprised by her calm demeanor.

"Well," recalled the Chief, "Mr. Lyell was at the hospital on the night that you were born. He called me and said that he had found you. He appointed each of us to look after you. We all vowed to help raise and protect you, until the day..."

"The day?" asked Emma. "What day?"

"Until the day Mr. Lyell was no longer with us," said Ms. Coraline. "He told us to gather and tell you your true destiny."

"My true destiny?" asked Emma apprehensively.

Mr. Sedgwick declared, "To protect the Grail and all humanity. You alone have been burdened with this task."

Emma suddenly felt a heavy weight upon her shoulders. However, she still did not understand what was really going on. She knew that the Grail was not real because Charles touched it with his bare hand. Regardless, she knew that they had to rescue Charles.

Though she was unsure of what she had learned about herself, she now understood why the stories of her father's death were so loosely put together. The Chief and the others did their best to protect her, but even they knew that it was just a matter of time before all was revealed.

Chief O'Brian said, "We think we know where they may have taken the Grail and Charles." He added, "Get your things and I'll brief you on the way."

Emma was hesitant. She still could not believe what was going on. Mr. Lyell had told her of the legend of the Grail, but she never really took him seriously. She now realized that he was not just telling her stories all this time, but preparing her.

Emma stood by the door as she surveyed her room. The hardest part was leaving her trophies and metals behind because she had worked so hard to get them. She did not know if she would ever see them again.

Susannah spoke with Emma in her room about how she felt, knowing that she was not her biological mother. Emma disagreed. She has only known one mother all of her life and it made no difference to her. Susannah was her mother and no one could convince her otherwise. Susannah was very happy to hear that.

The Chief told everyone that they needed to hurry. The helicopters were primed and ready to go. After making sure that the path was clear, he told Emma, Susannah and the others that it was safe to leave the house.

Chapter 24
The Deluge

The first thing Emma noticed, as she stepped outside, was the dark, dense patch of cloud that had settled over Silent Hum. She raised her hands to shield her eyes from the rain, as she made her way to the cruiser. Lightning lit up the pitch-black sky and the crashing thunder silenced everything else.

The skies opened up. It began to rain even harder. It was getting worse, with each drop of water striking the ground with a small explosion. Visibility was near zero, as a wall of fog advanced. Before entering the car, Emma saw a familiar face heading her way. It was Philip. He insisted on helping to rescue his son. Chief O'Brian agreed. Just then, there was an emergency call on the radio.

"Evacuate! Evacuate!" screamed the caller.

The Chief could barely understand what he was saying, with static interfering with the signal. He pressed the radio to his ear.

The caller warned, "Get everyone to higher ground! Hey, what are you doing here?" The caller suddenly hung up.

Emma then remembered the first letter and its warning of a deluge. She was scared. The Chief's expression failed to comfort her. Everyone looked to him to do something. He called into the police station to raise the alarm. Throughout the entire town, everyone understood the blaring sound. They knew that they had to get to Angel Bridge, as it was the highest point in town. While the bridge was not fully rebuilt, they would still be safe around it.

There was no panic, as everyone took to the streets. Just as they had practiced, the entire fleet of school buses in Silent Hum began driving through the streets, picking up everyone along the way. In all of the drills that they had practiced, everyone reached the bridge safely.

As the driver was about to depress the accelerator, Chief O'Brian asked him to wait. He opened the door and stepped outside. He then turned his head to the side as he seemed to be listening for something. While he couldn't see through the dense fog, he could hear a distinct rumbling noise. Something was heading his way. While fog normally settles in one place, the Chief could feel the chill on his skin as the wall of mist rushed past him. Something was pushing it forward. When he realized what it was, his eyes opened wide. He jumped back into the car and ordered the driver to step on it. His worst fears were realized.

The drills and simulations were not accurate. While the Chief figured that he had time to get everyone onto the buses, he could already hear the water rumbling. In front of them was a wall of fog and behind them was a wall of water.

The Chief screamed over the radio, "It's already here! Hurry!"

The Chief could only look on in the rearview mirror, as the torrent of water began to overtake the buses and those who were still in the streets.

"Drive! Drive!" he screamed, as the cruiser raced down the street. There was nothing that he could do for the people running in the streets. The wall of water was moving too fast for anyone to escape. First cars, then trees and eventually entire houses were being uprooted as the relentless force of the water swallowed the town. As quickly as fires erupted, the deluge drowned them out. The screams of helpless citizens were silenced only by the roar of the galloping wave.

Emma watched helplessly as people were running back into their houses for safety. But with the wall of water being two times higher than the houses, she could only pray for those left behind. Of all the school buses, only six were ahead of the police car that Emma was in. She could do nothing but hope that there were more buses hidden in the fog ahead of them. How is it that she is supposed to protect all of humanity when she can only watch helplessly as her town is being destroyed?

The police cars caught up to the buses but could not pass them. The wall of water was gaining on them. They were close to Angel Bridge. The driver steered the vehicle to avoid the people and animals running in the streets. Some people were grabbing onto the windows of the buses as they drove by, hanging on for their lives. The people inside the buses tried to hold onto them. Most, however, were not so fortunate. Several cars sped past the buses and police cars, driving on the sidewalk as people began to panic. They did whatever was necessary to get to Angel Bridge.

As the wall of water towered over them, the police cars sped up the hill towards Angel Bridge. Garbage cans, trees, cars, and other debris crashed onto the slopes of the bridge. The water rose until it lapped next to Emma's feet. Only a few hundred people and animals were beside her in the pouring rain. Crying and screaming were the only sounds heard. As Emma turned around, all she saw was debris and water where her town once stood. While everyone important to her was beside her, she felt the agony of mothers and fathers calling for their children and not hearing any response. There was nothing that she could say or joke that she could tell, to make them stop feeling the agony that they were going through. She had never felt so helpless, as she did now. Everywhere she turned, all she saw was despair.

She now understood why it was called Angel Bridge, for she felt protected. She only wished that all of the others could be with her. She vowed that she would never let this happen again if indeed she was meant to save the world.

When they had all gathered together, one person was missing. They could not find Mr. Sedgwick. Joseph told them of how he was swept up in the deluge, as he bravely tried to help others. Everyone silently thanked him for his sacrifice, Emma most of all.

After speaking with the mayor, the Chief gathered Joseph, Ms. Coraline, Susannah, Emma, and the other officers. They made their way over to an inconsolable Philip. He could not find his wife among the small crowd of people. The Chief asked him if he wanted to continue or stay behind. Reluctantly, he agreed to help save his son, knowing that his wife was still out there.

As everywhere was inundated with water, the Chief radioed for the helicopters to come to them. Rather than taking all six helicopters, he asked that two remain to help with evacuation and rescue efforts. Within minutes, they were airborne. They all marveled at the scale of destruction. Save Angel Bridge and Old Oak, everything else was under water. No one could tell that a town ever existed there, for it looked like a lake.

As difficult as it was, they had to keep moving. The Chief knew that they had to rescue Charles and get the Grail back. He explained where they were going. Emma thought that it was a simple plan. They would land within a few miles of the Base and trek through the swamp. They would use infrared devices to detect where Charles was in the Base.

They went undetected as they landed. It was about four in the morning, according to Emma's watch. Ms. Coraline and Susannah remained with the helicopters, while the others advanced towards the Base.

Before them, lay uncharted territory, somewhere in Florida. The swamp was filled with insects, snakes and alligators. As they walked, everyone felt as though they were being watched. Every unknown movement around them startled everyone. Several times along the way, they stopped to make sure that it was safe to proceed. The darkness was teeming with blinking eyes and croaking and hissing noises. They proceeded cautiously every time they approached a pool of water. Several times they were chased away by female alligators guarding their nests.

They were almost through the swamp when one of the officers raised his left hand up, bent at the elbow, fist closed. Everyone stopped. They were all completely quiet. They could see the Base, but it was surrounded by a moat. Everywhere in the moat were piercing eyes. There was no safe way around the alligators. The only way to the Base was through them. They could see only six people inside, with their infrared devices. There were four adults who stood together and two isolated smaller individuals. Emma knew that one of them must be Charles.

The Chief quickly gathered everyone together to go over their options. Half of the officers said that they were not going any further. They were afraid to approach the moat.

On the opposite side of the moat, was a dock with a small paddle boat. The Chief explained that someone needs to go over to the dock, untie the boat and bring it back. Eventually, one officer agreed that he would try. Everyone else admired his bravery. However, they needed a way to distract the alligators without alerting those inside the Base.

On the horizon, the sun was beginning to rise. If they did not act now, it would be too late. Phillip stood up and walked over to the water's edge. He looked at the officer who volunteered to go into the water. He was going to distract the alligators long enough for him to reach the boat. They had only a few minutes of darkness before the sun rose and left them exposed.

Suddenly, Philip dove into the alligator-infested moat. All eyes in the moat focused on him. The alligators began to congregate at his location. Seeing this, the officer dove into the water. After a few seconds, there was a commotion across the moat. The officer surfaced and climbed over the side of the boat and rolled safely inside. He quickly untied the boat and began to row in the direction of Philip. He stood over the spot where Philip dove in and plunged one oar deep into the water. While fending off the alligators with the other oar, he moved the oar back and forth in the water.

Then, something grabbed onto it and tried to pull him into the water. He held onto it as tightly as he could, not knowing how big the alligator was. With all his might he pulled the oar out of the water, fearing the worst. A hand grabbed onto the side of the boat. The officer hit the water with the paddle to fend off the hungry alligators, as Philip pulled himself on board. Suddenly, a giant alligator lunged out of the water and locked onto Philip's left hand. As it rolled, it ripped the limb from its socket. Philip was not injured as the alligator swam away with his prosthetic arm.

No one could believe that he had stayed under the water for more than five minutes, with so many hungry alligators within inches of him. They knew that he did it for his son. The officer and Philip quickly rowed the boat to where the others were. The Chief commended both men for their bravery and courage.

With everyone safely across the moat, the Chief led the charge as they stormed the Base. Emma headed for Charles, based on the infrared information. Peering through one of the doors, she noticed him. Emma removed the pin that locked the door. Charles was extremely happy to see her. She was happy to see him, too. Emma looked at the device over his mouth and tried to open it. She could not. He could not speak.

"Where's the Grail, Charles?" asked Emma.

He pointed in the direction that he wanted for them to go. They ran towards the cell that Charles believed contained the Grail. Charles opened the door and pointed to the vault at the far end of the room. In front of the vault was a large hole in the ground, occupying most of the room. Charles carefully navigated himself around the hole and made his way to the vault.

Emma did not follow him but kept watch at the entrance. She peered into the hole. It was a natural cavern, a dark place where no light could be seen. She could not see the bottom.

The vault was not closed. Charles simply swung the door open, took out the goblet and brought it back to where Emma was. He did not immediately hand it over. He looked at it, not just at its surface but through it. His gaze fixated upon it.

"Hand it to me," said Emma.

Charles hesitated to hand over the goblet. His grip was secure upon it, as he admired it. After a moment, he extended his hand, holding the goblet in front of Emma. As she reached to get it, something was stirring at the cell's door. It was Gilbert. Emma withdrew her hand from the goblet.

Gilbert ran past Emma and lunged himself at Charles, tackling him at the midsection. The goblet slipped out of Charles's hand and flew high into the air. Charles stumbled backward as Gilbert's momentum pushed him to the edge of the hole. Emma lunged forward to catch the goblet.

Charles tried to stop himself but he could not. He slipped into the abyss, locking eyes with Emma for the last time.

The goblet hit Emma's fingers and slipped out of her hands, rolling to the edge of the pit. She rose to her feet and lunged again to stop it from rolling into the hole. Gilbert screamed for her not to touch it. He got to his feet and rushed over to Emma, just in time to grab her feet as half of her body was in the pit.

Emma rolled from her stomach and onto her back, clutching the goblet in her bare hands. She attempted to pass it to Gilbert, who was standing over her. He refused to take it.

Emma sat up, holding the goblet in her hand. She peered over the edge. Charles was gone. She could not comprehend what just happened. Emma turned to Gilbert.

"I could not let you take the Grail, Miss Emma," confessed Gilbert. "Charles was going to kill you."

"How?" questioned Emma, who was irate at Gilbert.

"Miss Emma," asked Gilbert, "how is it possible that you can hold the Grail with your bare hands?"

"It's not real, Gilbert," replied a frustrated Emma. She did not know how to explain to everyone what had happened, especially Charles's father.

"It is real, Miss Emma," revealed Gilbert.

Emma asked in frustration, "Then explain how I can hold it with my bare hands?"

Gilbert did not have to think. In awe, he answered, "Because you are The Chosen One! You are the Christ and Charles is the Antichrist. They told me everything." Gilbert was referring to the four individuals at the base. Tears fell from Gilbert's eyes. He cried out, "They made my parents and Fitzroy's parents touch the Grail. Now they are all gone."

Emma was shocked. She could not believe what she was hearing. Worse still, she could not come to grips with the reality that Charles was the Antichrist.

"How did you get here?" asked Emma.

He replied, "After my dad took me out of school, four men came to our house. They ordered us to get into their truck. It was the last thing I remembered."

"Promise me, Gilbert," insisted Emma, as she recalled her vision, "promise me that when you see the Colossus, you will run away. When I tell you to run, you must run away."

Gilbert nodded but he did not know what she was talking about.

Emma looked around the room before they left. In the vault, she noticed something. She carefully made her way over and retrieved it. Emma took off her outer coat and wrapped the Grail in it, as Gilbert led her out of the room.

As Emma and Gilbert reached the others, Gilbert told everyone that they must get out of the base immediately. Without questioning him, the Chief ordered everyone out. Just as they began to run, the structure began to shake, as though there was an earthquake. There were small explosions from the top of the structure. Pieces of the ceiling began to fall. A large chunk of rock fell in front of the entrance, partially blocking it.

"We don't have much time!" screamed Gilbert.

The Chief could see a small opening at the top of the pile of rocks. He knew that the Base could implode at any moment. He told Emma to head for the opening. An officer raced past Emma. She begged him to help her, but he simply sneered at her, "You are the reason we are in this mess. Help yourself!"

Emma was shocked by his reaction. As the officer continued up the pile of rocks, a piece of the ceiling came crashing down on him. He screamed in pain. Emma was the first one to get to him. She began to remove pieces of rocks that had fallen on him.

He looked at her and asked, "Why are you helping me when I would not do the same for you?"

"All we have is each other," she humbly replied.

He marveled at her, before succumbing to the weight of rocks, "You *are* the Christ."

Chief O'Brian grabbed Emma's hand and rushed up the pile of rocks and climbed out of the Base. Gilbert followed with several of the officers. As they tried to crawl out, there were more explosions, causing more rocks to fall, completely blocking the entrance, but not before Joseph pushed Gilbert out and leaving himself trapped with several of the officers.

Everyone that got out made their way across the moat and into the swamp. Emma noticed that only about half of those who had entered the Base were able to escape. Gilbert wanted everyone to keep moving. The Chief did not want to leave. The explosions continued until a final massive rumble completely leveled the structure, dooming all who were inside.

They could not go back to search for survivors because Gilbert told them that there were even greater dangers. He told them that there were others at the Base. They knew of the four helicopters heading their way. They planned to hijack the helicopters. They were planning on assassinating the president of the United States who was in Florida. He also told the Chief that there would be other attempts around the world. Once these world leaders were assassinated, the response of each country would result in a global war.

With a heavy heart, the Chief ordered everyone back to the helicopters, knowing that Susannah and Ms. Coraline were in danger. Philip said that he could not leave knowing that his son was still inside. The Chief pleaded with him but Philip was adamant that he was going back. Chief O'Brian told him that he will send back help. Emma did not say anything of what had happened to Charles.

They all hurried to get back to the helicopters. When they got there, Susannah was huddling with Ms. Coraline, trying to keep her warm. Ms. Coraline was gasping for air. Her pulse was very weak. Susannah explained how the two of them were attacked and overpowered by four masked individuals.

The helicopters were gone.

The Chief radioed to warn of the assassination attempts and for assistance. Within a few hours, they were all picked up and heading home. A small search party headed back into the swamp to search for survivors.

Ms. Coraline was taken in a separate helicopter with Emma, Susannah, Chief O'Brian, and Gilbert. Two of the officers joined the pilot in the cockpit. Emma sat next to Ms. Coraline, holding her hand.

"I am sorry, Emma," whispered Ms. Coraline. "I wish I could have seen you grow up to be the beautiful woman you are becoming."

"Don't talk like that," said Emma, encouraging her to conserve her strength.

With that, however, she closed her eyes and breathed her last breath. Susannah shook her head in disbelief and wept. Gilbert sat quietly in the corner, witnessing something that he had never seen before. He curled his feet up and wrapped his hands around them before resting his head on his knees.

Emma was beginning to understand the sacrifices that everyone was making. Not only had they suffered much, but each willingly gave their lives for her, from Susannah's husband, Mr. Lyell, Mr. Sedgwick, those at the Base, and now Ms. Coraline. She understood the importance of her task, though she could not comprehend it.

Emma clenched her fist as tightly as she could over Ms. Coraline's hand, realizing that she was gone. A single tear rolled down her cheek and dropped onto Ms. Coraline's hand. Like a bolt of lightning, Ms. Coraline jolted from her resting place. Emma gasped and pulled herself away from Ms. Coraline, dropping her coat in the process. Susannah's head flung upwards and Gilbert simply smiled as though to say, "What it is!"

Emma's heart raced. She wondered how it was possible. She looked down at her coat. A piece of the Grail was visible. It was just as Mr. Lyell had told her. The Grail can bring death, but in the right hands, it can also give life. Emma was overcome with joy. She approached Ms. Coraline and lay like a babe in her arms. Ms. Coraline did not know what happened to her. She felt as though she was dreaming. She simply wrapped her arms around Emma, gently embracing her.

As they flew in the helicopter, the pilot patched the radio into the speakers. There was a news bulletin on the radio: "Although this is only preliminary, it appears that the leaders of the United States, Great Britain, China, India, and Russia have all been assassinated today. Please stay tuned as these stories develop."

There was nothing that Emma could do now. She knew that the world was about to change, drastically. She thought about Charles and wondered if he had survived. In her vision, he lived to be an old man. But how could he have survived? She wondered about the new power that had been given to her. Was it a gift or a curse? For the moment, it did not matter. She was surrounded by everyone that she cared about and loved.

As they flew, Emma could only wonder as to what was happening below. Her vision showed worldwide destruction. Yet, she knew that the world and humanity would survive even this test. Just barely, however.

As they headed home, Emma opened the envelope that she had retrieved from the vault. She took out the letter and looked at what was written in it. It was a letter from Charles. He wrote it in the language that she had created. Emma instantly understood the message.

CHAPTER 25
Australia

As they flew, everyone listened to the radio broadcast for regular updates of what was happening around the world. Canada, the United States, Europe, Asia, most of Africa, Central and South America were all listed as no-fly zones. They could not go back home. They knew that they had to find a safe haven elsewhere. There were few places that they could go.

There were already violent riots all around the world. It was not simply looting and protesting, but hand-to-hand combat. Hundreds of thousands of casualties were already reported. The assassinations were the spark that the gunpowder barrel needed. The pent-up anger of all oppressed peoples was released.

Emma took a pen and wrote on the back of the piece of paper that contained Charles's letter. She handed it to Chief O'Brian, saying, "This is where we should go."

He looked at her and again at the latitude and longitude that she wrote down. He did not question her. He simply instructed the pilots of their new course. The Chief had made friends in Australia during the police conference. They were in need of a safe haven and he knew that they would find it in Australia.

As they flew, the pilot informed everyone that they were being followed. He was unable to shake the three pursuers. Whatever maneuvers he and the other pilot tried, they were able to copy them and gain ground. Again and again, they fired at the defenseless helicopters. Yet, the pilots were able to avoid being hit each time.

They were not able to elude their pursuers. The other helicopter began to sustain damage. He knew that he had to give Emma a chance to get away. He struggled to maintain control, as he aimed his crippled helicopter directly in the path of two of the fighter jets. As they approached, he swerved into the lead jet, clipping its wing with the helicopter's rotor blade. With only one wing, the crippled jet cart-wheeled all the way to the ground and exploded in a ball of fire. Upon impact with the jet, the rotor blade snapped off and spiraled into the second jet, cutting a deep gash into the jet's fuselage. After losing control, the jet followed the first one to the ground. There was still one aircraft in pursuit.

Emma and the others watched in dismay as the brave pilot sacrificed himself and the others. By now, they were almost over the coast of Florida. The helicopter was dangerously low on fuel. Even if they were able to escape the jet, they would not get very far without fuel, informed the pilot.

As Emma looked out her window, she noticed that the clouds around her were beginning to turn orange. She remembered a story that Mr. Lyell had told her. As she peered deeper, she noticed a tornado-like cloud forming on her side of the helicopter. The tornado was on its side, like a tunnel.

She unbuckled her seat belt and quickly made her way to the pilot. He instantly turned around and followed her instructions. They began to fly in the same direction as the approaching aircraft. They were on a collision course. Yet, he could not bring himself to doubt her orders. He thought that it would be easier to die an instant death than face the ravages of the open ocean if her plan did not work.

Onwards they flew, knowing that it may lead to certain death, as bullets were being fired at the helicopter. Emma pointed the way. The pilot repeatedly kept looking to her for reassurance. She was unwavering, her finger aimed at the target. As the helicopter and the jet sped towards each other, Emma saw the orange haze again and pointed straight ahead. Everyone held on tight and braced themselves. The pilot closed his eyes, but Emma held firm. The aircraft and helicopter were mere seconds from colliding with each other and as they were about to hit, the oncoming aircraft vanished.

Assuming that they should have already collided, the pilot opened his eyes. He didn't know what happened, only that they were still alive. It was only after he pinched himself that he came to this conclusion. Without saying a word, the pilot looked at Emma. She pointed at something in the distance. With almost no fuel left, he headed for the object. He told everyone to brace themselves for a rocky landing, with the helicopter weaving back and forth before they safely touched down.

They had somehow managed to find an American refueling vessel. The Chief explained their situation to the ship's captain, and soon after, they were refueled and given food and water.

When they were in the air again, the Chief sat down with everyone onboard. He said, "According to the ship's captain, we are somewhere around Christmas Island in the Indian Ocean. This means that we have traveled more than 11 000 miles in 10 seconds with no fuel."

Without saying a word, everyone looked at Emma. She simply smiled and shrugged her shoulders. Gilbert knew what she meant. She knew that they were waiting for an explanation. Yet, she was not prepared to offer one. She silently recalled the stories Mr. Lyell told her of people who have flown into the Bermuda Triangle and entered into wormhole-like clouds and seemed to travel through time and space. She distinctly remembered him saying that even Lindbergh claimed to have passed through one.

Even the pilot could not explain what happened. All he saw were his instruments acting erratically. However, he knew that he had just witnessed a miracle. Everyone else sat quietly as they flew. The pilot relayed to the Chief that it would only be a few hours before they reached their destination.

Australia was the only safe place left in the world, according to reports on the radio. Everyone listened to the news and wondered if the world would ever be the same again. The smoke from the fires burning in Africa and elsewhere could be seen from the helicopter. No one could believe what they were witnessing. From the radio description, it seemed as though the world was on fire, save Australia. Emma and the others learned that hundreds of millions of people, all around the world, were making their way to the oceans and other waterways to avoid the fires.

The Chief had met a few locals on his recent trip to Australia. He radioed to them to meet with him at the location that Emma had specified. They were completely out of fuel when the helicopter landed. They were instructed to quickly make their way to a nearby river. There were several people waiting for them at the river's edge to take them to safety.

They needed to cross the river. However, the small boat could not take everyone over at one time. The pilot and two officers decided to wait with Gilbert while the others paddled to the other side. The boat would return within a few minutes. Everyone was surprised to see that Gilbert had left Emma's side. It was the first time since they began their journey that he did so. In fact, it was Gilbert who volunteered to wait for the boat to return.

Once everyone was safely on the other side, the rower quickly tried to make his way back across the river. As he was almost halfway there, everyone looked down the river. They could see something coming their way. Before the Chief could yell, "EVERYONE, TAKE COVER!" a massive explosion sent the boat and a plume of water high into the air. Several other explosions could be heard across the river where Gilbert and the others patiently awaited the boat's return. Australia had caught up with the rest of the world.

The Chief quickly gathered everyone together. They had to find shelter. Everyone wondered about Gilbert and the others, but there was nothing that they could do to help them. The locals knew of a safe place that was not far away. They had enough food and water to last for a few days.

Throughout the night, Emma and the others could hear explosions. They all huddled together in the cold. The Chief did not want to light a fire, as it would attract unwanted visitors. He assigned everyone to watch duties.

The next morning, everyone woke up to rustling sounds outside. The guards had fallen asleep. Everyone was surprised to see Charles, Philip, Joseph, and the officers who were trapped at the Base. Emma was the most excited but the least surprised one to see Charles. They were happy to find out that Helen had been rescued along with several hundred others. They found refuge in the branches of Old Oak, the only structure, along with Angel Bridge, that was not covered by water.

Charles told everyone how they managed to escape from the Base. Although he had fallen into the pit, he landed on a soft surface below. It was some kind of escape route that was planned by those who had inhabited the Base.

When the Chief asked how he was able to find them, he told them that Emma had left a note at the Base. Emma, however, interjected. She said that she did not leave a note for them. She explained that the reason she guided everyone to their present location is because she was following the directions that Charles left her in the letter. She showed Charles the letter. It was written in the secret code that she had created. However, Charles was adamant that he did not leave any secret messages for her.

Emma countered with the same claim. However, they were happy that American VTOL fighter jets were able to bring them to Australia so quickly.

As they discussed the letter, they soon found themselves surrounded. From every direction, came mercenaries with guns drawn. Everyone was ordered to put their hands up.

"I told you," a familiar voice echoed, "I am smarter than you are."

Now, it all made sense to Emma, as she peered between two mercenaries to see Gilbert emerge. How he survived, she did not know. While Emma had blamed it all on Charles, it was the one person that she would never suspect. How could she have been so naive?

Gilbert looked at her. He was not injured. But he was also not alone. From behind Gilbert emerged Fitzroy.

He quipped, "Surprised to see me, Emma?"

Nothing made sense to her, anymore. The one person whom she truly cared about was holding a dagger to her heart. She had shared everything about herself with him. He knew about the cases, the secret codes, her vision, and the Grail. He was the only one who was aware of everything that was going on, but the last person that she would suspect.

Within minutes, everyone had their hands tied up and being led away to a waiting plane. Only Emma, Charles and Fitzroy remained with a few mercenaries. Emma was still in shock and filled with guilt. She blamed Charles for everything and was even about to suspect Gilbert, yet her heart would not let her see beyond her feelings.

Fitzroy said nothing else to Emma. He simply took the Grail away from her, still wrapped in her coat. Raising it above his head, he said to the mercenaries, "The power source for the Ridge Breaker is now ours." They cheered loudly and fired their weapons into the air.

As Fitzroy walked away, Emma simply asked, "Why?"

He did not say anything at first. He simply glanced at her and then at Charles. Emma knew that it had something to do with Charles. But knowing how she felt about Fitzroy, she was surprised by his suggestion that she and Charles were more than friends.

Shaking his head, Fitzroy said, "I never thought that the two of you would end up together." Again, he glanced over at Charles.

"What are you saying?" questioned Emma. "How could you think that there is something between me and Charles?"

"I don't have to think!" he snapped. "I know!"

"What do you know?" questioned Emma.

Fitzroy replied, "Just before Mr. Lyell died, he told me about a vision of the day the two of you got married."

"You are responsible for Mr. Lyell's death?" accused Emma. She was infuriated with him. She screamed, "There is no legend!"

"I guess he didn't tell you," said Fitzroy.

"Tell me what?" asked Emma.

Fitzroy suggested, "If you and Charles can touch the Grail with your bare hands and survive, what does that make you?"

"Listen," pleaded Emma, "I am not the savior of the world and Charles is not going to destroy it."

Fitzroy laughed cynically upon hearing Emma's explanation. He asked, "Mr. Lyell did not tell you, did he? You honestly don't know."

Turning to Charles, Fitzroy said, "Why don't you tell her."

With the guards standing over him, guns pointed, Charles stammered, "Em...Em...Emma, the truth is that the two of us are the only ones who can touch the Grail with our bare hands, now that Mr. Lyell is gone."

"I've heard this a million times before," said Emma in frustration.

"Tell her the rest," encouraged Fitzroy.

Charles continued hesitantly, "Except, that I am going to save the world."

With a shallow breath, Charles closed his eyes and lowered his head. He wished that he had not been the bearer of such news. Emma finally learned the truth. It was time and Charles knew that she needed to hear it. No more lies. It was a fact, which Mr. Lyell had revealed to him and Fitzroy.

Emma took a few seconds to digest what she was told. All of her life, Mr. Lyell had lied to her, she now realized. He was not preparing her. He was keeping an eye on her. He told her what she wanted to hear, in the hopes that she would never realize who she really was.

Charles explained to Emma that he and Fitzroy knew all along. Mr. Lyell had told them about his visions. Charles had seen it for himself. Charles further explained that Mr. Lyell tried to hide her true identity. He wanted to believe that she could choose for herself. She used her faith to save Ms. Coraline. Perhaps, when the time comes, she could do the same for the world.

Emma and Charles were held back as the others disappeared out of sight. No one else heard the conversation, but they were all wondering what they were talking about.

Fitzroy came forward with someone standing beside him. Charles recognized him from the retirement home. It was Thomas.

He looked at Charles and said, "So, you are The One."

Fitzroy asked, "What should we do with him?"

"If he is The One," suggested Thomas, "we need to get rid of him. Only then can we succeed."

Thomas signaled to two mercenaries to remove Charles and take him into a nearby cave. They grabbed Charles and proceeded to drag him away.

Emma interrupted, "You can't do this."

"And why not?" questioned Thomas.

Emma thought quickly and replied, "The legend."

He asked, "What do you know of the legend?"

She explained, "The legend said that The One will have a vision of coming events. Charles has seen the future. Don't you want to know how it all ends?"

With the wave of his hand, Thomas signaled to the two mercenaries to take them with the others. They gathered all of the food and water that was in the caves and took it with them. As they got to the waiting plane, the pilot warned that there was too much weight on the plane. He said that he would not be able to lift off. At least three people needed to stay behind. After scanning the crowd, Fitzroy instructed that Emma and Charles should be left behind. Besides, he had the Grail.

He also knew the legend. He could not directly destroy the Christ. But maybe wild animals could. Fitzroy knows that Emma will never love him the way she will eventually love Charles. It only made sense that they should be left behind in the wilderness. Without food and water and no one around for miles, they would not be able to survive.

Following Fitzroy's orders, a mercenary escorted Emma and Charles off the water plane. Seeing this, Joseph broke free of the others and rushed to Emma's side. Before he could reach her, a shot rang out. Joseph fell at Emma's feet, with one hand still inside the plane. With his foot, Thomas pushed the limb off the plane and onto the ground.

He laughed at Joseph, saying, "Thank you for volunteering."

Susannah and the others looked on in dismay as the plane took off. They could not believe what had happened to Joseph. Susannah had never been this far away from her daughter before.

Emma and Charles were still in shock at seeing the body. Emma's eyes were wide open and her chest heaved with rapid, shallow breaths. Charles shook her to wake her from her trance. While Joseph's face was to the ground, his hands were moving. Charles tried to roll him over. He was successful with Emma's help. Joseph was still breathing, but barely.

Emma looked at him helplessly. She cried, "I'm so sorry Joseph." She put pressure on his wound but she could not stop the bleeding. "There is nothing that I can do. They have the Grail."

"There is one thing," requested Joseph, as he gasped for air.

"Tell me," begged Emma, who was in tears.

"Don't," he said, gasping. "Don't call me Joseph."

It was an odd thing to say.

Emma asked, "Who are you?"

"Call me," begged Joseph, with his last breath, "dad."

"Dad!" cried Emma.

With satisfaction on his face, he closed his eyes for the last time. Emma had wondered what burdens Joseph has had to endure to protect her. She never realized just how truly heavy they were. For so many years, he knew who she was and said nothing. Yet, for a moment she knew who he really was and could not be more proud.

Chapter 26
The Outback

As the plane flew out of sight, Charles began to worry. The sun was rising fast and they needed shelter. If they were caught outside, they could easily dehydrate. However, they also needed to find food and water. They could not drink the water from the river as it was littered with dead animals. They had a dilemma. Go back to the safety of the caves and risk dehydrating or venture out into the unknown to find food and clean water. Vultures were already beginning to circle overhead.

Their first task, however, was to give Joseph a proper burial. They surrounded his body with rocks so that animals could not get to it. With each stone, Emma thought of how difficult it must have been for Joseph to keep his secret all of these years. After Emma had placed the last stone, she said a short prayer and her final goodbye.

Emma decided that this was not a safe place to be. Charles was excited to go forward. However, this was the Australian Outback. The farthest Charles had ever been away from civilization was when he and his father went camping in their backyard. When it started to rain that night, they both ran inside the house. Charles simply did not understand the dangers.

As far as Emma could figure out, they were somewhere in the Mitchell Plateau and possibly along the Gibb River. If they were able to make their way to Mitchell Falls, they may be able to find people there. Emma knew that it was a popular tourist attraction.

The decision was made. They had to venture forward. Charles thought that it would be safer to walk along the river's edge. With each step, the sun grew hotter. Charles was completely exhausted after a few hours of walking. The heat was unbearable. Emma decided that they needed to rest. As soon as they sat down in the shade of the large rock, Charles fell asleep.

It was late in the evening when Emma sprang from her slumber. She had fallen asleep next to Charles. They slept the whole day. Emma quickly woke Charles up. They had not found clean water to drink or anything to eat. They were exposed to the elements and whatever dangers lurked nearby. Now, the sun was setting fast.

Charles told Emma that while he was a little hungry and thirsty, he would be alright. The long nap was enough to rejuvenate him. Jokingly, she suggested that he use his powers to make water come out of the surrounding rocks. Although he knew that she was just joking, he tried in vain to make a miracle happen. No such luck.

Emma knew of another way to get water. The sun was extremely hot all day. As the sun set and the winds picked up, it began to get cold very fast. Emma knew that it would get foggy very quickly. Within an hour, the fog had settled on the nearby grass. Emma looked for something to collect the fog. She then noticed Charles's pants pocket. Something was sticking out of it. Emma asked Charles for his handkerchief. He had never used it before. Now he understood why he carried it around all of these years. There is a reason for everything, Emma told him. She began to walk in the grass with the handkerchief spread in front of her. Soon, it was soaked. They twisted it and took turns drinking the water that dripped from it.

Although they had no food, the water was refreshing. As the sun completely disappeared beyond the horizon, they knew that they faced an uncertain night alone. Emma thought about starting a fire, but they did not want to attract unwanted attention, even though it could also mean that they could be rescued.

The only light that they could see was coming from the full moon. In every direction they looked, the stars studded the sky. Neither of them had ever seen so many stars in the night sky. It was the most amazing thing that Charles had ever witnessed. He even pointed out the edge of the Milky Way to Emma. To her, it just looked like clouds.

Charles stood up on his feet. Emma wondered what he was doing. He reached out his hand to her. Hesitantly and delicately, she placed her hand in his. He helped her up to her feet. Emma was not sure what he was doing.

Charles gazed into her eyes and asked, "Can I have this dance?"

"But there is no music," protested Emma.

"Listen," he said, "there is music everywhere."

As he pulled her closer to him, she remembered that tonight was the night of their school dance. She thought of Max and his pow wow dance.

Although it was quiet, she could hear the music that Charles spoke of. The one thing that Emma was never quite good at was dancing. So, she followed Charles's lead. Although they only danced for a minute, it seemed like an endless song. Emma finally understood why Charles always wanted to go to the school dance. He would say, "Anything can be expressed through dance, even love."

Their dance was interrupted by rustling in the bushes. Emma grabbed onto Charles. He tried to act brave, though he was shaking. Whatever it was, it was getting closer and closer until it emerged from the bushes. They both thought that it was a wild animal but were surprised to see two older men.

Charles figured that they were Aboriginals, given their appearance. They each had a walking stick in their hands. Their faces were covered in white and yellow paint. One of the men tossed a baobab fruit to Charles. He shared it with Emma. The men were not surprised to see Emma and Charles. On the contrary, it seems that they were looking for them.

Without saying a word, the men turned and began to walk back in the direction from where they came. Emma and Charles looked at each other momentarily and made up their mind without saying a word. They knew that it was better to follow them than to be left behind. As they walked, the men explained that they had a vision. A visitor appeared to them the night before. They were instructed to follow the stars until they found Emma and Charles.

When Emma asked about the vision, she was told that an African-American man appeared to them and gave them instructions. Emma and Charles immediately thought of Mr. Lyell. From the description offered by the two men, they both knew that Mr. Lyell had somehow led them to safety.

Emma summoned the courage and said, "I am sorry to tell you that Mr. Lyell has passed away."

Neither of the men seemed surprised as they looked at each other, but wondered how Emma knew of Mr. Lyell or his passing.

One of the men replied, "We know he passed away. We performed his burial ritual almost fifteen years ago. Chief O'Brian was here, too."

Fifteen years ago? Both Charles and Emma looked at each other.

One of the men continued, "See that giant baobab tree over there?" He pointed in the distance. "That is Mr. Lyell's final resting place."

Now Emma was truly scared. Who has she been talking to all these years? Who was in his casket at the funeral?

One of the men suggested that it was Mr. Lyell's son, Malthus. Malthus and the Chief were good friends, Emma was told.

Emma stumbled backward and fell to the ground upon hearing the names of Malthus and Chief O'Brian together.

One of the men explained, "Malthus was a gifted stage actor. He impersonated his father all too well. He and Chief O'Brian had a very colorful and troubled history. They were involved in criminal activity. The Chief had no choice but to follow Malthus. If he didn't, Malthus threatened to reveal incriminating evidence."

That explains why Mr. Lyell did not attend the sentencing of Malthus, thought Emma. That also explains why they could not find Malthus after the judge released him. He could disguise himself to look like anyone. Chief O'Brian may have helped him fake his death. That is why there was no viewing of the body at the funeral. She wondered if the officers putting up the police tape at Mr. Lyell's home were also in on it. Malthus could have been at the fishing grounds, the museum, the police station, the church, the Home. He could be whoever he wanted, whenever he wanted, wherever he wanted.

It now made sense to Emma. Malthus was able to kill the judge and all twenty-one officers because the Chief led him to them. Chief O'Brian knew that Mr. Lyell had died, yet said nothing to her all of these years. Malthus and the Chief were keeping an eye on her all along. They wanted her to lead them to the Grail.

As they walked, the men told of how Mr. Lyell found a wandering infant in the Outback and adopted him. How Mr. Lyell trained and guided him. How Mr. Lyell loved him. How Malthus betrayed Mr. Lyell.

They were told about the secret scrolls. On one of his meditation journeys, Mr. Lyell traveled to a distant cave in the heart of the Outback. There he wrote down in scrolls things that were revealed to him. In it, he described the Christ. When Malthus read the scrolls, he knew he could never touch the Grail, see angels or be the next Christ. In a rage, he struck down his father and stole the scrolls.

One of the men said, "Malthus still has the scrolls. He is the only one who knows what is written in them. He has been using this knowledge to guide you and Charles, and to build the Ridge Breaker."

Emma added, "Don't forget about Gilbert and Fitzroy." She could only imagine what Malthus may have revealed to them.

Emma and Charles were told of how Malthus escaped and traveled to Brazil where he lived as a rancher in the jungle. He was married and had two children. They were also told about the fire, how Malthus lost his entire family and livelihood, and his quest for revenge. He then returned to Canada and pretended to be his father.

One of the men said, "Malthus grew up thinking that he could help humanity. He was such a good boy and student. He wanted to make things better, like his father. When he was told that he could not be the next Christ, he became angry. When his family was taken from him, however, it filled him with rage. He became disillusioned with the world. He only wanted revenge and destruction. With the power of the Grail, he can now finally carry out his plans."

Neither Emma nor Charles asked any questions as they walked throughout the night. As day was about to break, they had finally reached where they were going. Charles did not bother to ask where they were or why they were there. He was simply too exhausted to stay awake. He crawled onto a small mattress and immediately fell asleep. Emma joined him.

Chapter 27
The Death of Malthus

It was almost noon when Emma and Charles were stirred from their sleep by the sound of a helicopter blade twirling. As they looked about their surroundings, they saw toothbrushes and other toiletries. On a small table was a platter of food. After they ate, they emerged from the tent to investigate where they were.

One of the men who led them throughout the night was sitting outside their tent to greet them. They both recognized him and politely smiled.

"Thank you for everything," said Emma.

He smiled at her.

"What is your name?" asked Emma.

Charles was prepared to hear a deeply-rooted Aboriginal name with meaning and essence, perhaps something that had significance in nature. However, he was somewhat disappointed when the kind man said, "John."

Emma introduced herself.

"I know who you are," said John, smiling. "Mr. Lyell had predicted many years ago that you would come."

"What about me?" asked Charles excitedly. "Did he talk about me?"

John replied with a straight face, "I know nothing about you."

"Oh," replied Charles disappointedly.

John laughed loudly. "I'm just messing with you. Of course, I know who you are, Charles."

"You knew Mr. Lyell?" asked Charles.

"We were very good friends," said John, a man about 80 years old. "Mr. Lyell knew this day would come. We have everything prepared and awaiting your orders."

"Orders?" asked Charles.

John nodded. He said, "Mr. Lyell had said that when the time was right, Emma would know what to do."

Seeing that John thought that Emma was The One, Charles said nothing. He and Emma had agreed not to tell anyone anything about who they are or may be. John did not suspect anything and Charles saw no reason to reveal any. Mr. Lyell had told them who the Christ would be, but it seemed that he did not mention the other. Maybe Mr. Lyell knew something that no one else knew.

Charles instructed, "We have to go to Iceland. At the Base, I overheard them saying that they are going to open up the Mid-Atlantic Ridge with the Ridge Breaker. It will cause a global flood. Iceland is where the ridge can be seen above the ocean. The assassinations are just a distraction. While everyone is fighting against each other, Malthus and his mercenaries are busy carrying out their plan."

John said, "I already have brave men and women in Iceland searching for the Ridge Breaker."

Emma finally understood the reason for the fires. If Malthus can cause tsunamis, then the edge of the ocean would not be the safest place. Everyone was heading for the oceans. Emma knew that they had to act quickly. They had to recover the Grail.

"Can you get us to Iceland?" asked Emma.

John begged Emma, "Maybe you should stay behind. You know the legend. We cannot allow anything to happen to you."

Emma reminded him that he promised to follow her orders. Reluctantly, he agreed. As Emma emerged from the tent and stepped into the sunlight, she could not believe her eyes.

John, walking behind her, said, "This war has taken its toll." He was talking about the children staring at Emma. Pointing to one of the children before them, he said, "Little Mary has lost everyone and everything."

Emma walked over to her and knelt down.

The dirt-smudged-face little girl asked, "Are you going to bring back my mommy and daddy?"

Emma could only offer her a consoling hug.

John walked up to Emma and said, "We have hundreds of orphans to care for and many more come every day."

The sirens began to wail all around the compound. Everyone began to usher the children to safety underground.

"What's going on?" asked Emma, as she and John began to run towards the helicopters.

She was told that there was an army of mercenaries heading towards the compound.

"We can't just leave them," protested Emma.

"No," she was instructed, "we have to leave now."

As they ascended towards Iceland, John sent an army of his own to face the mercenaries.

It was a small army, Emma thought, as she looked behind her. There were several dozen helicopters filled with individuals who had dedicated themselves to this mission. It was something that Mr. Lyell had been planning for many years.

"Mr. Lyell had visions of the final battle," explained John. "While he traveled the world to raise up armies, Malthus was organizing mercenaries. For years, we have been secretly training ground, sea and air troops to prepare for this day. We have tens of thousands around the world ready to join us. This will be the greatest battle the world has ever seen."

As they flew across the Indian Ocean, they witnessed the destruction of numerous ships. Many were rendered to mere wood, while the majority were in flames. They could not bear to witness the scale of destruction. No one could grasp what was going on below. All of the nations of the world had risen up against themselves and each other.

Throughout their trek across the African skies, they saw nothing but fire and smoke. The continent was set ablaze. How quickly the violence spread. It was incomprehensible to Emma. Yet, she knew that this would not result in the end of the world. She could only imagine what a battle it would be when such a day does come.

The scene was equally dismal over Europe. To everyone's surprise, they were the only ones in the sky. None of the other pilots that John spoke of had survived, except those who traveled with them now. Their deaths were not in vain, however. They had cleared the way for Emma to get this far.

As they approached Iceland, they were met with heavy resistance. The first wave was a squadron of fighter jets, whom they easily defeated. Emma could not believe the skills of the pilots that John had trained. In the fight, they lost two helicopters and fourteen brave men and women.

No sooner were the fighter jets scattered in the ocean, they encountered a fleet of bombers. Once again, the helicopters were able to out-maneuver the bombers and laid waste to all of them. Six helicopters were taken down. Emma prayed for each of their souls as they made the ultimate sacrifice.

The only thing between them and the Ridge Breaker were gunships that littered the ocean below. They were not prepared for them. As the gunships were firing at them, they had to keep their distance. Most of their ammunition was already spent and taking out just one gunship would require massive amounts of it or a miracle. Since they were almost out of ammunition, Emma looked for a miracle.

While there was no air support, John learned that several of their ships were making good progress. They had already destroyed three gunships. They were speeding towards Emma's location, but they were still several hours away. Despite heavy casualties, the ground forces were also making great strides. They had broken into the heavily fortified base and were attempting to dismantle the Ridge Breaker. When Emma learned of how many brave men and women had been lost, she was devastated.

Everyone watched in awe as something was happening in the ocean below. Steam began to rise over the ocean and in mere moments, all of the gunships were surrounded by the mist. The mist rose higher and higher until the water and the gunships could not be seen anymore. The shock waves from the explosions below could be felt in the helicopters. Plumes of water spouted from the ocean.

Then, there was silence. When the mist finally lifted, the entire fleet of gunships rested at the bottom of the ocean. John learned that a team had entered the underground bunker and destroyed the Ridge Breaker. However, they could not celebrate, because the explosions under the ocean sent tsunamis hurtling in every direction. There was nothing that they could do to stop it. John frantically radioed to all of the ships to turn around. He knew that the ships could not outrun what was coming their way, but he still desperately tried to warn them.

As Emma and Charles looked on helplessly, they realized that their helicopter was the only one left from the original fleet. They were surrounded by several mercenary helicopters. Even though the Ridge Breaker was destroyed, its purpose was fulfilled: to create tsunamis to drown the world.

With machine guns pointed at them, Emma watched as Fitzroy and Malthus (no longer disguised as Thomas) boarded the helicopter with Gilbert. Once inside the helicopter, Malthus pushed Gilbert towards Emma before disconnecting the bridge. The other mercenary helicopters flew away.

As Malthus looked below towards the ocean, he declared, "My Ridge Breaker may have been destroyed, but in mere moments, the world will be cleansed."

Fitzroy held onto the goblet. Malthus handed him several pieces of rope and ordered him to tie up Emma, Charles and everyone else.

Fitzroy approached Emma and Charles but walked past them. He then turned around and stood between them. Malthus realized that he had been tricked. Fitzroy had switched sides. He handed the goblet to Emma. Charles and Gilbert were happy that he did.

"What are you doing, Fitzroy?" begged Malthus. "We are so close to achieving our goal."

Fitzroy accused Malthus, angrily yelling, "You lied to me! You told me that my parents would be safe. I know that they are both gone. I can't forgive you for that." Fitzroy reached into his pockets and pulled out a cloth bag and threw it at Malthus. The bag hit the floor of the helicopter next to his feet. Several pieces of gold coins rolled out of the bag.

Charles looked at Emma. The look in her eyes told him that she had a plan. Emma knew the fate of hundreds of millions of people who were unaware of what was heading towards them at the edge of the ocean.

"Even with the goblet," teased Malthus, "there is nothing that you can do to stop what is going to happen." He looked at Emma. He stretched out his hand and encouraged her to come to him. "I know who you are, my dear. Accept your destiny. Join me and we can share power together. I have been preparing you for this since the day you were born." He suggested, "You are eventually going to enslave the world. I can help you. Just bring the Grail to me."

Emma looked at Charles for one last time and whispered, "I can't let him do this. Stay alive. I will find you." She leaned forward and kissed him on the cheek.

It was something that Charles had waited for his entire life. Yet, he wished it would not be at this moment. For he knew that it may be the last time that he will look upon Emma. He painfully removed the thought from his head.

Emma lowered her head as she took a few steps towards Malthus.

"That's right," he insisted. "Come to me. Do you not feel the connection between us?" asked Malthus. He lifted his shirt to reveal a scar below his left rib cage. Emma felt her side, knowing that she too had a scar, in the same position.

Charles, Fitzroy and Gilbert begged her not to listen to him.

"I have no choice," said Emma, as she walked to within a step of Malthus, her head still down. Her friends begged her to stop.

"You have made the right choice, my child," reassured Malthus, reaching out his hand.

Gilbert approached Emma from behind. She turned around. She could see that he was scared.

Emma cried, "Gilbert, I need a miracle."

He replied, with tears in his eyes, "You don't need a miracle, Miss Emma. You are the miracle."

Emma, Charles, Gilbert, and Fitzroy all cried out: "Together, for each other!"

Emma spun around, dropped down in a running-back stance, protected the Grail against her chest and with all her might, charged Malthus. Her shoulder dug into his midsection, forcing him towards the door. With two steps backward, Malthus and Emma slipped out of the helicopter.

Perhaps no one would ever know why Emma made the decision that she did. Maybe she, at last, believed in the power of the Grail and herself. Maybe she finally believed that one person can change the world. Gilbert knew that Emma was special.

John radioed to the ships below. His calls went unanswered. Again and again, he radioed, but no one answered. The captain of one of the ships, his son, he was sure would reply. Again, no answer. As brave and fearless as he was, eventually John's eyes betrayed him. He continued to send messages, crying, "Please, answer! Please!" John put his hands over his eyes and shook his head. The others could only watch helplessly.

But those tears turned to joy when he heard, "Just...surfed...the biggest...wave...of my life, dad." The celebration and shouts of jubilation were well received over the radio. They were all still alive.

The helicopter headed for the ships below. It was hard for Charles, Fitzroy and Gilbert to celebrate on the ship, even on the

Earth's finest hour. Without Emma, there would be no celebration. Charles, most of all, was inconsolable. This is not how the angel told him it would end. As everyone hugged and laughed, danced and celebrated, he found little satisfaction. He scanned the crowd, waiting to glimpse Emma. After everyone came and went, he stood alone, realizing that, perhaps, even the angel can be wrong.

Later, as they all gathered on the ship, Gilbert told everyone what he saw, being the only witness to it. For while everyone else closed their eyes, his eyes were wide open. He saw it all and recounted it with tears and a heavy heart. "As she fell, there was a huge explosion beneath the ocean. The plume of water reached Emma high up in the air. It swallowed her up as it fell back. I saw towering waves speeding towards land on all sides of the Atlantic Ocean. I was sure that they were going to hit Canada, the US, the Caribbean, and South America. Tsunamis were heading for Greenland, Europe and Africa. They were so big, I was sure that they could reach Antarctica. But as the water from the explosion fell back to the ocean with Emma and the Grail, all of the tsunamis, one after another, began to calm and crashed onto the shore as little ripples in a bathtub. Some had grown as high as skyscrapers, but before they crashed onto the shore, even these became like a droplet in your palm."

Gilbert could only imagine the fear that people who stood in its wake were going through. Their prayers were answered and their lives were spared because one person was willing to sacrifice their life so that others may live. While the survivors were celebrating in the streets, they did not know why they were spared or by whom.

After Gilbert had told of what he had witnessed, Charles wanted to search for Emma. He believed that she was still alive. He told John of the day he and Emma will be married. The angel had revealed this to him. She must still be alive, he argued.

Everyone was willing to help him look for her. They began immediately. By nightfall, they had scoured the ocean but found no trace of her. Everyone was sure that she was gone, but Charles was defiant. So, they continued to search. Word had spread that Emma had saved the masses. The next morning, all available ships from all around the world were out looking for her, but to no avail. After three days with no sleep, Charles was too tired to continue.

Sometime that morning, after only a few minutes of sleeping on the deck of the ship, Charles was startled. As he rolled and looked over his shoulder, someone laid beside him. He rushed to his feet and stood over the body. His eyes were wide open. He could not contain his excitement. Immediately, he began to yell for help. Within seconds, everyone on the ship crowded over Emma. The search was called off as the message was relayed. All of the other ships convened close to the one that Emma and Charles were on. Susannah and Philip were on one of those ships. John reported that Chief O'Brian had shot himself. Ms. Coraline, however, was nowhere to be found.

A doctor onboard quickly checked her pulse and vital signs. They were faint but detectable. No one knew how she had managed to get onto the ship or how she found the one that Charles was on. The only thing they knew for sure is that Fitzroy could not stand to be in her presence. As soon as he found out that she was onboard, he asked to be transferred to another ship. Charles could not convince him to stay.

Emma did not wake up. They all waited by keeping vigil over her for the next three days as she rested and recovered. They remained on the ship and a news crew broadcast the coverage around the entire world. On every corner of habitable land on Earth, everyone tuned in to see her progress. Those who could not see it on handheld devices watched it on television, while some tuned in to the radio or read about it in the newspapers.

After visiting Emma, Charles called John aside. He was bothered by something that Malthus had said. If it is true that Malthus and Emma share a similar destiny, if Emma is alive, should the same not be true for Malthus?

John seemed uncertain of what to tell Charles. Looking around to make sure that no one else could hear him, John whispered, "He is on the ship."

"Show me where he is!" demanded Charles.

"This way," said John, leading the way. They scaled the ladder to the top deck of the ship. John pointed to a half-closed door. Upon entering, Charles was faced with a subdued, shirtless Malthus in the center of the room. He was surrounded by armed guards. How he survived the fall, Charles did not know.

Malthus began to laugh as Charles moved closer. "You cannot kill me," he teased, looking down at the scar below his rib. "If you do, you kill the girl."

A glove snapped onto the hand of someone looking away from Charles. He began to roll a sheet-covered cart towards Malthus. Charles only recognized him after he removed the mask from his face. It was Samantha and Madison's father.

"What is Dr. Wallace doing here?" asked Charles.

John replied with certainty, "He is here to fix things."

Malthus laughed again, semi-sedated. His head began flailing from side to side.

"Thirteen years ago," said a remorseful Dr. Wallace, "I did something unforgivable. When Emma was born, Malthus, disguised as Mr. Lyell, gathered all of those charged with protecting Emma at the hospital. He foretold that she would be in great danger if I did not perform emergency surgery on her and him. So, I did. Little did I know that the device I put inside them would also unite them. You see, if one dies, so does the other."

"I always win," interrupted a smiling Malthus, in a drug-induced haze.

Looking at Malthus, Dr. Wallace whispered, "I also implanted a tracking device in you. That is how we found you in Brazil. That is how we found you in the ocean. You are not the only one with secrets, Malthus. You remind me of a coward named B. Wrester Pioners from Napa Valley in Alberta, Canada."

Malthus was enraged.

Dr. Wallace continued, "For the past 13 years, I have dedicated myself to finding a cure for Emma." Pointing to the cart, he added, "Today, I will cure her."

He removed the sheet from the cart to reveal a device with many tubes. There were wires and tubes protruding from an inner glass dome. The entire contraption was encased in a larger glass housing. Next to the dome, were a variety of surgical tools.

"What is that?" questioned Malthus.

Dr. Wallace explained, "I have come to a profound realization..."

"...that I cannot be killed?" suggested Malthus, laughing hysterically.

"No," said Dr. Wallace, shaking his head. "I have come to the realization that to rid the world of you and to save Emma, you must die."

"If I die," screamed Malthus, "she dies! I have taken your daughters from you and you can do nothing about it. My men are coming for me. When I get out of here, I will personally slaughter all of you!"

"My daughters have paid for my mistakes," agreed a calm Dr. Wallace, "but Emma will never suffer the same fate."

Malthus screamed, "You are all dead! Do you hear me? Dead!"

Dr. Wallace pressed a button on the device. A red substance began to swirl around the apparatus, filling every tube as it circulated. Dr. Wallace declared his sentence, "Malthus, for your crimes against humanity, you are sentenced to die."

Malthus could only laugh at his suggestion.

Dr. Wallace then revealed, "Now, let me tell you my secret. The device inside you was never meant to keep you alive. It was to keep you from harming Emma. She does not need you to live. She only needs your heart. My contraption will keep your heart beating for as long as Emma needs it."

"NO! NO! NO!" screamed Malthus, upon realizing what he had heard. He fought to free himself, kicking and screaming.

Everyone began to leave the room, except Dr. Wallace. He gathered several surgical tools and approached Malthus. Charles closed the door, hearing Malthus screaming out loud, a piercing, throbbing scream; a scream of terror, of fear.

Chapter 28
The Awakening

Gilbert never thought that there would ever come a day when there would be *perfect peace* over all the Earth. Yet, it was the only way that he could describe what he witnessed. For three days, there were no wars, no crimes and no evil to be found. All over the Earth, everyone patiently waited for any news from the ship. Even the animals in the trees and barns seemed to keep watch.

This was an event that everyone wanted to be part of. Most of them had never met Emma in person. Most never will. Yet, they all felt a shared connection. The cameras rolled anytime someone emerged from her room. For three days, the news was always the same: "She is resting peacefully." It brought a sense of relief to the masses. Even hearing these simple words was a cause for celebration.

Then, on the fourth day, she began to move. Noticing the twitch of her fingers, someone quickly called for a doctor. Within seconds, the room was filled with a doctor and nurses, followed by several other people. Everyone clamored into the small room to see the miracle. No one ever thought that she would ever wake up, much less be able to move her fingers. Most had resigned to believe that she would never walk or talk. This was also the opinion of the doctors. However, there were a few who believed otherwise. They never gave up on her. They knew that her purpose was far greater than to simply lay in a bed all of her life. They knew the fighting spirit that embodied her.

The first words Emma heard when she opened her eyes were: "Welcome back." She did not know who spoke the kind words, but it was a familiar voice. As she opened her eyes for the first time, all she could see was white light. After a short while, out-of-focused grey figures began to fill her view. Not long after that, her eyes began to focus. To her dismay, she did not recognize anyone in the room. However, they were all excited to see her. While she did not know where she was, the smile on their faces reassured her that she was safe.

No one said anything else. The doctor and nurses began to conduct tests on her to make sure that she was alright. They removed the tubes attached to her face and arms. They checked her heart rate, blood pressure and other vital signs. She was patient with them, as they tugged and pulled at her limbs. Only when they were completely satisfied, did they leave her alone. They all stood back and admired her. Slowly, she pressed her hands into the mattress and raised herself into a seated position.

Everyone was amazed and speechless when Emma asked, "Where is Charles?"

One nurse uttered, "Oh my God, she can speak!"

Emma wondered what all the excitement was about. It was just a simple question. Yet, everyone else in the room reacted as if they had just witnessed a miracle. Emma was puzzled.

The doctor smiled, knowing that everything would be alright. All of the nurses were ushered out of the room. There were only eight people left, including Emma. Then, the doctor herself left the room, saying to the rest, "Call me if you need anything."

Emma looked at everyone and they, in turn, did not take their eyes off of her. No one moved. No one approached her or retreated. They simply stared. Emma felt a little uncomfortable with all of the attention. There were many questions that she wanted to ask, but she was not the first one to speak.

"Do you know what your name is?" asked a woman, the oldest person in the room. Standing next to her were three young girls, another woman and a young man. They were all neatly dressed as if they were getting ready to attend church service. They seemed anxious to meet her, but no one approached.

"Yes, of course," she said with certainty. "My name is Emma."

The woman smiled at Emma as tears rolled down her cheeks. She then asked, "Do you know who I am?"

Emma responded with a simple shake of her head, indicating *no*.

The woman then inquired, "Do you know anyone else in the room?"

Emma looked at everyone, one at a time, studying each one closely. Sadly, she did not recognize anyone and shook her head indicating so. She felt as though she should know them, but she was sure that she had never met them before.

Emma was shocked by what the woman revealed next. In tears, she said delightfully, "I am your mother, Emma."

Emma was speechless when she was introduced to her brother, three sisters and an aunt. She was suspicious of the woman and screamed for the doctor. The woman and the others tried to calm her down when the doctor came rushing into the room.

Emma demanded to know where she was and who these people were. She asked if Charles and Gilbert and the others were alright and if the world was safe.

What she was told next absolutely mortified her. The doctor informed her that everyone that she asked for did not exist. These were not names that anyone in the room was familiar with. No one had ever heard of Ms. Coraline, Susannah, Charles, Gilbert, or Fitzroy. Regarding the assassinations, they explained to Emma that there were no assassinations of any world leaders. The president of the United States was speaking on the television in her room. The war that Emma spoke of did not happen. Nor were there any people in the wastelands or fires and tsunamis that threatened the world. She even learned that she had never been to Australia. In fact, she had lived her entire life in a hospital bed.

"What's the meaning of all this?" questioned Emma. She was beginning to get scared. Though she was frightened, she listened to the woman who claimed to be her mother. Her every word was corroborated by the doctor and everyone else in the room. To her surprise, she found out that everyone called her Emma, even though her real name was Elizabeth. She had spent the last 12 years in a hospital bed. While watching her brother playing football, there was an accident in the stands. She fell and has since been in a coma in the hospital. She was only one year old at the time.

Emma also learned that her father had passed away just before she was born. He tried to protect her while still in her mother's womb from a would-be robber. After he handed over his wallet, he was still shot. Everyone else in the room looked sad. They all remembered the painful memories.

Some of what they were saying was beginning to make sense to Emma. Every day, her mother told her stories when she came to visit. The life that she dreamed was a mix of these different stories, it would seem. Emma figured that when she was levitated by the light, it could have coincided with someone picking her up to change her bedsheet. Her mother had told her stories of when her siblings had gone fishing, to the museum, to the police station to report her father's death, and the accident at the football game.

For a moment, it all made sense to her. Although she was in a coma, she could still hear what was going on in the world. Her imagined life took all the stories that she had heard and blended them together.

In the end, she found this life to be better than the one that she had imagined, though she was sad because now she had to conform to rules. In her dream, she was a legend on the gridiron, the savior of the world. Here, she was just Emma. At the very least, the world was safe, she thought. Yet, she was sad that Susannah, Ms. Coraline, Gilbert, Charles, and the others were not real. Even so, she still missed them dearly.

Later that day, the doctor told Emma that she could go home with her family. Her siblings crowded around her in the van, listening to how she saved the world. They hung onto her every word. Some laughed, some had tears in their eyes and others just listened quietly.

"How did you get back on the ship?" asked Emma's younger sister.

She said, "After I fell into the ocean, an angel rescued me. She took me to Atlantis, deep beneath the ocean. There, Atlanteans tended to me for three days, until I regained consciousness. I met Prince Ari. He is next in line for the throne. He is the most amazing person that I have ever met and he is only 14 years old. When I was ready, the angel took me to the ship and placed me next to Charles. Before she left, I saw her face. It was Ms. Coraline. She was my guardian angel."

They were all surprised and in awe when they learned who Ms. Coraline was.

Another sibling asked, "What happened to the Grail?"

Emma answered, "It is back where it belongs in Atlantis. It was the source of their power. Prince Ari will use it to raise the city of Atlantis from the bottom of the ocean."

While it didn't matter to her what they thought of her story, Emma was happy to have a family that loved her. They, in turn, told her of each of their lives, so that she got to know them better. She was blessed to have such a wonderful family.

It was only when they exited the highway, that Emma noticed the Black Wall. No one else seemed concerned about it. Malthus, disguised as Mr. Lyell, had predicted that only those with the *gift of sight* could see it. It was an odd sight; a shapeless black wall towering above everything. There were no discernible features - no doors, no windows, just a glass-finished, black wall. It was the tallest structure around and extended as far as the eye could see. It reminded her of the Black Gates that the angel spoke of. She stared at it but did not ask what its purpose was. No one else seemed to know that it was even there. Differing thoughts crowded her head. Was it meant to keep something from coming over onto her side or prevent her from seeing what was on the other side?

Emma's new home was not far from the hospital. As the van pulled into the quiet neighborhood, there was a gathering in the driveway. When Emma got out of the van, she saw a large banner that read: Welcome Home! Everyone was cheering and celebrating when they saw her. She couldn't believe how many people there were. She felt as though she had just won the championship game. They must have brought presents, she thought, because she could see a new bicycle wrapped with a ribbon.

Emma felt a little uncomfortable with all of the attention that she was getting. Everyone was coming up to her and asking her how she was doing, how she felt. But mostly, people were coming up to her and telling her that she was a miracle.

It was only later, when the food had been eaten, the candles on the cake blown out, the presents opened, and everyone went home, that Emma was most afraid. The last of the envelopes was in her hands. She had saved it until she was alone in her room. Unlike all of the other envelopes, there was no mention of whom it was from. There was no writing on the front or the back, other than: Attn: Emma. She knew that there was no card inside because she could feel none.

The white envelope was strikingly similar to the ones that she had seen before. She began to open it by tearing a small piece along the edge, next to where the stamp would be. After inserting a pencil into the hole which she had created, she opened the envelope. She slowly peered inside. Seeing only a small piece of folded paper, she debated if she should take it out and read it.

Nothing good had ever come from the other white envelopes that she had opened.

Emma could hear her brother and sisters in the next room laughing and having fun. This was a life that she could get used to. She thought of Susannah, Charles and the others. She wondered what had happened to them. It reminded her of the *what-if* world that Gilbert talked about. Even though they were merely in her head, they were still real. She wondered if they were waiting for her, if they missed her as much as she missed them.

She continued to listen to her siblings laughing and playing as she reached into the envelope and took out the piece of paper. She was surprised and shocked by its contents. It was a letter from a most unexpected source. Although there was no mention of whom it was from, the letter was written in the form of a crypt that she was familiar with. It contained the following:

I know a secret about you. It is something you need to know. I will not tell you what it is, but I will give you clues to help you figure it out.

7and10 Tipty 184143 177329 20nOdashs8463

train oinOnest jEfferson

1	1	2	2	7	7	7	7	7	9	1	1	1	1	1	1	1	1	1	1	1	1	1	1	1	1
8	9	4	5	0	1	2	9	9	0	0	1	1	2	2	2	3	3	3	3	4	4	5	6	6	6
			3	3	6	4	6	4	0	1	2	6	9	9	1	6	6	8	9	9	9	1	2	9	
							2	7	3	1	1	2	2	2	6	1	3	6	5	2	4	2			
1	1	1	1	1	1	1	2	2	2	2	2	2	2	2	2	2	2	2	2	2	2	2	3	3	3
7	8	8	8	8	9	9	0	1	1	2	2	2	3	3	3	3	4	4	4	4	5	5	2	3	4
1	8	8	8	9	3	3	1	3	5	0	2	8	2	6	8	8	0	0	0	2	3	5	6	0	4
3	1	2	3	2	5	6	1	3	4	1	4	4	4	1	2	3	5	6	9	2	1	3	3	1	1

Emma immediately recognized the clues and ran over to the computer in her room. She searched the internet for the document that pertained to the clues. She began to translate the numbers into letters. When she finished translating it, she was puzzled by what she uncovered.

There was a thump in her room. The whole house trembled like it was being shaken. It was followed by another tremor, only bigger this time. The tremors continued with the gap between them getting shorter and shorter.

The rumbling of the house continued. She could hear car alarms sounding outside. Her siblings were frantically calling for her. The door to her room flung over. Emma's younger sister stood just inside her room.

She demanded, "Who are you?" She did not sound like the sweet little girl in the van earlier listening to how Emma saved the world.

Emma did not answer. She simply held onto her chair as the tremors almost knocked her to the floor.

The little girl screamed defiantly, "How can I be your younger sister if your father died before you were born?"

Emma looked scared as she realized that this was not her family. The little girl was right. How could she have a younger sister? She looked down at the chain around her neck and knew for sure that something was not right.

"They are coming for you, aren't they?" calmly asked the scared little girl.

Emma shook her head, indicating yes.

The closet door slid open due to the tremors. The little girl signaled for Emma to get inside. As Emma dove into the closet, the roof was peeled off the house. Emma could hear the little girl screaming. Two large red eyes stared back at her from above, as bright as the full moon. Mechanical arms tossed the roof onto the road. An army of machines followed, leaving a trail of destruction behind them.

There was an opening at the back of the closet, which led to a tunnel. In a panic, Emma hustled into the tunnel and found herself at the back of the house. As she looked up, she could see the towering Colossus uprooting trees and demolishing homes. Suddenly, it stopped, spun around and looked directly at Emma. An alarm began to sound from a red dot on its head. The Colossus began to walk through the house heading for Emma.

"Surrender!" it demanded, in its mechanical voice.

Emma, instead, ran towards her new bicycle. She jumped onto it and headed for the back gate, down the path along the river. The other machines congregated at Emma's house. The one that noticed her began to clear a path, as they all pursued her. Nothing stood in their way as trees and homes were leveled by explosions. Emma rode as fast as he could, staying just ahead of them, weaving and dodging her way.

In front of her, Emma could see a small orange light that appeared to be getting larger. The light was moving towards her at an incredible speed. Only when it got closer, did she know what it was. She swerved to avoid being hit. She fell to the ground. The orange light sped past her and incinerated the Colossus upon impact. It was followed by several others, each targeting a different machine.

Emma scanned her surroundings to look for her bicycle. In the dimly lit space, she noticed the silhouette of someone. He held her bicycle in an upright position. He reached out his other hand to help her to her feet. When she looked at him, all she heard was: "Heaven-o, Miss Emma."

Emma was happy to see Gilbert but she knows that he should not be here. She had warned him to stay away from her. She did not know why he would not listen. There was no time to argue, however, as the Colossus trailed them. She remembered the words of the angel on the bridge. On her way home from the hospital, she noticed the sentinels that watched over the sea. The river she rode along filtered into the sea. She did not know why but she knew that she had to go towards the Black Wall.

Emma could see the outline of the wall as she and Gilbert approached the sea. From behind the wall, another orange light appeared. It was aimed at the raging machine. The light missed its mark. They were still being pursued. Emma searched for an entrance along the wall but could see none. Gilbert wondered what she was looking for. He could not see the wall. He only saw the edge of a cliff and the sea below.

As the Colossus got closer, it emphatically repeated, "Surrender! Surrender!" Weapons raised and pointed at Emma and Gilbert.

They both stood with their hands up.

Gilbert looked at Emma and, referring to the wall, asked, "Is it real?"

Emma nodded and smiled with tears in her eyes. Malthus, disguised as Mr. Lyell, had told Gilbert about the Black Wall. Emma had warned Gilbert to stay away from her. She knew what would happen if he was with her. Emma was well aware that Gilbert could not see the Black Wall. What she was most fearful of is that he could not walk through it to the other side. Yet, of his fate, she could not discern.

"Gilbert," pleaded Emma, "you have to run. You promised me that you would run."

"No more running, Miss Emma," he said, standing beside her bravely. With closed fists, he put up both hands in a fighting stance. He would fight beside her to the very end. Emma could not prevent it. She would have it no other way.

He reassured her, "If I am here only to bear witness, then it is enough."

Even if he wanted to run, there was no place for him to run. In front of him was the Colossus, and behind, the sea.

"Step away from the wall," ordered the Colossus.

The wall began to morph. Emma glimpsed a huge gathering of people on the other side. They were trying to prime the cannon for another blast. A portion of the wall extended towards Emma. The Colossus immediately fired all of its weapons. As the wall enveloped Emma, she yelled out Gilbert's name. The bombs exploded upon impact with the wall.

After the smoke cleared, Emma could see the Colossus turning around and walking away. Immediately, an orange beam of light struck the Colossus and it fell to the ground. There was no trace of Gilbert. Tears filled Emma's eyes. She began her journey with a band of protectors. She watched as each made the ultimate sacrifice. Now she was all alone.

As Emma grieved for Gilbert, the wall began to morph again. Slowly, a shadowy figure emerged through the ash-covered wall. Emma's eyes opened wide. She immediately ran to Gilbert and embraced him. Though dazed and somewhat disoriented, he managed to remain standing. Emma knew that only those worthy enough can walk through the wall. Gilbert had proven himself plenty worthy.

The one person who was there from the very beginning was still providing her with strength. With Gilbert by her side, she somehow knows that everything will be alright. She cannot see his future because he is unlike anyone whom she has ever met before.

Behind her, Emma could hear a rumbling. She turned slowly, wiping tears of joy from her eyes. As far as she could see, there stood a gathering reminiscent of the words of the angel on the bridge. Emma stared at the people of the wastelands.

A voice came forth out of the mist and proclaimed loudly, "People of the wastelands, I give you your savior!" Immediately, the multitude fell to their knees, head to the ground, ten million strong.

Emma immediately recognized the voice. She had heard his voice since the day she was born. It was a voice that she could count on, depend on and lean on. Emma sprinted as quickly as she could to embrace the grey-bearded one, standing by himself at the front of the crowd. He was very happy to see her. As they turned to the crowd, one inquisitive little eye looked up. Emma signaled with her hand for her to stand up. Everyone followed her lead. Emma smiled. She felt like she was finally home. The crowd erupted in cheers as they approached to greet her and Gilbert.

Chapter 29
Silent Hum

Emma had many questions, the least of which was how Mr. Lyell was still alive. But that would have to wait.

"Take cover!" shouted Mr. Lyell.

Emma looked up to see the sky filled with Winged-creatures, with claws and beaks resembling eagles. Their multitude blocked out the Sun. Everyone scattered to find shelter as rocks and balls of fire rained down from the sky.

Mr. Lyell grabbed Emma's hand and led her into a vehicle. Gilbert followed and sat beside her. They drove as quickly as they could, with dozens of creatures attacking the vehicle, pecking and scratching at the roof and windows. Emma looked back to see the devastation. There were vast numbers of people lying motionless on the ground.

"We need to help them," cried Emma.

Mr. Lyell knew that there was nothing that they could do to help. His main concern was Emma's safety. With so many creatures following them, he knew that they could not turn back. As they reached the fortress walls, the vehicle suddenly started to levitate. The creatures struggled to lift it up. It was too heavy. They dropped it to the ground. It rolled several times before coming to a stop a short distance from the fortress gates. Mr. Lyell, Emma and Gilbert managed to crawl out through the windows of the overturned vehicle. They were surrounded by several creatures.

They gnashed their beaks at Gilbert's limbs and squawked at each other. He was terrified. One of the creatures lunged itself at Emma. Suddenly, orange beams of light shot forth from behind the wall and destroyed the invaders. The gates opened and Emma was quickly ushered underground, into the Viewing Room.

"Do not let her out of your sight," shouted Mr. Lyell before shutting the door closed. Gilbert remained outside. He tried to ask what was happening but with a hive of activity, no one had time to respond to him. Someone pointed to a corner for him to go and sit.

As Emma surveyed the dimly lit room, there were hundreds of holograms floating in the air, showing war and fighting around the globe. At the helm were two individuals about her age, scrolling through the holograms with the swipe of their fingers. As she approached one of them, Emma felt as though she was looking into a mirror.

"Welcome home, sister!" said the stranger excitedly, as she greeted Emma with an embrace. She clearly knew who Emma was. "Father and I thought that we had lost you."

"Sister?" asked Emma.

"I am Mira," she said excitedly. "Do you not remember me?"

Emma shook her head indicating no.

"Maybe you were gone too long," suggested Mira.

"Who is our father?" asked Emma hesitantly.

Mira was confused at first. Then she remembered that the effects of transporting through the wall had not worn off yet.

She said, "Well, you know him as Mr. Lyell. Around here, we call him Father."

Emma was stunned.

"But don't worry," reassured Mira, "when the effects wear off, you will see his true form and mine and yours, too."

Emma began to get scared.

"Ok, ok," said Mira, trying to calm her down. "Now stand still," said Mira as she reached behind her, brought forth a needle and stabbed Emma in the arm, injecting serum into her.

"What have you done to me?" screamed Emma, as she dropped to the ground in agonizing pain. A silent hum could be heard as scales began to protrude from Emma's hands. She began to panic. Webbed feet sprang forth. Nails and fangs grew. A slender tail extended behind her. Her long, shiny black hair was replaced by two antennae-like structures. Gill slits grew out of the side of her head and her nose retracted. Bulging eyes popped out of her eye sockets.

"What did you do to me?" wailed Emma as she turned to Mira. "Ahh!" she screamed again. Mira looked completely different, transformed into an unrecognizable creature.

Emma stood up and approached Mira. She touched her face gently. Memories began to flood her mind, as she grabbed onto her head in endless pain. After her breathing calmed, Emma whispered, "I remember now. I remember everything. You are my sister. This is our true form."

"Oh," said Mira as she embraced Emma, "I am so happy to see you again."

"What is happening?" asked Emma, as she looked at the holograms around the room.

"The holograms track the humans," said Mira. "The more holograms there are, the more humans there are. Father has gathered as many humans as he could in the wastelands. We are ready to start the breeding program, to save them."

"What has happened to them?" asked Emma as she followed Mira.

"They are on the brink of extinction," explained Mira. "From eight billion, there are less than ten million left. They have been ravaged by diseases and they have destroyed their world beyond recovery. Father wants to try and save them by creating a captive breeding program. Of the three species of intelligent life left in the Milky Way, humans are next to become extinct."

"If we are trying to help them," asked Emma, as she points to one of the holograms, "why are we attacking them?"

"They are stubborn," said Mira, scrolling through the holograms. "We have to try and save them, even if they resist."

As Emma looked at a different hologram, she asked, "Where did all of these creatures come from?"

"In the North," said Mira, "Father has created the Frost Giants. In the South, the Jaguars round up the humans. In the East, are the Dragon-kinds. In the West, where we are, are the Winged-creatures.

"Father has unlocked the mysteries of dark energy and converted it to physical matter with the power of the Grail. Just like you once looked like a human, he can control the shape we take. Imagine a hologram with physical properties.

"Our Father sent you into the world to save the humans. When you were on the ship, all humans paused to pray for you. Father was hoping that they would stop fighting each other if they had a worthy enough reason. But once you were alive, they started to fight each other again and continue to pollute and destroy the planet."

Emma asked, "Did you hear a hum when I transformed?"

"Yes," replied Mira. "That is why Father named the town Silent Hum."

"Have you ever been in the human world?" asked Emma.

"Many times," replied Mira. She showed Emma a hologram, saying, "I was the one who put the Grail back into the box at the Wallace Institute."

Emma asked, "Were you conducting experiments on dark energy?"

"Yes," she replied. "Samantha Wallace was helping me."

"So you created the angel that stood before me on the bridge?" asked Emma.

"Yes," responded Mira. She swiped through many holograms as she spoke, reliving the memories. "I was there during the Aldaine case. I was the one who dropped the laptop on the floor at your quiz tournament. I was the jumper on the bridge. I was Aunt Bessie. I tried to steal the Grail at the museum when you stopped me. I was at the dam when they tried to warn you. I was your little sister. My job was to steer you in the right direction, to lead you here. Father even made the Winged-creatures attack you, so he could separate you from the humans. He is always two steps ahead of everyone."

"Who are these?" asked Emma, pointing to one of the holograms.

Mira said, "That is Prince Ari and the Atlanteans coming to stop Father and take back the Grail. They are the only ones Father has no control over."

Emma did not immediately recognize Prince Ari with his helmet, shield and armor.

The door opened and someone walked in. Emma heard a hum. She could not see who it was as it was dark. An officer walked up to Emma, pointing a weapon at her. She put her hands up and stepped back. The officer ordered the guard who was monitoring the holograms to report for duty. She did as she was told. The officer then locked the door from the inside, while still aiming the weapon at Emma. The officer then put the weapon down and injected a needle into his arm in haste. The scales quickly retracted from his body, to show smooth human skin and a human face.

"Charles!" shouted Emma.

"Hi, Emma," he said with a smile on his face. "We don't have much time."

"Now that the guard is gone," said Mira, scrolling through the holograms, "the truth is that Father has killed countless humans. He is setting a trap to eliminate the rest and take over this planet. There is no resettlement or breeding program. He just wants to destroy the humans. We have to stop him."

"How can we stop someone who has harnessed dark energy?" asked Emma. "Have you even found the Grail?"

"No," replied Mira. "But I know Father has it. I just don't know where he keeps it. But, at least, I have the vials."

"Without the Grail," stated Emma, "there is no hope."

"Regardless," insisted Mira, "you are the only one who can save them. That is your purpose."

Emma said, "Then help me save them. I have seen goodness in them." She thought of Gilbert. "Even for one, they are worth saving."

Charles agreed. Mira stabbed Emma to transform her into a human.

Gilbert sat quietly in a dark corner of a far wall. The door opened and Emma stepped outside.

"Miss Emma," shouted Gilbert, trying to get her attention.

Several guards, in human form, noticed Emma. They hit the alarm. The blaring sound echoed throughout the fortress.

Gilbert had made a grave mistake by alerting the guards to Emma. He was immediately taken into custody.

"Stop her!" yelled Mira, bursting through the door.

Emma ran as quickly as she could up the stairs. Several guards followed her. She ran up several flights of stairs, with a hoard of guards pursuing her. Seeing a window, she headed for it at full-speed and leaped shoulder-first, in a football-style tackle position. Breaking through the window, she fell several stories and landed in the raging rapids below.

The guards turned around and headed back down the stairs.

Mira cried, "I am sorry for letting her get away, Father."

"Sir," said one of the guards in fear, "the prisoner has escaped. She is in the river."

"Well, find her!" screamed Mr. Lyell. He began to transform into Malthus without the use of serum.

The guards rushed out of the fortress, heading for the river.

"She could not have gone far," said Malthus. Turning to Mira, he ordered, "Go back inside and track her down."

Mira did as she was told. Her father followed her. In his rage, he began to transform into a creature resembling Mira without using the serum. Mira quickly detected Emma on one of the holograms.

"Look," she said to her father, "she is in the river."

He ordered, "Send troops to her position." Speaking into the microphone, he commanded, "Kill her if you must!"

"But father," reminded Mira, "she is your daughter."

"She is my daughter," he agreed, "but you are my favorite. That is why I did not send you into the human world. She has spent too much time with them. They have corrupted her."

"But father," begged Mira.

"No!" he insisted in a loud voice. "You know the legend. One of you will save our kind and one of you will save the wretched humans. Her death is necessary. You know how much I love you," he said, pointing at his rib cage. "As long as you and I are alive, our kind will survive."

"I know, father," said Mira. "No one can harm us. If they kill either of us, our entire species will die. You were wise to place implants in every citizen."

At the thought of what is to come, Mira put her head down and stared at the holograms in sadness.

Emma bobbed up and down in the rapids as she struggled to stay afloat. Splashing and kicking, her body is thrown wherever the rapids steered her. From the shore, she could see guards tracking her from both sides. She swam as hard as she could, as the water began to rush with exceeding force. Something was compelling it to flow faster. A waterfall was the first thought that came to mind. With no choice, she headed for the bank of the river. Immediately, guards surrounded her.

"Sir," a voice echoed over the microphone, "we have her."

Other voices reported, "Humans are now extinct in the Northern Quadrant."

"Humans are now extinct in the Southern Quadrant."

"Humans are now extinct in the Eastern Quadrant."

"What is happening in the Western Quadrant?" demanded Malthus.

The commander of the Western Quadrant announced, "The Atlanteans are here."

Malthus screamed as loud as he could in disgust, "Direct all troops towards the Atlanteans! Do not let them breach the walls. We will deal with the pesky humans later."

As the Atlanteans approached the fortress wall, they were met by the Winged-creatures. They were joined by the Frost Giants, the Jaguars and the Dragon-kinds who were transported through the Black Wall.

The Atlanteans, too, had weapons of magic. Prince Ari dug his gloved hands into the ground to raise up a forest of mighty trees to surround his army and confuse the enemy. The Winged-creatures flew into the forest with many of them getting tangled in the ever-expanding branches of the trees. The Dragon-kinds, the wisest of all creatures, dared not enter the forest but circled above looking for a way in. Some tested the strength of the trees by attempting to set them ablaze.

The Frost Giants of the Northern Quadrant laid ice deep into the ground with each step that they took into the forest. The frost stifled the trees, freezing their trunks and leaves. The Jaguars entered the forest with stealth and silence.

Prince Ari and the Atlanteans were surrounded on all corners. The Dragon-kinds roared as loudly as they could to signal all troops towards the Atlanteans. Prince Ari blew on the war-horns to prepare the Atlanteans for the oncoming onslaught. The rustling leaves of the trees let Prince Ari know that they were under attack. All creatures from all sides penetrated the forest and engaged the Atlanteans, even the Dragon-kinds from above.

"It is almost finished," cheered Malthus. "First, we destroy the Atlanteans and then we rid this planet of the humans."

One by one, the Atlanteans fell. By the frost, they fell. By the fire, they fell. By the claw, they fell. Pick up by the wing and soaring high into the sky, they fell. Valiantly and bravely, with courage and heart, they fell until Prince Ari stood alone. Stripped of his glove and armor, he was stomped on, struck by and beaten down until he was broken and could no longer stand. The forest around him withered away.

"Bring him to me," ordered Malthus. "Bring her to me also and send all of the troops to the humans. It is finished." As Mira looked on, one by one the holograms faded, until there were only two remaining.

All of the troops raced to the humans. The sky darkened and the ground trembled like a quake. From a distance, the humans could hear the deafening roar of the Dragon-kinds. Defenseless, they awaited their faith. The creatures formed a wall, surrounding the humans on all sides, corralling them into a tighter and smaller circle. They awaited their final instructions.

Emma and Prince Ari were brought before Malthus outside of the fortress gates, along with Gilbert.

"Humans," began Malthus, "have done unimaginable harm to this planet. It cannot be allowed to continue. For thousands of years, I have watched over you. I have shared my knowledge with you. I have given you technology. From the very beginning, you have only sought to use it for evil. I should have never brought you out of that valley."

"They still have goodness in them," argued Emma.

"Silence!" shouted Malthus.

All of the guards began to transform into their scaly and leathery forms. Gilbert stood alone among them, terrified. Emma and Prince Ari were bound and on their knees. One guard, Charles, came forward and pointed a weapon at Prince Ari. Malthus signaled for him to fire. Gilbert ran over to shield Prince Ari and Emma.

"I commend your courage little one," said Malthus. "If only the rest were like you. Now, it is finished."

Malthus commanded the troops to attack the humans who stood bravely with nothing but raised clenched fists. The troops closed ranks around the humans. They attacked with a ferocity that was both swift as it was lethal. The commander of the Western Quadrant announced that all humans were now extinct.

Gilbert was devastated as he heard the news.

Only one hologram remained.

With all humans, except Gilbert, now extinct, the fortress began to rumble. The roof opened and spaceships began to lift off in the hundreds and filled the sky, including their monolithic mothership.

Malthus then took the Grail out from inside his garment and held it up high. He took the weapon from Charles, and before he fired at Prince Ari, said, "I do this for my kind!"

Emma lunged forward to protect Prince Ari. A shot was fired. She fell to the ground.

"No!" screamed Gilbert, reaching out to her.

Mira wept.

Unphased, Malthus held up the weapon to fire again at Gilbert. He asked, "How does it feel to be the last of your kind?"

Gilbert replied, defiantly, "I am not the last of my kind, you coward. I am the first!"

Before Malthus could fire again, the weapon fell from his weakened hand. He looked at Charles just in time to see him fall to the ground. One by one the others fell, too.

The Winged-creatures could not control themselves in the air and crash into each other before plummeting to the ground. The Frost Giants froze where they stood. The Jaguars were motionless. Finally, the Dragon-kinds succumbed and fell out of the sky.

"What magic is this?" asked a scared Malthus looking at Mira. He fell to his knees.

"You were the wisest of us all, father," said Mira. "You saw to protect our species by connecting all of us, so we can be stronger. It is something the humans lacked. But our strength is also our weakness. By killing your daughter, you have doomed our species."

"No!" cried Malthus. "You and I cannot die. I don't understand."

Mira took a needle out of her pocket and inserted it into her arm. She began to transform into a human. She transformed into Emma.

"You killed the wrong daughter," said Emma. "Mira saw what you were becoming. She saw, like I did, that there is still goodness in humans, especially Arianne Aldaine and Gilbert. She used what you created to transform into me and I into her. She knew that only you could kill her. By doing so, you've doomed our entire species, just like you almost did on our home planet. I know what you did."

Feeling unsteady, Emma grabbed the left side of her rib and winced in pain. Her knees gave out and she lay motionless on the ground.

Malthus fell to the ground. The fortress began to crumble. Without him, the entire structure began to implode. So bent on survival and destruction he was, even the fortress was set to be destroyed if he dies. Without pilots, all around them, the spaceships began to plummet to the ground in spectacular balls of fire.

The Grail slipped from Malthus's fingers and rolled before Prince Ari.

Gilbert ran to Emma.

"How is she?" asked a worried Prince Ari.

"She is not breathing," cried Gilbert. He looked at Prince Ari and the Grail. He begged, "Use the Grail to save her."

Prince Ari was bound and could not move, as he struggled to free himself. "Gilbert," he said, "take the Grail to her."

"I cannot," cried Gilbert. "It will kill me."

"No, Gilbert," reassured Prince Ari. "You can wield its powers if you are worthy."

Gilbert summoned all his might and picked up the Grail with his bare hands and brought it to Emma. In one hand was the Grail and in his other hand, he held Emma. He clenched both tightly. Nothing happened. Gilbert sobbed. It was foretold that he would be there by her side to the very end if only to protect her. He had failed in his mission.

"It's not working!" screamed Gilbert. He cried, "I am not worthy!" as tears fell from his eyes. Prince Ari struggled to fight back tears as he looked on helplessly.

As Gilbert was the only human left, he was both the Christ and the Antichrist. The forces within him fought for dominance. Gilbert refused to give up as tears flowed down his cheeks. He squeezed Emma's hand even tighter. Memories flooded his mind with all of the times that Emma was there for him. She protected him. She brought great joy and purpose to his life. She was more than just a mentor and a protector. She was his friend. Then, the hand he held, softly and gently caressed his. As Gilbert looked down at Emma, the only words he heard were: "What it is!"

Gilbert was overjoyed.

As Emma opened her eyes, she felt as though she had awakened from a dream. Gilbert freed Prince Ari as Emma quickly ran over to Mira and untied her. She took out a needle and inserted it into Mira's arm. Life sprang into her body. Gilbert did not understand how Mira was still alive until she showed him her implant which she had removed. Mira quickly took out two small vials of orange and blue fluorescent liquids from her pocket and poured them into the Grail. Immediately, Emma heard a silent hum as the Grail began to vibrate and flew high into the air. There was a loud sonic boom as the sky was filled with the mist of the liquids. The sky became clearer as everything else faded.

Now that Malthus was gone, the illusion created by Mira disappeared to reveal the world exactly the way it was, including Silent Hum. She had created a *what-if* world to fool Malthus. She could not get him to reveal the Grail unless he was sure that all humans were extinct. The illusion felt so real, it fooled everyone, especially Malthus.

As the illusion faded, they found themselves in Silent Hum. They were standing in front of Samantha's workplace, where it all began. Suddenly, someone bumped into Prince Ari. When he saw them, especially Emma and Mira in their otherworldly form, Snevyl dropped his pencil and notepad as he screamed and ran away. They all looked at each other in bewilderment, as Gilbert shrugged his shoulders. At the entrance of the building was Samantha, who complained, "We don't have all day!" Two aliens, an Atlantean and a human walked into the institute. Indeed, what it is!

Silent Hum: The Challenge

It's now your turn to become a detective. You may submit your answers to: **silenthum@yahoo.com**

1) On what day of the week does the novel begin?

ANSWER:______________________________________

2) Almost all of the names found in this book were taken from a specific time period in history. They are all connected with one particular individual.

Names: Emma, Charles, Lyell, Fitzroy, Gilbert, Susannah, Coraline, Malthus, O'Brian, Sedgwick, Mayr, Beagle, Abbey

Who is this person? Hint: rearrange the following letters to form this persons title and name (4 words in total): **a whet cerb lion said rrrrs**

ANSWER:______________________________________

3) What is Gilbert's last name? Hint: the answer is on page 9.

ANSWER:______________________________________

4) Imagine that you are flying a plane. At fifteen thousand feet, you experience turbulence. So, you climb five thousand inches higher. You encounter a gaggle of geese and climb two thousand meters more. The radio tower informed you that you are on a collision course with another plane and that you should descend by five kilometers. Instead, you only descend by 2 miles. How old is the pilot?

ANSWER:______________________________________

5a) There are three As, two Bs, two Cs, three Es, one F, one G, two Hs, two Is, three Ls, one M, three Ns, one O, one P, one R, and two Ss.

1: For letters occurring more than once, only the two Hs are next to each other;
2: The two Bs and two Ns are each separated by one E;
3: The two middle letters are N and E in alphabetical order;
4: The last I is separated by an S and a P;
5: The two Ss are only separated by two letters;
6: H and R are end-letters;
7: The letter E also occurs in the 3rd and 7th positions;
8: The I that directly follows the L are both directly preceded by the first E;
9: There is an A before the R;
10: The letter C precedes three letters before the second N and two letters separate the first and second N, one is the fourth vowel in the alphabet and directly following this is the fourth consonant in the alphabet;
11: The last S comes directly after the P;
12: Of the 5 letters that separate the Ls, one is a C;
13: Two letters separate two As, one is an M and one is a G;
14: Two As come before the two Ls;
15: The M precedes the G;
16: An A and an L occur directly next to each other, twice;
17: The P is closer to the C than the I.

ANSWER:______________________________________

5b) Now that you have solved the puzzle, use the hint below to uncover the mystery as to what these letters could represent.

Hint: Einstein, Curie, Bohr, Nobel, among others, are all there.

ANSWER:______________________________________

Manufactured by Amazon.ca
Bolton, ON

20868476R00122